Praise for th[e]
Sweet Pepper [...]

Playin[g ...]

"Cook's second Sweet Pepper Fire Br[igade ...]
engrossing a[...]

"I love the s[...]
wait, I may j[...]

"The characters are a lot of fun [and] the town is a place you'd
like to visit."   —*Kings River Life Magazine*

That Old Flame of Mine

"Dark family secrets, a delicious mystery—and a ghost! What
reader could ask for more?"
                              —Casey Daniels, author of the Pepper Martin Mysteries

"This book was so difficult for me to put down, and even more
difficult for me to have it end. I could have continued reading
this series forever! Oh, to live in that same small town tucked
away by the great Smoky Mountains, and to have neighbors
such as these, would ensure that I would be a happy camper
forever."   —*Cozy Mystery Book Reviews*

"A fascinating, successful mystery. It's hard to go wrong with an
intriguing mystery involving a ghost, a strong female character
in a role normally reserved for men, and a spark of romance.
J. J. Cook is kindling a sizzling good mystery series, beginning
with *That Old Flame of Mine*."   —*Lesa's Book Critiques*

"A good read with the usual 'm' words of any paranormal
mystery: Murder, Mystery, Motives, Messy relationships, and
unique to this book, a Motorcycle and accidents."
                                                   —*Meritorious Mysteries*

In Hot Water

J. J. Cook

BERKLEY PRIME CRIME, NEW YORK

THE BERKLEY PUBLISHING GROUP
Published by the Penguin Group
Penguin Group (USA) LLC
375 Hudson Street, New York, New York 10014

USA • Canada • UK • Ireland • Australia • New Zealand • India • South Africa • China

penguin.com

A Penguin Random House Company

IN HOT WATER

A Berkley Prime Crime Book / published by arrangement with the authors

For information, address: The Berkley Publishing Group,
a division of Penguin Group (USA) LLC,
375 Hudson Street, New York, New York 10014.

ISBN: 978-0-425-25262-8

PUBLISHING HISTORY
Berkley Prime Crime mass-market edition / January 2015

PRINTED IN THE UNITED STATES OF AMERICA

10 9 8 7 6 5 4 3 2 1

Cover illustration by Mary Ann Lasher.
Cover design by George Long.
Interior text design by Tiffany Estreicher.

*To our wonderful readers and
the joy they bring us each day!
Thanks for being there!*

Chapter 1

~~~~~~~~~~~~

.

Sweet Pepper Fire Chief Stella Griffin stood between a bulldozer being loaded off the back of a truck and the log cabin where she lived. Her temper was as hot as her mid-length red hair.

She'd spent more than a year living in the cabin—a perk from the town council for her service to the community. She'd always known it wasn't meant to be permanent. The property belonged to the town. But she didn't expect to be kicked out either.

Stella glared at councilman Bob Floyd, who'd purchased the property that day. She'd known it had been for sale, but until now, no one had wanted it.

Bob didn't want it either. He only wanted to destroy the last remaining vestige of the first Sweet Pepper fire chief, Eric Gamlyn.

"I can't believe the town council is sanctioning the cabin being demolished," she said to the man she'd come to dislike. "It's part of Sweet Pepper's history."

She was playing for time. They both knew it. Stella was hoping someone would show up and stop this from happening.

She'd called everyone she could think of in town—from the police to local businessmen. So far they were all a no-show.

"I can do what I like." Bob waved his deed in her face. The wind blew off the Smoky Mountains, moving his curly gray hair like an old mop on his head. "And I want this cabin down *now*!"

Stella had already looked at the deed. She knew she had to have *some* rights. Surely he had to give her time to move out.

"I have to get my things out of the cabin," she stalled.

He laughed. "I'll give you twenty minutes. Get out or get trampled."

She ducked inside the old cabin and closed the door. She needed a minute to think, to come up with a plan. It wasn't just her things and the cabin she was protecting. The actual, ghostly embodiment of the former fire chief was waiting in the kitchen.

"What's going on?" Eric Gamlyn asked. "Can he really tear down the cabin?"

Eric was as tall as he had been in life, well over six feet. He was a big man with broad shoulders and narrow hips. His arms were strongly muscled from years of hard work. He'd built the log cabin and the original firehouse down the road. Then he'd created the Sweet Pepper Fire Brigade.

That had been more than forty years ago.

His longish blond hair would forever be held back from his face with a leather thong, as it had been on the day he'd died. He wore a red Sweet Pepper Fire Brigade T-shirt and jeans.

Stella had gotten used to her ghostly roommate after moving here from Chicago to help train the new fire brigade. It hadn't been easy. Believing in ghosts, despite her Irish father's tales of ghostly ancestors, hadn't been on her bucket list. Eric had made a believer out of her first and then a friend.

"I don't know." She picked up the phone, glad that she'd had the landline installed. She didn't have time to run back to the main road where she'd get cell service. "I'm not running away. He may tear this place down, but it won't be without a fight. I've called everyone I can think of. Bob owns the property, but there must be some loophole or law that says he can't show up here and force me out on the same day."

She could hear the bulldozer out front revving its engine. No doubt courtesy of Bob's impatience to get rid of the cabin, and Eric's ghost.

Bob, and most of the people who lived in the Sweet Pepper area, believed the cabin was haunted. They'd warned her about it when she'd first moved there. It wasn't a legend type of thing either—they firmly believed Eric's ghost was there.

Stella knew she'd made a mistake threatening to send Eric's ghost to get Bob. She could see that now. She'd only wanted the short, ambitious barber to back off. He'd hired someone to burn the woods around the cabin. She wasn't going to put up with that.

Not like she could really "send" Eric anywhere. He was trapped in the cabin that had been his home. But Bob didn't know that. He'd been terrified by the idea.

Before the old firehouse he'd built had been destroyed, Eric had at least been able to appear there as well. Not anymore. That was what worried her. What would become of Eric if his cabin was destroyed?

Part of the problem was that Eric and Bob hadn't exactly been friends before Eric died. The other part was that the cabin was on valuable land that fronted the Little Pigeon River. Thousands of people came to go rafting and tubing every summer now that Sweet Pepper had become a tourist stop in the Great Smoky Mountains National Park.

Stella had planned to buy the place herself after this year's three-day Sweet Pepper Festival was over. Nothing went on while the festival was in progress—as it was now. It took over the small town. Bob must have heard something about that and decided to put a stop to her plans. Nothing was a secret here for long.

It had been a hard decision for her to leave her life in

Chicago behind and stay here as the permanent fire chief. She wasn't going to start by losing the cabin she'd come to love, and Eric.

"What's that?" He nudged the blue ribbon she'd put on the table. "Did we win something in the recipe contest?"

"Not that it's important right now, but yes, we won first place in the festival for the candied, stuffed pepper recipe yesterday," she told him.

He'd done most of the cooking in that effort. She was a toast and Pop-Tarts girl. Eric loved to cook. It was weird watching bowls and pots whizzing through the air as he worked.

"Really?" He looked surprised. Sometimes he became stronger, more visible—more *human* in appearance. Most of the time, he was a little see-through and tended to float above the hardwood floor. But he'd been real enough to save her life when the old firehouse had been destroyed.

"Didn't you think we'd win?" She couldn't believe they were even talking about this when they were both about to be evicted.

"Not really. I never won while I was alive."

It was her turn to be surprised. "I can't believe it. And after all the ladies in town thought you were so hot. I assumed they'd let you win just to spend time with you."

"My charms with the female population of Sweet Pepper have been greatly exaggerated," he quipped. "You might've guessed that since I was still alone when I died."

"Or I might've picked up on that from all the other greatly exaggerated stories about you. According to local legend, you single-handedly felled all the trees needed to build this cabin and the old firehouse in one day. You climbed mountains in single leaps. I think there was even a story about you changing the course of the river by wading into it."

He laughed. Despite the fact that he was a ghost, Stella could make out laugh lines around his bright blue eyes. He had a hearty laugh too. He could scare the birds off the roof sometimes.

"Chief Griffin!" Bob Floyd yelled at the cabin. "I'm only giving you another five minutes."

Stella looked out the window. Bob was careful not to get too close. None of her friends had arrived. No police officers had shown up either. Where was everyone? Were they afraid to deal with Bob?

"Don't worry about it," Eric advised. "Like I said before, if the cabin goes, I'll wander the woods. It's okay. Maybe you should get your stuff out. I don't think he's bluffing with that big bulldozer. I don't want you to get hurt."

"No. I'm not taking anything out and running away. There have to be eviction laws here, even if he owns the property. I must have ninety days or something. Where is John, for God's sake? He should be here by now."

Officer John Trump was one of Sweet Pepper's finest. He was also a member of the fire brigade. He and Stella had an on-again, off-again romantic relationship, although recently it had been more off than on. But no matter what, he'd always helped her when she needed it.

She needed it *now*.

The sounds of the bulldozer and the large truck that had brought it were almost deafening in the usual quiet of the woods on the mountaintop. It was part of why Stella loved the spot. There were crickets, and bats that swooped down on the wide deck in the back of the cabin. On quiet nights, she could even hear the river murmuring as it went by.

"I'm sorry," she said to Eric. "I should've taken care of this right away when I got back from Chicago. I knew I was going to stay in Sweet Pepper. I should've secured my position before Bob had a chance to do this."

Stella had gone home to Chicago after training the fire brigade, but it had only been to get her things. She'd known she was staying before she went back.

"Spoken like a fire chief."

"Why aren't you upset? I've seen you more upset over the outcome of a game of *Jeopardy* on TV. Can't you do something ghostly?"

"You know my perimeter only extends about fifty feet from the cabin." He shrugged. "Maybe once they move in here closer I can do something. Right now, all I can do is stand here and talk to you. What do you think we should make for the next Sweet Pepper Festival now that this one is all but over?"

"That's a year away. I think we need to fix this problem first."

Stella heard barking and knew Hero, one of the fire brigade's Dalmatians, was outside. He was a large puppy with long legs and a sweet disposition. They were training him, and his mother, Sylvia, to be rescue dogs.

Maybe he could use his cute face and sweet nature to divert Bob and his wrecking machine. She wished it were that easy. Bob didn't seem to be the kind of man who'd care about the puppy, one way or another.

The sound of a police siren also got her attention. Maybe John was here too. She hoped he had good news about Bob's claim on the property.

"Looks like one of your white knights is here to save you." Eric nodded toward the window in the kitchen that faced out from the front of the cabin.

It was John. He was followed by two members of the fire brigade in the Jeep Cherokee the town had bought for the group. Former Sweet Pepper police chief Walt Fenway was there too.

"Don't worry." Stella opened the door. "I won't let anything happen to this place."

As she went out, Hero ran into the cabin. He and Eric had a special relationship. Hero seemed to be able to see and hear Eric. He spent most of his time at the cabin.

Stella ignored Bob and his bulldozer. She ran to John, who was getting out of his police car. Kent Norris and the mayor's son, Bert Wando, were already out of the Jeep Cherokee.

"John! Did you listen to the message I left you? Is there something we can do to stop this?" Stella asked.

"Legally, he can evict a tenant from this property," John said. "But he has to give you ninety days."

John was one of the fire brigade's most valuable members. He had ten years on the police force and was good in emergency situations. His dark brown eyes were steady and serious in his good-looking, square-jawed face.

Stella liked the tiny dimple in his cheek when he smiled. It reflected his sense of humor. She enjoyed John's company, even though they frequently argued over what seemed to be petty things. Some of those arguments had slowed down their budding romance.

"Can you tell him?" she asked. "Bob has seriously lost it over this."

"I can do more than that. Excuse me, Chief." John sauntered over to where Bob was staring at the old cabin.

Kent and Bert joined Stella quickly. She noticed Walt was getting around a little better after a recent injury, but still limping.

"What the hell is going on now?" Walt demanded with his usual fierceness. "Can't a man get any rest?"

Walt was barely five feet tall with a heavy pelt of yellow-white hair that looked like it hadn't seen a comb in years. He was nearing seventy but was still a tough character.

He'd been friends with Eric when the old fire chief was still alive. He liked to visit and talk with Eric, though he couldn't hear or see him. Walt relied on Stella to translate what Eric had to say.

"Thanks for coming," Stella said. "How are you doing? I haven't seen you in a while."

"I knew I should run for police chief again," Walt grunted. "You and Eric are like family to me. If that jackass tries to tear down your home, I'll give him a whack in the head with my cane!"

Walt swung his cane to show her what he meant. Stella caught his arm before he could fall.

"Can he really tear down the cabin?" Bert Wando had recently graduated from high school and started at the community college in Sevierville, the nearest large town to Sweet Pepper.

He'd been with the present fire brigade since it had

started, when he was still the star quarterback for the Sweet
Pepper High School Cougars. He'd hoped to go on to a big
college with an important football program, but his grades
weren't good enough. His skill with a football was heroic for
Sweet Pepper, yet no scouts had offered for him.

Bert had taken it in stride with a maturity that had
impressed Stella. He reminded her a lot of the Dalmatian
puppy—leggy and sweet, cute and good-natured.

"I don't know yet," Stella admitted. "Bob says he can.
John says no."

Kent Norris was a forty-something over-the-road trucker
who drove the fire brigade's pumper-tanker. He was trying
to get rid of the stomach he'd built up from his wife's good
cooking, without much luck. "They're hashing it out over
there. That means there's a gray area."

"Or John is too scared of Bob to put his foot down,"
Walt said. "Where's Don Rogers? He should be up here at
a time like this."

Don Rogers was the Sweet Pepper police chief, and not
exactly Stella's biggest fan. He'd been angry since she'd
first came, not expecting a woman, or someone from outside the community, to take the position.

"You know we don't get along so well," Stella said. "He
might've put Bob up to doing this to get rid of me."

"That shouldn't matter," Walt told her. "He swore an
oath of office, same as I did, to enforce the law. He should
be here."

"It looks like you've got more company, Chief." Kent
glanced at the older Volkswagen Beetle that had chugged
up the mountain road. "The Smittys are here."

The Smittys were Pat and John Smith who ran the *Sweet
Pepper Gazette*, the only newspaper in town. They got out
of their car, both of them with cameras, to find out what
was going on. As usual, they were dressed the same—tan
trench coats, sneakers, and jeans. They were both about the
same height and weight and had gray hair.

Stella was glad to see them. She hadn't thought of calling them, but it was good to have them there. Whatever Bob

chose to do would be recorded and read by a lot of people in town. He might think twice before he did anything completely stupid. He might want to run for reelection again.

"So, what have we got going on up here now?" John squinted at the old cabin. "Somebody gave us a call about the situation. Care to elaborate, Chief Griffin?"

Stella gave them the whole story, from her point of view. The Smittys, both in their mid-fifties, took pictures and nodded. The Smittys absorbed what she had to say and then walked over to where John was still arguing with Bob.

"I think John might have the upper hand now," Kent observed. "He's sending the bulldozer driver back home. If Bob's face turns any redder, he'll explode for sure."

"What's that darn fool doing *now*?" Walt asked.

Stella watched in disbelief as the driver of the bulldozer climbed off the machine and Bob took the controls.

"Hey!" the driver yelled at Bob. "You're not licensed to drive that machine!"

"Get down from there, Bob!" John yelled loud enough to be heard over the noise from the truck and the bulldozer.

"Leave me alone," Bob screamed. "Get out of here. I can take care of this myself."

"Bob is crazy, Chief," Bert said. "I think he's gonna drive the dozer into the cabin."

"Somebody, besides Bob, better do something," Walt muttered.

John moved quickly out of the way as the bright yellow bulldozer began to jerk forward again only a hundred yards or so from the cabin.

"He's gonna do it," Kent said. "He's gonna ram the cabin."

"Shoot him, John," Walt demanded. "Take out your gun and shoot him in the leg!"

The Smittys' cameras were flashing, like paparazzi following a famous movie star. They got as close as they dared when Bob started moving faster toward the cabin.

Stella gritted her teeth, her hands clenched in tight balls. She ran to John's side.

"I don't know what else I can do," he said. "I can arrest

him after it's over, but that won't do much good now. I called Don. He's on his way."

"I understand that Bob's on the council and he owns an important business. You can't just shoot him."

"I'm sorry, Stella."

They all waited for the impact of metal hitting logs. Stella scanned the front windows in the cabin but couldn't see Eric. What would be left of him when the cabin was gone? Would he disappear for good?

The bulldozer was close to the front steps. The frenzied look on Bob's face was frightening. Everyone stood completely still as the heavy scoop blade reached the stairs.

Then the bulldozer shuddered and shut down.

The quiet after that moment was startling. Bob tried again and again to restart the engine. It didn't work. That gave John the opportunity to jump on the dozer and take the keys from him.

"I think that's enough for one day, Mr. Floyd. Come on down now. We don't want this to go any further."

Stella let out a long breath of relief, and her pager went off. There was a fire in Sweet Pepper.

Chapter 2

❝I want that cabin torn down," Bob yelled as John escorted him to the back of his police car. "I want that ghost laid to rest once and for all."

"I'll have to take care of this first," John told Stella. "I'll come out to the fire, if I can."

Stella wanted to know if Eric had stopped the bulldozer. There wasn't time to find out. She was going to have to wait until after the fire brigade had answered the call.

"Do what you have to do," she said to John. "We can handle it."

"Going down with us, Chief?" Kent was already behind the wheel of the Cherokee.

"Yes." She jumped in the front seat beside him. Bert was in the back. "Let's go."

Most of the volunteer firefighters were already getting in their gear by the time Stella and her supporters reached the firehouse at the end of the long road from the cabin. Eric had built the cabin close to the firehouse for his convenience. The fire brigade had been his life, and ultimately, his death.

"The fire is out at Sweet Pepper Lake," Tagger Reamis said when they got inside. He'd been on communications when the call came in.

He was a Vietnam veteran, one of the members of the original fire brigade. Tagger didn't go out on calls, but he was pretty good at communications, now that he'd stopped drinking. "215 Half Moon Road. I think that's old Barney Falk's place at Sunset Beach again."

"This better not be another speed test. I don't care if he used to be the state rep from this area or not. Some of us have better things to do than run after him every month or so," JC Burris said. He was a thin, wiry black man who worked at the Sweet Pepper canning plant. He used to drive a cement truck, which made him perfect for driving the engine.

Stella agreed and knew the rest of the volunteers did too. These people took time out from their daily lives to service the fire and emergency needs of their community. They were passionate about what they did, and they didn't like being played.

Barney Falk had dragged them out to his house several times to gauge their response limits and ask ridiculous questions about what they did and how they did it. He had once been a powerful man, according to everyone else in Sweet Pepper.

To Stella he was just an annoyance.

"I'm with you." Stella put her gear on as she ran out to the engine. She climbed up on the passenger seat and closed the door. "If this is another wild-goose chase, we'll turn the hoses on him."

Everyone who heard her knew she was joking, but they enjoyed the idea. Whether Barney Falk was powerful or not, the volunteers knew the chief was dedicated to a code of conduct.

The rest of the volunteers scrambled into the back of the fire engine. Stella saw Hero running down Firehouse Road from the cabin to turn out for the fire. His mother, Sylvia, barked a greeting to him, and he jumped in the back of the pumper-tanker with her. Volunteers Kimmie and David Spratt welcomed him.

The pumper-tanker followed the engine/ladder truck down the main road into Sweet Pepper. They continued their high rate of speed past dozens of small shops and the town hall. People waved when they saw them go by. Folks in Sweet Pepper and the surrounding areas, who had been left high and dry when the county pulled their fire service, loved the fire brigade. It had meant lower house insurance premiums as well as knowing their emergency needs would be met.

"Looks like they finally got around to paving the road," Stella observed as they started up the steep slope into the Sunset Beach community. The road had been deeply rutted and sparsely graveled, making it difficult to get the two large vehicles into the area where the expensive houses were located.

"Yeah, after you gave them hell at the town council a few times," JC said. "Then they made the rich folks who live out here take care of it."

"Whatever—it's a lot better than it was the first time we came out here."

"I wouldn't have had any problem with it. It was Ricky Junior driving back then. He was good for a young upstart. I've got experience with these babies."

Which was why Stella had asked JC to drive when Ricky Hutchins Jr. had to leave the fire brigade. She'd hated to see Ricky go. He was one of her first volunteers. He was young and a little wild, but he was the best mechanic she'd ever seen. The fire brigade still missed him.

He'd had to quit the fire brigade to help his mother at the family restaurant after his father had gone to prison. It had been a hard time for them. Everyone from Sweet Pepper had done what they could to make it easier on Ricky and his mother. There was only so much to do with a bad situation.

Both the pumper-tanker and the engine/ladder truck rolled smoothly into the heart of the lake community. There were no old-lady gingerbread houses here from a hundred years ago to give the place character, as there were in town. Everything had been built in the last ten years. The houses were new, huge, and modern—several of them worth millions of dollars.

"Doesn't look like much to me." JC parked the engine on the street in front of Falk's home. "I think that old dude is bored or something. Maybe you can get an injunction against him. I left my little girl's birthday party to be here, Chief."

"We need to get out and take a look around." Stella got on the radio with Tagger. "Who called in the fire?"

Before Tagger could answer, a loud explosion ripped through the house that stood three stories above the lake. The entire area shuddered. Flames and debris were everywhere. The house became an inferno in an instant.

"Get the pumper in back," Stella yelled at Kent Norris, who was driving that vehicle. "We have to get water on the house from all sides. Tagger, call the police and get someone out here."

"Chief?" Tagger waited for her response. "The phone call wasn't routed through 911. I have the cell number on the computer."

"Hold on to it. This may be arson."

JC already had the engine pulled up to the house. He jumped out to help Kimmie and David Spratt, Royce Pope, and Allen Wise get the hose attached to the shiny new fire hydrant.

"Where do you want us, Chief?" Bert Wando asked, pry ax in hand, face mask pulled down. "I can go inside and look for Mr. Falk."

Stella thought a lot of Bert, but she didn't think he was ready to go into the house. He'd missed a lot of training the last few months of high school. "Not this one. This is bad. Get the thermal imager. Let's see what's going on in there."

She was missing some of her most experienced volunteers. Ricky was gone. John wasn't there. Banyin Watts was too pregnant to work. Petey Stanze had been injured in another fire.

Stella was going to have to take Allen and Kent into the house. The two men were hard workers. She needed JC and Royce's strength and calm outside to make sure the hoses remained stable enough to fight the fire.

Bert was disappointed but didn't disagree with her. He got the used imager the town had recently purchased and brought it to her as she directed the hoses. Kimmie and David put the hydraulic ladder up to the third floor.

"We have to get the roof vented," Stella told them. "Allen and Kent, I need you inside. Put on your packs and let's go."

The fire was so hot that it had scorched the new trees and grass around the house. Debris had totaled the Mercedes that was parked in the drive. People from other houses in the neighborhood walked up to see what was going on. Drivers stopped to point and stare from their cars as the fire ripped through what was left of the structure.

Stella looked at the thermal imager. It was clear to see where the heart of the fire was located, but not if there was anyone inside. "I can't tell if Barney Falk is in there."

"We're gonna look for him?" Allen asked with some trepidation in his voice. He wasn't used to being backup for the core members who were gone.

"That's what we have to do," Stella said. "Are you okay with that?"

Allen frowned. "I'll give it my best shot, Chief."

"That's all any of us can do."

"We're not looking for a *living* person in there, right?" Kent grabbed his pry ax.

"I don't know," she confided. "There's always a chance. Watch your backs. Keep your masks on, and be careful going in. I'll be right behind you. When I say get out, get out fast."

Stella got her gear set up and gave last-minute instructions to everyone before she joined Kent and Allen in the inferno.

So much damage had been done to the interior of the

house from the explosion and the fire that followed that it was difficult to tell what rooms they were walking through. It looked like a foyer and an office of some sort. The heat and sound of the flames made it hard to concentrate.

They wouldn't have much time before the house came down. They were going to have to split up to search the three floors, if they had a chance of finding anyone alive. While she wanted to protect Allen and Kent, she needed each of them to walk through the flame and smoke alone.

"I'll take the second floor." She knew the fire was hottest there. "Kent, you take the top floor. Allen—the ground floor. Look for survivors. That's it. Make a quick sweep of the place and get out, whether you hear from me or not. Just get back outside."

The two men nodded, grim faced, their eyes filled with fear. They each held their pry ax in a death grip before them.

Stella ran up the burning stairs to the second floor. If she hadn't turned away, she would have lost her nerve as she looked at them. Everyone was scared, even her. It was different back home, where she'd been a firefighter for ten years. Chief Henry had made these decisions. He'd been responsible for what happened to the men and women who worked for him.

Here in Sweet Pepper, that was her job. It was the hardest thing she'd ever done.

Kent quickly used the radio to report from the top floor. "Just melting piles of furniture, Chief. The windows are gone or bubbling. No sign of anyone up here."

Stella liked and trusted Kent. Even though his inspection seemed fast, she knew he'd thoroughly checked the area.

She could hear her volunteers on the roof trying to vent the fire to allow some of the heat to escape through the roof. What went out through the roof wouldn't blow back on them.

"Okay. Go outside."

There was a huge hole in what was left of one of the rooms on the second floor. Whatever had caused the blast had destroyed everything around it. The rest of the floor wouldn't last much longer.

Stella hoped Barney Falk wasn't home when this happened. If he was, she had no doubt that they would find his body later.

As she descended what was left of the stairs, Royce called her on the radio. "Chief, we're out of water in back. The pumper is empty. I thought maybe we could stretch a hose down to the lake and draw from it, but it's too far. I'm sorry."

"Not your fault," she told him. "Get the equipment out front. See what you can do to help everyone else."

"The police are here," Kimmie called in. "They want to know if we have survivors. Do we need paramedics or the coroner?"

"Tell them to take care of the bystanders and call both. We don't know yet what we're dealing with," Stella replied.

"Chief!" JC's voice sounded frantic. "I think the left side of the house is coming down!"

"Get everyone out of that area. Work where it's safe. We'll be out soon." Stella ended up on the ground floor with Allen.

"No sign of Mr. Falk so far, Chief," he said.

"I don't think we can search much longer."

The left side of the house began falling backward, toward the outside, taking what looked like a fireplace and a whole room with it. Stella turned to run, but Allen was gone.

She called out to him on the radio and finally found him on his knees by what was left of a human being. The hole from the second floor, where the blast had gone off, appeared to have dropped the body into what was left of the kitchen.

Allen was desperately trying to give CPR to the dead victim, who had been burned beyond recognition in the fire.

He'd removed his helmet and face mask. "Chief." He was coughing and trying to catch his breath. "I can't get him up to carry him outside. I thought I could help him here. I can't do that either."

"Get your gear on now, Allen, and get out of here. You can't help him."

"Chief—"

"Get out now!" she yelled at him.

He was crying as he put on his hat and mask. He ran outside and Kent got him away from the house.

Stella knew Allen had never witnessed anything like this before. They'd only had two fires with fatalities in the time she'd been there. Neither of them had been this bad. He wasn't prepared, not that anyone could be. This was beyond anything she could have explained to them. Only their tough training got them through it. There was just a moment or two left to get the victim outside before there was nothing remaining of the house.

Kent put his mask back on and grabbed a rug from the front porch. He and Stella wrapped the rug around the victim and got him outside.

"The roof is going! The roof is going!" JC's words exploded over the radio.

As Kent and Stella reached a safe place away from the house, JC's prediction came true. The large red roof folded into what remained of the structure.

The sound echoed across the lake and into the heavy forest that surrounded the community. Debris and ashes flew up into the bright blue sky. The image of the fire reflected on the still waters of the lake behind the house.

"Anybody live through that, Chief Griffin?" the lead EMS tech asked.

Stella shook her head. "We have a victim. Not sure who it is. We need the coroner. I hope no one else was inside."

Kimmie, who was a bit timid, tapped Stella lightly on the shoulder. "Chief? I think Allen needs help. I tried to get him to take some oxygen. He won't."

Stella turned toward Allen. He was sitting on the ground with Sylvia and Hero beside him. Hero's training to be part of the fire brigade had included gently taking a victim's hand in his mouth and guiding him to safety. He was trying his best to help Allen to his feet, but the stubborn volunteer was refusing.

"Allen?" Stella shouted as she walked toward him. "Get over there and get some oxygen. You'll ruin your lungs. I don't know how long your mask was off, but it only takes a few minutes to cause permanent breathing problems."

Tears were running down his face from his red eyes—another issue. His eyes had been exposed to the heat and chemicals in the house. They needed to be washed out.

"I can't, Chief," he told her. "I keep thinking about that man in there. Do you think it was Barney Falk?"

His voice was hoarse and gritty. Stella wanted to be sympathetic to his first experience finding a fire victim, but that would have to come later. Right now, he needed treatment.

She got him to his feet. "You need help. We take care of the survivors first, right? Then we deal with everything else."

"Right, Chief." He coughed as though his lungs were coming out of his chest. "Thanks."

Chapter 3

~~~~~~~~

The cleanup took hours. There was only a burned-out shell left of the house. The fire brigade had put up crime scene tape around the perimeter, and the Sweet Pepper police added caution tape for good measure.

The hot spots had already been hosed down by the time the coroner had finally arrived. Stella had sent the pumper and her crew back to the firehouse. The engine crew was getting ready to leave as well. There was nothing else they could do with the crime scene until an investigation could be launched.

"We've done what we could," Stella told her volunteers. "Good job, everyone. Let's go home."

Two part-time Sweet Pepper police officers were assigned to stay at the site to keep anyone from getting hurt. Stella hadn't seen John. She had to assume dealing with Bob Floyd had taken longer than he'd thought.

"I'll need a report from you on this, Chief Griffin," coroner Judd Streeter remarked as he walked by. He was a round, gray-haired man who seemed more likely to play

Santa in a department store than to examine dead bodies. "Sooner rather than later."

"I'll have it on your desk tomorrow." Stella was exhausted and didn't stop to talk. She climbed up into the front seat of the engine. Hero shot in before she could sit down. He claimed his rightful seat between Stella and JC.

"That was a bear," JC said as he drove back toward the firehouse. "You think Allen will be okay?"

"I hope so," she replied. "You never know until something happens that you can't get over."

"You ever have a time like that?"

She nodded. "I had to take a few days. I was lucky. I had my father, grandfather, and assorted uncles who'd all experienced the same thing. When you come from a family of firefighters, you know the ins and outs."

"I suppose so."

"We'll have to be Allen's family on this. Only people who do the job really understand. We have to stick together."

He agreed. They didn't speak again as they returned to the firehouse, where the pumper crew had finished putting away their gear and cleaning the truck. They'd already refilled their water tank from the big cistern behind the firehouse.

No one left the firehouse even though they'd finished their responsibilities. Some stayed to take a shower. Others had something to eat and drink, or talked to Tagger.

Stella knew they were waiting for words of wisdom and comfort from her. She remembered doing the same thing with Chief Henry back home.

Bad things happened. She wished it could be as easy as that. She didn't think of herself as wise or profound. She just did her job.

Being chief required more. She'd signed the contract. She had to find some words of comfort for what her volunteers had gone through.

Sylvia and Hero were running around the firehouse, barking and carrying on. Everyone was watching their antics and laughing. Stella laughed at them too as she went into the kitchen area.

As soon as they saw her, Kimmie and David, their light brown hair almost meshing, pulled the two dogs close and kept them quiet. All the laughter and talking abruptly stopped. The volunteers stared at her, waiting for what she had to say that would help make sense of what they'd been through.

Allen had breathed in some oxygen and had his eyes rinsed—he still looked rough. He got to his feet and apologized to the whole crew. "I don't know what happened back there. I just lost it."

"There's nothing to apologize for," Stella said. "Most of you haven't been in the position of finding a victim yet. I can tell you now—it never gets easier. It's part of our job, but no one needs to apologize for falling apart. You wouldn't be human if you didn't."

Allen was usually the one who kept everyone's spirits up with his funny jokes about his life as a barber in Sweet Pepper. Now he bowed his head and asked permission to say a prayer for the person they'd taken out of the burning house.

Stella was good with that. It was the best way to end her speech about finding victims. They'd each have a turn at that, the hardest part of their job, if they stayed with the fire brigade. It was inevitable.

When Allen was done with his prayer, Tagger asked, "Do you think it was Barney Falk?"

She hated to speculate. "I don't know for sure. We won't know until we have word from the coroner. The body was close to the blast and badly burned."

"I think it was old Barney." Allen's voice was quiet with despair. "You know, he did a lot of good things for this town when he was our state rep. He brought in jobs and found money to do upgrades at the pepper factory."

"He paved a lot of roads and helped get us started in the tourist business too," Tagger added. "He was a good man. He'll be missed."

"Let's make sure *our* ID of the body doesn't go beyond this room," Stella warned them. "I don't want to see a headline in the paper tomorrow about firefighters saying it was Barney Falk that died. Everyone understand?"

They all agreed.

"What was that explosion, Chief?" David asked. "Was it something already in the house that went off from the fire, or was it a bomb?"

"I don't know," Stella admitted. "We won't know until the investigation is complete."

The group began to break up. Tagger was going off his communications shift, and Allen was scheduled to stay in his place.

"Are you sure you're up for it?" Stella asked Allen.

"I'm as good here as I would be at home watching TV," Allen replied. "Thanks, Chief."

She let him stay. "I want to remind everyone that the town bought those dress uniforms for us to wear at Chief Eric Gamlyn's memorial tomorrow at noon. I hope you can all attend. It's part of being a firefighter. We honor the ones we lose."

Everyone agreed to try to be at the cemetery the next day when a new statue, dedicated to Eric, was being unveiled. The mayor was going to say a few words, and the town council would be there. She'd received a reminder text about it on her phone while they'd been fighting the fire.

It was good, she thought, opening the door to the Cherokee and waiting for Hero to jump in. She hoped it would allow everyone to see Eric more as a man and less as a folk hero. Not that she had anything against all the crazy stories about him. He'd saved her life. He was a hero in her books.

But she thought they should respect that he gave his life for the town too. He really was only a man, but he'd given everything he had to make Sweet Pepper a better place.

Stella drove up Firehouse Road, wondering again if Eric had stopped the bulldozer, and if everything was going to work out to save the cabin. Bob was certainly within his legal rights to tear down the cabin. She wanted to make sure all avenues to prevent that had been explored before she gave up.

For tonight, it was just nice to go home. She may have grown up in Chicago, but Sweet Pepper had her heart now.

It had only been a fluke that had brought her here. She'd been injured and had a falling-out with her boyfriend. The ad she'd seen in the station newsletter in Chicago, asking for an experienced firefighter to train the new fire brigade, had seemed like the perfect opportunity to get away for a few months.

Coming to Sweet Pepper had definitely taken her mind off her problems—and added several more she hadn't expected. But for good or bad, she was now the fire chief. Sweet Pepper was her home, and she planned to keep living in Eric's cabin.

Stella parked the Cherokee outside the cabin next to her Harley. The large truck, and the bulldozer it had brought, were gone. She hoped it was a good sign.

The porch light was on. Eric always turned it on when she left. It was the first of many clues that had led her to believe that something strange was going on when she'd first come here. She'd thought it was a prank at first, not willing to believe people were right about the cabin being haunted.

The door was open, and the smell of something wonderful cooking wafted into the evening air.

Hero ran in, almost knocking her down to get inside first. He barked and jumped at Eric, as he always did.

"You're hungry, aren't you?" Eric asked the puppy who twirled around and kept barking. "That's what I thought."

It was still amazing to Stella that not only did she live with a forty-year-old ghost, he could cook. She had to buy groceries every week. On the bright side, it saved her from eating junk food all the time.

"Whatever that is smells really good." She shut the door. "I'm starving."

"Help yourself," Eric said as he fed Hero. "It's rice with almonds, vegetables, and peppers."

"Of course. Doesn't everything have peppers in it?"

Eric sort of hovered in the small area around the rough-hewn wood table where Stella ate and kept her laptop. The cabin wasn't large, though it had a small second story that was used for storage.

It still looked like an old hunting lodge, made of large, smooth logs that were stained a light brown color. There were three big rooms—living room, kitchen, and bedroom—with a large stone fireplace.

She'd managed to get rid of most of the deer antlers that had been everywhere when she'd arrived. They'd been used as cup holders in the kitchen and as lamps on the tables Eric had made.

Now there was only the ceiling light fixture in the living room, made from huge antlers. Eric really loved that piece, willing to compromise on her other changes if he could keep it.

The living room had a large brown leather sofa and matching chair with colorful Native American rugs and prints. The single bedroom had an oversized log bed in it with two dressers and a side table.

Tall windows overlooked the porch in back, the Little Pigeon River running by hundreds of yards below. The Smoky Mountains rose up beyond the river, their majestic face changing with each passing hour.

Stella loved sitting on the porch. The town had even put in a hot tub for her.

"What happened with the fire?" he asked.

"We had a victim. It was probably Barney Falk."

"That's what I was afraid of when I heard the address." Eric monitored police and fire calls. "He was a good man. He did a lot for this area. He was too filled with his power and ego at the end, but he did a good job for a long time."

Stella complimented the rice. It was delicious. Too bad ghosts didn't eat. "He was one of the old guard, according to my grandfather. He said Barney was more dangerous than anyone else in Sweet Pepper."

"Ben Carson should know. He's as dangerous as Barney. Maybe a little worse."

One of the many surprises waiting for Stella in Sweet Pepper had been finding out that her mother's family was from that area. Her mother, Barbara Griffin, had never told anyone that she was a pepper heiress from Tennessee—at least not until Stella had already arrived there.

Stella had gone in blind. Her mother had called it not prejudicing her opinion against her millionaire grandfather. Ben Carson owned a significant part of the town, and all of the Sweet Pepper canning factory operations. He lived on a large estate a few miles away. Stella had found out quickly that almost everyone feared him—some actively hated him.

"Do you think someone got angry enough to kill Barney?" Eric asked.

She told him about the blast at Barney's house. "It may have been a bomb."

Chapter 4

"I think it's possible," Eric said. "I hope you can figure out who's responsible. No matter what Barney did, he shouldn't have died that way."

"I know. I'm a little nervous about doing the investigation on this. I'm not really qualified. I could put what I know about bombs in my pocket. There's bound to be fallout from this. He was an important man in the state."

"You'll be fine," he reassured her. "There's no one else. You'll have to do the best you can. You could check with Ben first and make sure he isn't responsible."

"I don't know why you and John are so against him. He's been as good to this town as Barney Falk! He set up the canning operation, which employs most of the people here. He started building the vineyard. I haven't seen him do anything but work for the town since I've been here."

"Maybe it's because he knows you're watching him."

This wasn't a topic they could agree on. Stella knew that. Sometimes it enraged her, and she got into the old argument again anyway. But not tonight.

"Your memorial is tomorrow," she reminded him, changing the subject.

"You'll forgive me if I don't attend."

"I'll take pictures for you. There should be a good turnout."

"Thanks. At least since you've been here, I know what's going on outside the cabin. Before that, well, let's just say CNN doesn't have much information about Sweet Pepper."

Stella put her plate and glass in the sink and sat in the comfortable brown leather chair near the fireplace, slinging one leg over the arm. "Did you stop the bulldozer?"

"No. I didn't have to. After everyone left, the driver was looking at it. It was out of fuel. He was cursing his partner, so I guess that's what happened."

"It was a close call. Do you think you *could've* stopped it before it took out the cabin?"

He shrugged. "I don't know. I'm not sure how strong my 'ghostly powers,' as you call them, are. I've never put them to the test. I hope I don't have to. Did you hear anything from the police about Bob?"

"No. John never made it to the fire. I don't know what happened."

"Is there anything that can be done about it?"

"I'm going to find a lawyer. I noticed Hugh Morton is next door to the town hall. I was thinking about asking him."

"You know he's the town attorney, right?" Eric hovered toward the laptop she'd left sitting open on the table. "He went to school with Bob, Mayor Wando, and Nay Albert. They're all still chummy."

"Did you go to school with them too?"

"Part of the time. I left home before I finished high school." He'd already started looking in the area Yellow Pages online for a lawyer. He'd become well acquainted with the Internet.

"No way! You didn't finish high school? What happened?"

"My father died, and I had to get a job to support my family. I was the oldest son. That's what I was supposed to do."

"I guess it doesn't matter. You're famous anyway."

"It was a different time, Stella. A lot of young people around here dropped out to go to work. Very few went to college. I was lucky—I left Sweet Pepper. That was an education in itself."

"Yeah, that's right. You worked as a lumberjack up north, didn't you? That's what your legends say, anyway."

"I went up to Canada and did some work as a lumberjack. I also did some gold mining, and worked as a brakeman on a train. I learned to do a little of everything before I came back here. I was glad for it."

"So you're self-taught. You were a good fire chief, besides building the cabin and the firehouse and starting the fire brigade. What made you decide to start the first fire brigade?"

He looked at her over the top of the laptop screen. "Are you saying a few words on my behalf tomorrow? You're usually not all that interested in my past."

"Yes," she admitted. "I thought someone else, someone who actually *knew* you when you were alive, would want to do it. Instead, they passed it to me with the lame excuse about me being the fire chief."

"That makes sense to me. I'd rather have you talk about me."

"So why the fire brigade?"

"Well, there was a loose group of men who did the work before the fire brigade. They never practiced and had no real firefighting equipment. When someone called to tell them there was a fire, they got in their trucks and met at the location."

Stella was amazed. "You're not talking about a bucket brigade, are you? What was the population of Sweet Pepper back then?"

"It was more like the garden hose brigade. All the men had really long garden hoses. They brought them along and attached them to nearby houses when they got to the scene so they could put out the fire."

"This sounds like the kind of stuff my great-grandfather

back in Chicago talked about when I was growing up. He was with the fire department back in the 1930s. Were you part of the garden hose brigade?"

"Yes. When I got back home and found out about it, I joined. I had a big black hose that I kept in the back of my pickup for emergencies. We had CB radios back then to get in touch with one another."

"Any good stories you'd like to share?"

He thought about it and smiled. "The best story might be the time I went to answer a call and there was a six-foot black snake wound around my black garden hose. I had picked up the whole thing and taken it to the closest open spigot I could find. That's when I noticed that part of my hose was moving and hissing."

Stella shuddered. She hated snakes, and really most wildlife. Eric had taught her to appreciate a few of them—owls, bats, and deer. She couldn't get into snakes or southern scorpions. They were right up there with large, hairy spiders in her book. He, and most of the members of the fire brigade, teased her about being a city girl because of it.

"I'm going to look at hoses in a whole new way," she promised. "Anyway, don't worry. I'll do a good job talking about you. I wish I could mention that you saved my life too. I know everyone from Sweet Pepper would believe me. But I don't know if I want to explain it to the local TV station."

He looked up again, excitement in his bright blue eyes. "You didn't say it was going to be on *TV*. Find out what channel. I'd like to see it."

Stella agreed to do that.

"Someone's here to see you," Eric said. "John Trump might have some information on what happened with Bob. Take the kissing, if there is any, outside please."

John's rap at the kitchen door made it open for him. "You know, Chief, you really need to get that fixed. The door shouldn't open because someone knocks on it."

She shrugged. "It's not the door. You know this place is haunted."

He took off his gray police hat. "Know it? I'm the one who first told *you*. But I don't think the door has anything to do with the ghost."

"Coffee?" she asked.

"I believe I'll have one of your Cokes, if you have an extra. You've gotten me hooked on the things. There must be ten cases of them at the firehouse."

"I don't like to run out." She took two cans of Coke from the refrigerator.

"That stuff is addictive," Eric commented. "Coffee's better for you. It's natural."

Stella paused a moment, as she always did when Eric spoke and someone else was present. She always expected other people to hear him too. It had never happened, but she was always surprised by it.

When John didn't ask who else was speaking, she went on. "I hope you have some good news for me about the cabin."

They both sat on the brown leather sofa that was worn as smooth as butter from years of use. It had belonged to Eric, as had the rest of the furniture in the cabin. Stella hadn't brought any of her furniture back from Chicago when she'd decided to settle here.

"I suppose it all depends on what you think is good news," John said. "I was able to charge Bob Floyd with disorderly conduct. Anyone else I would've charged with assault on an officer too. He took a few swings at me, but that's not gonna stick."

Stella digested his words. "So he owns the property?"

"He signed the papers with the real estate company yesterday. You know the town has been trying to sell the land and the cabin. No one was sure if you were coming back from Chicago."

"I know. I didn't think about it. Everyone's told me that it's been for sale or rent for years with no takers."

"He'll have to give you ninety days to get your stuff out. You've got that long to buy it from him, I guess. Like I said—good news and bad news."

She sipped her Coke, thinking about it. "Can't the town

council change their mind about selling the property since I'm staying on as fire chief?"

"Your guess would be as good as mine. I suppose it might be possible, but don't forget that Nay Albert will vote with Bob. Probably the mayor will too. You might be able to win over Willy Jenkins and Danielle Peterson. That still puts you short on votes."

Stella thought it was possible that Mayor Wando might be willing to listen to her argument about selling her the log cabin. He liked to do whatever he could to keep the fire brigade happy. The other two council members, Willy and Danielle, might be convinced to vote her way.

Willy Jenkins owned Beau's Bar and Grill. They were sort of friendly. Danielle Peterson was a retired schoolteacher from Nashville who would definitely side with Stella. Her biggest problem with small-town life was a lack of services. She loved the fire brigade.

"It's worth a try."

John scanned the small cabin. "I can't figure why you care if you stay here. I know it's close to the firehouse, but there are newer, nicer houses just as close. Wouldn't you rather live somewhere more modern? I'm sure the town would help you with that."

A cool breeze swept through the cabin, making the antler chandelier sway and papers fall to the floor from the table. There were no windows or doors open.

"Tell him to mind his own business," Eric said.

"I like it here." She ignored her roommate's outburst of "ghostly power." "It's quaint, and sturdy."

John shrugged. "It could use something to keep the draft out. I think I've heard you complain about the shower always running low on hot water too."

"Well, a few repairs here and there." Stella wanted to change the subject before Eric showed off again.

"Anyway, that's what you're up against. You could always ask your grandfather to intervene. I'm sure he'd be able to persuade Bob to sell you the place. I don't like to think what you'd have to promise him for the favor. Or maybe the old man asked Bob to take care of the problem for him. He's wanted you to move into the mansion with him since you got here."

Stella knew she had to consider the source. John hated her grandfather. He blamed his alcoholic father's suicide on Ben Carson. If John were able to see and talk to Eric, they would have a field day talking crap about him.

"Thanks for the information. I'm going to consult a lawyer," she said.

"A lawyer who doesn't live in Sweet Pepper?" Eric snorted.

She ignored him. She'd gotten good at ignoring him around other people.

"Not to change the subject," John said, "but I hear you found a dead man out at the fire today. Sounds like it was Barney Falk."

"Did you hear that from Chief Rogers, or Judd Streeter?"

"Neither one. It's a logical guess."

"Then let me repeat what I told everyone else at the firehouse today," she said. "We don't comment on this type of thing until the coroner has released his findings."

John smiled in the slow and sexy way that Stella liked, his dimple appearing to enchant her. "There's only one problem with that right now. When I'm in this uniform, I don't work for *you*. You can't tell me what to do."

"Well, Officer Trump, I won't forget your insolence." She grinned. "You could try to persuade me to feel otherwise. I'm open to your best shot."

It felt like their on-again, off-again romantic relationship might be on-again. Stella was never quite sure with him. He could kiss her until the room spun around them one minute, and leave her the next with a scathing reminder that she was part of the Carson family.

Sometimes it was an exciting game to play. Other times, it was annoying. He wasn't the only man in Sweet Pepper that she'd dated, but he was the only one she was really interested in so far.

"Oh brother." Eric groaned. It sounded like the wind blowing through the eaves during a storm. "Didn't I ask you to take that stuff somewhere else?"

John leaned closer to her. "I can be pretty persuasive when I need to be."

As their lips met, there was a loud knocking at the front door.

Stella couldn't see Eric, so she glared at everything around her. He usually chose to be invisible when he was being obnoxious.

"It's not me," Eric said. "You have another visitor. Maybe you'd like to flirt with Walt for a while."

Before she could get up and let the former police chief in, Eric opened the door for him. John sprang up from the sofa. He swallowed half of his Coke at one time and choked a little, coughing and sputtering as Walt came in.

"Glad to see you're here, John." Walt hobbled to the cabinet and got everything he needed to start a pot of coffee. "Have I got some news for both of you."

Chapter 5

~~~~~~~~~~~~~

While the coffee was brewing, the three of them sat at the kitchen table. Eric was sitting on the stairs to the second floor behind them.

"I heard on the way over that the coroner made it official." Walt's eyes were bright with excitement. He loved to gossip. "Judd said the body the fire brigade recovered out at the lake is Barney Falk. I've been hearing rumors about it all day. I guess they were true."

Stella shook her head. "They better not have come from my volunteers."

"They could've come from anyone from the police to the medics." Walt shrugged as he started to get up for his coffee when it was done perking. "What I can't figure is why you didn't call me, Stella. I thought we were friends."

"Stay there. I'll get the coffee." She put her hand on his shoulder. "You're still having a hard time getting around."

"I'm doing just fine. Don't try to change the subject. You're the fire chief. You knew who you'd pulled out of that house."

Stella poured coffee into a mug that was shaped like a

deer head. It had been Eric's mug when he'd been alive. Walt had told her that he and Eric had sat around this same table many times drinking coffee and discussing the problems in Sweet Pepper.

"I can't give out that kind of information." She brought the coffee back to him. "That's *because* I'm the fire chief. We're not supposed to spread gossip and rumors. We wait for the facts."

Walt laughed. "Nobody ever told *me* that when I was the police chief. I got no complaints. People wanted to know what was going on. I told them."

John agreed with Stella. "The chief has to be careful in her position. There are lawsuits and such now. Things weren't that way when you were police chief. That's why Don keeps such a tight lid on what's going on in town."

"Sounds like hogwash to me." Walt held up his cup as though he were toasting someone before he slurped some of the hot brew from it. "Here's to you, buddy."

John looked around. "Are you talking to me?" He picked up his can of Coke.

"Don't be stupid. I'm talking to Eric. It's rude to ignore him."

"Are you telling me you can *see* Eric Gamlyn?" John's disbelief mingled with astonishment in his tone.

"I can't see him or talk to him," Walt said. "But I *know* he's here."

Stella took a big gulp of Coke, hoping Walt would drop the subject before it went any further. Then he dropped the bomb she'd wanted to keep from exploding.

"It doesn't matter, 'cause Stella can see him and hear him too." Walt nodded at her with a big grin on his thin face.

She suddenly had the feeling that this was payback for not calling him after the fire. He knew she didn't want to discuss Eric with John.

John's head swiveled to face her. "Is that true? Can you see the ghost right now?"

"No." That was true. She had her back to the stairs. He'd been sitting there when she'd come back with Walt's coffee. She didn't have eyes in the back of her head. He might not be there now.

Maybe it was a technicality, but she didn't want to be known as the fire chief who saw ghosts.

John looked relieved.

Walt wouldn't let her get away that easy. "We have long discussions here, the three of us. Eric talks to Stella. She tells me what he says and then I answer. He's listening right now. I've learned a bit about the afterlife since Stella got here. Did you know you need your own place to haunt? I was grateful when my cabin was rebuilt after the fire since Eric said you need your space."

Stella fumed. Walt winked at her and slurped his coffee.

John got up and walked around the room. "Seriously? We've all told stories about Eric Gamlyn's ghost. Can you really tell if he's here, Chief?"

She wished someone else would arrive unexpectedly. She didn't want to lie to John. He might find out on his own someday. And like he said, everyone in Sweet Pepper knew the cabin was haunted.

It had taken her a while to deal with it. She wasn't comfortable discussing her ghost with many people. John didn't seem like someone she wanted to have the conversation with.

"Walt is pulling your leg." She kicked Walt's good leg under the table. "Aren't you, Walt?"

The old police chief guffawed. "Gotcha!"

John appeared to be relieved. "You did."

Walt asked Stella to pour him another cup of coffee. "This thing about Barney is bothersome. I heard someone with the fire department thought it wasn't an accident."

"What do you have to do around here to keep gossip from spreading?" Stella asked as she got the coffee and sat back down.

"That's not gonna happen," Eric said. "It's as true now as it was when I was a kid."

John and Walt were discussing who would want to kill Barney, not hearing Eric's remark.

"You know Barney made a pile of enemies," Walt said. "People in politics don't make many friends."

John agreed. "Don said a special arson investigator is being appointed from the state. Barney was well-known. The state doesn't like it when one of their former representatives gets blown up."

That made Stella angry. "I didn't say he was blown up. There was a small explosion when we first got to his house. It could've been anything—aerosol cans, butane lighters, or hundreds of other things that people keep in their homes."

"I thought you'd be glad to hear someone else had to investigate that pile of rubble," John said. "This way the burden of proof won't fall on you."

"That's true," she agreed. "What I don't like is that something as important as this is already fruit for the grapevine."

"Relax," Walt said. "I doubt if it was any of your people. They follow you like zombies. I can't imagine one of them going against you."

Stella raised one red brow. "Zombies? Really?"

"They love you. That's all I'm saying." Walt sipped his coffee. "Back me up here, John."

"I love her." John grinned and then grew flustered when he realized what he'd said. "I mean, we all love Stella—the chief—you know what I mean."

"Thanks." Stella smiled, wondering what he actually meant.

"Anyway," John began again, "the special investigator will be here with a Tennessee Bureau of Investigation team tomorrow. We're to keep the site off-limits until they get here. I can't tell you how *excited* Don is about having a state investigator here."

Walt laughed loudly. "I can imagine. I was always glad to see the back of those people. Half of the time, they don't know their heads from a hole in the ground."

"I'm looking forward to working with a real arson investigator," Stella said. "Maybe I can pick up a few things for the next arson we have that's not important enough to warrant that kind of attention."

John got to his feet and put on his hat. "I have to go. My shift is over in an hour—unless Richardson doesn't make it in. I'll see you all later."

When John had pulled his patrol car out of the driveway, Walt raised his cup again. "That was pretty funny, huh, Eric?"

Eric agreed. "The look on Stella's face was priceless."

Walt rubbed his leg. "She darn near crippled me."

"I couldn't believe you said that to John." Stella put their empty Coke cans in the trash. "You know how he feels about me."

"Yeah. He loves you." Eric came down the stairs and sat in the chair John had vacated.

"Did he say something?" Walt peered around the room.

"We're ignoring him until he has something useful to say," Stella said.

"I know what he said," Walt guessed. "It was all about John loving you, right?"

"Can we move on to another subject?" Stella asked them both.

"How about what happened *here* today?" Walt asked. "What are you going to do to keep Bob Floyd from knocking down the cabin?"

Stella told him her thoughts and shared what Eric had added to them. "I don't know what we can do if the town council won't reconsider and agree to sell me the land and cabin. John said I should move someplace more modern."

"Don't worry, buddy," Walt said to Eric. "I'm old. I've lived a good life. I'll go to Bob's house with some C-4 strapped under my shirt. There'll be another arson investigation, but at least that snake won't take your home away."

"I think we can come up with a less violent plan," Stella said. "I'll talk to a lawyer and to the town council at their meeting tonight. We'll figure a way around this."

Walt wasn't entirely convinced. He said he'd be at the meeting too. He departed a short time later, leaving an invitation for Stella to visit him. "Wish you could be there too, buddy. It's not fair that you have to be trapped here all the time."

Eric agreed. He and Stella watched Walt leave in his old pickup.

"I have to leave early for the town council meeting," she told him. "I've been selected to help with the Sweet Pepper Festival planning committee for next year. We're getting together at the café before the meeting. I can't believe this year's festival is barely over and they're planning for next year."

"Lucky *you*. I always managed to avoid those situations. It's one thing to cook something for the recipe contest. It's another to hang around with all those crazy festival people. From what you've told me, I think the same people from forty years ago are still putting the festival together today."

Stella smiled. "That's something I wish you could experience for yourself. Maybe I'll invite the planning committee to have a meeting here."

"As long as you don't expect me to be a welcoming host." Eric had an evil grin on his handsome face. "I have been known to play a prank or two in my time."

"You mean like that sudden breeze when John was here? You and I are going to have a talk about interfering in my personal life."

"I'm available twenty-four/seven for your convenience."

"You're watching too much TV," she remarked with a laugh. "I'm changing clothes now. Don't come in the bedroom unless you want me to start playing some pranks on *you*."

Eric wasn't good with boundaries. He'd been a little better respecting her privacy since she'd decided to stay there permanently. She left him watching *Jeopardy* and closed the bedroom door behind her.

Was John serious when he said he loved her? Stella went over his words in her mind as she changed her jeans and fire brigade T-shirt for a calf-length brown skirt, knee-high boots, and a brown top.

She studied herself in the tiny bathroom mirror as she pulled her red hair back from her face. She'd gained about a hundred freckles since she'd come to Sweet Pepper. It was warmer here than in Chicago, and she'd spent a lot more time outside, hiking and rafting in the river over the summer.

She still had fewer freckles than her father. She grinned when she thought about his last Skype. He and her mother were still experimenting with that newer form of communication. It was a work in progress, but it had been nice to see their faces.

Stella pulled on one of two black blazers she'd had made with the Sweet Pepper Fire Brigade emblem on the pocket. It was a nice way to dress up a little, without wearing the stiff dress uniform she'd be putting on tomorrow for Eric's memorial. She didn't like the idea of wearing jeans and a fire brigade T-shirt to official meetings.

Eric made a whistling sound—not quite like a living human would make but equivalent—when she came out of the bedroom.

Hero had come inside the cabin while she'd been dressing. His ears perked up, and he made a growling sound when he heard Eric's whistle. He wagged his tail when he saw everything was all right, and went back to sleep on the rug by the hearth.

"I like the jacket. Nice touch. I wouldn't have thought of that. My T-shirt and jeans were good enough for everything."

Stella twirled around, her loose skirt swishing around her long legs. "That's because you're a man. Those clothes were probably all you had in the closet anyway."

"I never put clothes in the closet," he scoffed. "That's what the dresser was for. I kept my hunting and fishing stuff in the closet with my skis and snowshoes. Sometimes I put dirty turnout jackets in there too."

"Like I said." She grabbed her bag. "Don't wait up. I hear these planning meetings can take all night."

"Don't take the Harley out," he warned. "There could be ice later."

She frowned. "I haven't heard anything about that."

"You can't pay attention to the stuff they say on TV.

You have to listen to the birds and watch the animals. It's November. There will be ice later."

Stella didn't argue with him. For all she knew, he was right. Maybe ghosts could tell things about the weather.

She got in the Cherokee and headed down the mountain. There was no ice yet.

Chapter 6

The pepper festival planning board was made up of the same people who ran the festival. They'd probably been planning the festival since Eric's day. Most of them were at least in their fifties. They started planning for the next year's festival when the present festival was barely over.

Bill and Lucinda Waxman were there, of course. Perry Dumont, who owned the local cable TV station, was there, along with his wife, Lacie. Myra Strickland was smiling and presiding over the group. The pepper festival had been started by Myra and her late husband, who'd been the mayor of Sweet Pepper at the time.

The party room in the back of the Sweet Pepper Café on Main Street was brimming when Stella got there. Jill Wando, as the official mistress of ceremonies for the pepper festival this year, greeted Stella as she came in. Her husband, Erskine, was absent because he was the present mayor and was busy getting ready for the council meeting.

"You gave us quite a scare finding poor Barney in his house," Jill told Stella. "I think we're all a little more grateful right now to have the fire brigade with you as chief."

"Thanks." Stella gave up trying to fight the news until it was official. "I'm sorry Mr. Falk couldn't be saved."

Jill's blue eyes widened dramatically. "Well with that bomb exploding and all, what could anyone expect? Come have some punch, Stella. We're glad to have you here tonight."

Stella went willingly to the punch bowl, not even bothering to say that she didn't know if it was a bomb or not yet. There was a variety of Sweet Pepper Café favorites on the buffet, including sweet potato fries, stuffed jalapeños, and sausage biscuits.

Ricky Hutchins Jr. was there, smiling and making sure everyone had a clean plate. His mother and father owned the café, which was a town landmark. He was almost too busy flirting with Foster Waxman to notice Stella. When he did, his blue eyes fixed on her.

"Hey, Chief! It's good to see you. I heard about the fire out at the lake today. Wish I could've been there. Did they get that road fixed yet? Man, I miss being with the fire brigade."

"We miss you too, Ricky," Stella said, and meant it. "We've been spending a fortune on repairs to the pumper's engine."

"Yeah, I hate being stuck here cooking too. You know, I told those mechanics at the shop that they had to treat the engine right. You can't act like she's brand-new. I'm sorry I can't help. With Dad gone, Mom needs me a lot more."

Stella understood that his family needed him more since his father, Ricky Hutchins Sr., had gone to prison. They all hoped his sentence would be reduced on an appeal.

Ricky had been a good firefighter. She hoped this time away from the job wouldn't make him give up on it entirely. She was glad he was still interested.

"I know. Hero misses you too. He doesn't like the way JC drives the engine."

"JC?" Ricky shook his head, the blond curl that was always on his forehead moving back and forth. "He's no driver at all compared to *me*. I'm surprised you even got to the fire today. Don't worry, Chief. I'm coming back. Dad's gonna get his time reduced. Wait and see."

Stella said she hoped that was true, and put some food on a plate before she sat at a table.

"Chief Griffin!" Banyin Watts, the town librarian, was holding a plate of food too. "I'm so glad to see you."

Banyin tried to hug Stella. It was difficult getting close enough over her very pregnant belly. She'd been another good firefighter. She was on leave, awaiting the birth of her child. Banyin was tall and strong. She was calm too, able to assess situations and know what to do. Stella missed her.

"How long is it now?" Stella asked as they sat together at the table.

"Only a few weeks. I don't mind admitting that I'm a little nervous. Being a mother is even scarier than being a firefighter."

"Which you don't have to worry about anymore." Banyin's husband, Jake, sat beside them. Jake was a large man who always dressed like a lumberjack in plaid flannel shirts and suspenders. He was actually a lineman for the power company. "My wife is retiring from the fire brigade."

"Ignore him," Banyin said with a tight smile. "He's always grumpy."

Stella didn't know about the grumpy part, but she knew Jake hadn't wanted Banyin to be a volunteer firefighter in the first place. He'd fought her every step of the way.

"I'm serious about this, Banyin," Jake said. "You're going to be a mother. Women who are mothers don't go into burning buildings. Your days with the fire brigade are up. You can keep your job as a librarian. That's an appropriate job for a woman and a mother."

Stella ate her food and let the couple hash it out. These losses of volunteers were going to have to be addressed. She didn't want to replace Banyin or Ricky, but she'd have to find some new faces and warm bodies if the fire brigade was going to continue its work.

"Well, anyway, the baby isn't here yet." Banyin smiled at Stella. "I don't have to make that decision just now."

The rest of the festival planning meeting went as Stella

had thought it would. Myra made some speeches about this year being the biggest, best festival ever with some quick reports on how much money they'd made and how many people had attended. These were only preliminary and would be discussed at length later.

Elvita Quick and her sister, Theodora Mangrum, told everyone their plans for next year's pepper contest. There would be more categories, and they expected everyone involved with the festival planning board to enter a recipe too.

"We need a lot of recipes because we get so many duplicates that must be disqualified," Elvita explained. "Think new! Think outside the box."

"Or in this case, the pepper," Theodora quipped.

Everyone laughed. The sisters, attired as always in green dresses that almost matched each other, enjoyed the joke. Their bright green hats contained small bird's nests with different colored eggs inside them.

"It takes one heck of a woman to wear a hat with a bird's nest in it," Flo whispered as she took a seat opposite Stella. She owned the bed-and-breakfast in town and had been a friend to Stella since she'd arrived in Sweet Pepper.

Stella agreed. "I wonder if they'll hatch next spring and become birds."

Flo giggled, her blueberry-colored eyes mirroring her mischievous nature. She wore her poufy blond hair with a red bow in it. The bow matched her bright red dress.

"Heard about Barney, bless his soul," Flo said. "That's no way for a great man like him to die."

"I didn't know him well," Stella said tactfully. "I guess it's no way for *any* man to die."

"I heard you needed water at the back of the house during the fire." Flo took a folded picture from her pocket. "I was thinking you should ask the town council for money to buy a fireboat. I'm sure all those rich people up there by the lake would support you."

Stella looked at the picture. Of course she'd seen fireboats. She'd spent a tour on one when she was in Chicago. She hadn't thought about it for Sweet Pepper. The community by the lake was small. She didn't think the town would approve the money it would take to buy a boat and get it accessorized.

"That's a good idea. Thanks."

"Sure thing, honey." Flo bent close to Stella's ear. "And how's that handsome hunk of ghost treating you up at the cabin? He seems to have calmed down."

Flo was one of the few people Stella felt comfortable with talking about Eric. "He's difficult like always," Stella told her. "Will you be at the memorial tomorrow?"

"I wouldn't miss it. We should've done it long ago."

The brief planning meeting was winding down. Julia Grace, from the Sweet Pepper Presbyterian Church, was warming up the old piano in the corner. It was time for Stella to leave. She'd been assigned her position on the planning board—finding new people to enter recipes into the festival contest.

Stella knew Eric was going to laugh when she told him. The position meant she was going to have to go around asking everyone, at least twice, if they'd submit a pepper recipe. It was going to get old very quickly. Why they felt she'd be the perfect person for this task was beyond her.

Smiling and nodding at the people she knew, Stella left the café and headed toward town hall. A cold breeze had begun to blow down from the mountains. Maybe Eric was right about a change in the weather.

She didn't have far to walk. Police chief Don Rogers was going into town hall at the same time. He held the door open for her.

"Ms. Griffin." He inclined his head as she walked in the building. Opening doors was about the only courtesy he'd ever shown her. He never called her Chief Griffin, which would have been proper in their professional situation.

Chief Rogers was a difficult man—at least he had been for her. He'd thrown as many obstacles as insults her way. The fifty-something man with graying blond hair cut in a military style had started out as a fire brigade volunteer, he just hadn't continued.

"Chief Rogers," Stella acknowledged him. She tried not to make matters worse by antagonizing him. It wasn't always easy.

"Looks like ice coming down from the mountains." He searched the dark sky. "I hope you have supplies in so you're not trapped in that old cabin with no food. There are stories about people up here starving to death after a winter blizzard where they couldn't get out for weeks. If you like, I'll put you on our check-in list to make sure you're okay."

Stella faltered in the anteroom before she entered the main part of the town hall. Had she heard right? Was he offering to help her in some way?

She had to be coming down with something. There was no way Chief Rogers had just volunteered to do something *nice* for her.

"Thanks."

"While I have your ear," Chief Rogers said, "I wanted to let you know that I'm sending Officers Richardson and Schneider your way to become volunteer firefighters. I have a few part-time officers that are interested too. It seems to me that the fire brigade is getting a mite small after losing a few people. I hope that helps."

Chief Rogers smiled at her in a way that actually reached his pale blue eyes—the ones usually glaring at her.

Something was up. Stella didn't know what it was, but Chief Rogers had never shown her this kind of respect. Maybe it was a practical joke. She kept waiting for the punch line.

When one didn't come she politely thanked him for his help and wandered, dazed, into the meeting room where the town council members were on the dais. She was going to have to ask John what was wrong with his boss.

She'd expected some hostility from Chief Rogers because state investigators would be in town to examine Barney Falk's death. She knew he was going to have to put himself out, as she would, to accommodate them.

Maybe that was it.

Maybe he was afraid she'd say something nasty about

him to the investigators. He didn't have to worry. She'd been a team player for a long time. She wouldn't say anything to the state that could hurt him. He was annoying, but he did a good job for Sweet Pepper.

She picked up a packet of information created for officials by the town clerk. The documents and agenda gave her a heads-up about what was going on during the meeting.

Stella was expected to be at the meeting every month so she could give the fire report, which included expenses and calls the fire brigade had gone on. Chief Rogers did the same for the police department.

"Stella." Ben Carson, Stella's grandfather, sat beside her in one of the uncomfortable plastic chairs. He was tall and bone thin. His shoulders were stooped, and his gray hair was rapidly thinning.

The one feature that didn't show any signs of age was his eyes. The brown eyes he shared with Stella's mother, Barbara, were as sharp and clear as ever.

"Ben. How are you? It's unusual to see you at a town meeting." She hadn't been able to bring herself to call him Gramps yet, like she did her grandfather in Chicago. She didn't feel she knew him well enough. Maybe someday.

"True enough. I hate these things. Nothing gets accomplished here. The mayor and the council strut around for the public, but all the deals are done in the back room."

It was a cynical point of view. Stella was sure he had plenty of reason for it. As Walt, John, and Eric liked to remind her, Ben ran everything in town from the back room.

"I heard you had some trouble with Bob Floyd wanting to tear down your little cabin." He used his chin to point at the council member, who was on the dais examining his packet of information.

"Some." She wasn't surprised. Ben knew everything that went on in Sweet Pepper.

"Want me to take care of it for you?" he whispered.

Being from Chicago, Stella was well educated in under-the-table deals. She didn't want to get involved in whatever

Ben had in mind. She barely knew him as her grandfather. She didn't want to tarnish that relationship.

"No, thanks. I'm going to see a lawyer about it—if the town council won't reconsider and sell me the property."

Ben took her hand in his icy grip. "If a man can't use his position and fortune to help his only granddaughter, a heroine in the community, what good is having position and fortune?"

It was the same conversation they normally had. The subject varied—she should move into his mansion with him, she should work for one of his companies, she should let him set up her life in a manner that he found befitting the status of his granddaughter.

"I don't know the answer to that." Stella smiled and nodded at council member Danielle Peterson across the room. "But I can handle this. I'll appeal to the council first, and find the right lawyer if I need to."

"Okay." He patted her hand. "That sounds like a plan. Since you don't have a lawyer already, at least use mine. Is that too much collusion for you?"

Ben and Stella had a tenuous relationship. Neither of them wanted to antagonize the other. Stella had made it clear that she wouldn't accept expensive gifts from him.

On the other hand, she didn't have a lawyer. What could it hurt to use his? She'd pay for it, not him. "That sounds fine. Thank you. How should I contact him? Do you need me to fax or email information to him?"

Ben smiled tenderly at her. "Not at all. I think he can find everything he needs."

Mayor Wando slammed the gavel down once on the council table to bring the meeting to order.

"I think that's my signal to get out of here." Ben got to his feet after planting a kiss on Stella's cheek. "You'll hear from my lawyer in the next few days. Don't let that old blowhard Bob Floyd get to you. We'll get this settled."

"Ladies and gentlemen," Mayor Wando started the meeting. "It is with a heavy heart that I begin this meeting and announce to you that Representative Barney Falk has passed. We dedicate this meeting to him, and remember all of his good works through the years. I'm going to call on our fire chief, Stella Griffin, to say a few words about the terrible thing that happened out at Sweet Pepper Lake. Chief Griffin? If you will come to the podium."

Chapter 7

~~~~~~~~~

S tella glanced around the room in horror. What was she
going to say? Did he want her to describe the fire or what?

She adjusted the microphone at the podium. She kept
hoping someone would give her a clue as to what they
wanted to hear from her. She'd been expecting to talk about
the usual call and expense reports for the fire brigade. She
had her speech ready about Eric for tomorrow. This was
completely off the schedule.

She flashed to what Flo had said about the fire brigade
needing a boat. It seemed to her that this was a perfect time
to talk about it. She didn't know what else to say. They
probably wouldn't do anything about it, but at least she'd
have something intelligent to present.

"Mayor, council members, and fellow citizens of Sweet
Pepper, there was a horrific fire at the Sunset Beach community that claimed the life of Mr. Barney Falk. I'd like to
say that the fire brigade had a difficult time putting out that
fire because of the close proximity of the house to the lake."

Stella paused, and warmed to her subject. "I can't promise that we could have saved Mr. Falk's life with better

equipment, but we could have saved more of his house. And the next time a fire happens out there, it might mean the difference between life and death for someone. Our pumper-tanker ran out of water before the fire was extinguished. There was only one hydrant close enough to use. That hose wouldn't reach the back of the house."

People in the audience were nodding and whispering. She hoped that was a good sign. "I believe what's needed in that area is a fireboat. We had fireboats in Chicago to fight fires on the river. A boat equipped with a large stationary water cannon and a pump to draw from the lake would have been able to save property today—possibly lives tomorrow. We have to think to the future, as I've heard Mr. Falk always advocated. Sweet Pepper needs a fireboat. Thank you."

Stella stepped down, not sure if that was what Mayor Wando had wanted to hear, but it was the only thing she could think to say. There was a smattering of applause from the audience—probably from residents who lived on the lake.

The rest of the meeting went as planned on the agenda. Stella gave her report on calls the fire brigade had answered during the past month, and what those calls had cost the town. Chief Rogers spoke briefly about the state investigators who were in town to help look into Barney Falk's death.

"We're not anticipating any unusual circumstances regarding this fire," he said. "But you can be sure Chief Griffin and I will be on top of the situation."

Stella was glad when the meeting was almost over. There was only a short time left for comments from the council members. Then she could approach the council individually—minus Bob Floyd—and ask for their help.

When Mayor Wando called on Bob Floyd for his remarks, Bob was quick to let his thoughts out. "I realize a fair number of you are aware that there was a small ruckus up at the old cabin where Chief Griffin resides at this time. I would like a moment to explain how the town's interest is served by my purchase of this property."

A moment stretched to ten as Bob went on about how the town had paid county and state taxes on the property with no return for forty years. His purchase had ended the debt the town owed and would create a new site for rafting on the Little Pigeon River. He promised new jobs and a better life for everyone.

"I would like to extend an apology to Chief Griffin. She has inadvertently been caught in the middle of this dispute." Bob stared hard at Stella across the room. "I want to reassure you, Chief Griffin, I have a rental home that can be put at your disposal. You can move into it at any time."

Bob thanked the community for coming out for the meeting and cautioned everyone to be careful going home. "It looks like we're in for some rough weather. Thank you, and goodnight."

Stella was stunned by his words, as well as his offer of a new place to live. She knew she'd have trouble winning over any council members after that. What could she possibly say that would convince them to sell her the cabin?

She cornered Danielle Peterson anyway. Apparently the council had discussed the matter before the meeting. While Danielle was sympathetic, and wanted to keep Stella happy, she couldn't see why Bob should be stopped from tearing down the cabin and creating another public entry point to the river since he'd purchased the property.

"If it's a matter of a house, Chief Griffin, several of us have rental properties we'd be glad to have you use."

Stella thanked her. She was going nowhere fast with her arguments.

It was the same thing with Mayor Wando. She caught up with him as he was leaving town hall. He'd already made up his mind too. He thanked Stella for the moving words about the fireboat and commended her idea.

"I knew from the start that you were the one for this position, Chief Griffin. Keep up the good work." He shook her hand and smiled warmly before putting on a heavy coat that covered his barrel chest. He pulled a cap on to protect his shaved head. "Best get home now. The storm is settling in."

Stella gave up for that night. She had to hope her grandfather's lawyer would have better luck. She walked outside to the Cherokee to find everything covered with a thin layer of ice. It seemed Eric and the others knew better about Sweet Pepper weather than the National Weather Service.

The roads were slippery. The Cherokee's four-wheel drive meant nothing to the ice. There were chains in the back toolbox. She thought she might have to stop to put them on in order to get up the mountain to the cabin. She stopped at the firehouse for the task. Royce was monitoring communications. He was listening to some old jazz and drinking a large cup of coffee.

"Chief!" He jumped to his feet when he saw her. His weathered black face looked half asleep. He'd pulled his suspenders down from his shoulders, letting them ride at his hips.

"Just coming back from the town council meeting." She smiled as he quickly pulled up the suspenders and tucked in his red flannel shirt. "I thought I'd check to see how things are going."

"Well, there's bad weather." He grinned. "I guess you know that. No accidents or any word from the police or the sheriff's department that they need our help. It's quiet. I hope it stays that way. Most people got enough sense to stay in on a night like this."

"Some people have to be out."

"Oh. Sure. Like you coming home. Of course. You couldn't help it. Not saying that you don't have any sense. I was just saying to JC the other day that you're one of the most *sensible* people I know."

Stella laughed. "Don't worry about it. I get it. I'm going home. Carry on."

He thanked her a few times and asked if he could eat a few of the oatmeal cream pies that were in the cabinet. "My wife forgot to pack me a snack for tonight. Don't want to have her bring that over in this weather."

"Help yourself. If it belongs to someone in particular, their name should be on it. If there's no name, it's fair game. Goodnight, Royce. Thanks for your hard work."

Stella went out and opened one of the garage bay doors.

She pulled the Cherokee inside and started putting the chains on the big tires.

Royce saw her and immediately insisted on doing the job. Stella didn't argue. She was glad she hadn't brought the Harley down from the cabin. The Cherokee was better in situations like this. At least the weather here allowed her some sunny days to ride her father's motorcycle in the cold. In Chicago, it had to stay on blocks all winter.

Once the chains were in place, Stella thanked Royce for his help and then took the Cherokee up Firehouse Road to the cabin with no problem. The porch light was on, and the front door opened before she could put her hand on the doorknob. Hero ran into the kitchen to greet her.

"Ice," Eric said. "I told you."

"You were right. Can you use your ghostly powers on the stairs? They're kind of slippery."

"I think that's what the salt is for. You're starting to rely on me doing things you could do for yourself."

Stella took off her boots and frowned at him. "I'm keeping your cabin here. The least you could do is scare away some ice. That doesn't seem like too much to ask."

Before Eric could answer, Stella's radio went off. The house phone rang too.

"I was at the firehouse a few minutes ago. Royce said everything was quiet," she complained before she answered the phone.

"We just got word, Chief. There are hikers stranded on Dead Bear Trail, out near Big Bear Springs," Royce said. "Looks like we're going out, bad weather or not."

The hikers from Pigeon Forge were stranded on a trail that was high up in the mountains. A rockslide had trapped them there. The ice had started falling before they were able to free one of their fellow hikers from the debris.

"In other words, those hikers have been out there for hours before they bothered calling in," Eric said after Stella had hung up the phone and was changing clothes. "I'll never understand why people aren't smart in dangerous situations."

"Me either." Stella pulled on her heavy coat. "Keep the house warm. I'll be back when I can."

"I wish I were going with you. Be careful out there. It's going to be treacherous on that trail."

"You know me." She opened the door, and Hero ran outside.

"Yeah." Eric said to the closed door after she was gone. "That's why I'm worried."

Chapter 8

~~~~~~~~~

Big Bear Springs got its name from accounts of the 1800s when fur trappers in the area remarked at the number of bears living there. Those accounts brought more trappers and almost wiped out the bear population.

The bear title stuck. There was Big Bear Road and Bear Den Drive as well as the convenience store, campground, and rafting business, all named after bears.

Dead Bear Trail was no doubt a spot where someone had seen a dead bear. Standing about fifty feet above the trail and looking down, Stella wasn't surprised the hikers were in trouble.

The trail ran around the mountain, with sharp inclines and thin ledges where hikers were forced to hug the rock and shuffle across the trail, which dropped at least a hundred feet to a rocky ravine below it.

It was a difficult trail when the weather was good. With ice covering everything, it was a death trap.

"How are we gonna get down there, Chief?" JC asked.

"Two of us will rappel down. We'll tie our ropes around

the hikers and send them up two at a time." Stella looked at him. "Sounds like a plan, doesn't it?"

"A plan to get someone killed," he retorted. "I think we should wait until the ice melts in the morning. You know it won't take that long."

"The hikers said on the radio that two of them are injured from the rockslide. Another one has his foot trapped under some rock. We can't leave them down there all night."

JC didn't like heights, and everyone knew it. Normally, Stella could position him where it didn't matter. There was no way around it this time.

"You don't have to go down there." She was glad that John had been able to come out with them. He was an experienced climber. "John and I will go down. I need you, and everyone else, up here to pull out the hikers."

JC nodded. "Okay. I can do this. I'll stand back against the rock. I don't even need to see down there."

Stella patted his shoulder. "That's right. Let someone else look over the edge."

She wasn't sure who that was going to be. Allen was eyeing the edge with trepidation. Kimmie and David were doing the same. Kent didn't seem that nervous. Royce and Bert were both strong and up to the task.

"Okay." She loudly addressed her team as freezing rain fell on them, turning them all into human icicles. "John and I are going down. We'll send up the two injured hikers first. I hope we have an ambulance and medics by then. If not, keep them warm with the blankets we brought. "

"You didn't even say please." John was already preparing one of the ropes for the descent when she walked to the side of the rock. "You might've considered my feelings on the matter. You didn't make JC go down the the mountian."

"Quit teasing and let's go," she said. "I'm worried about this rockslide shifting again."

They both peered off the edge. From there down to the ledge where the hikers were trapped was an immense cascade of large and small rocks. They both knew it could shift again at any time. Later, the forest service would come in, clear the slide, and shore up the ledge. Until then, anything could happen.

"Are you sure you're up to this?" John asked her. "I could go down by myself."

Stella had practiced rappelling down the sides of the mountains almost since she'd come to Sweet Pepper. She'd realized right away that this would be a requirement of her job. She felt confident in her abilities. She wasn't afraid of heights, and she knew the team she left behind at the top would work well together.

"I'm good." She tightened the rope around her waist. It was already slick with ice.

"Okay. See you down there." John saluted her.

They both went off the side. The ropes were fastened into metal spikes that had been driven into the solid rock. These would bear the brunt of their weights. It wouldn't be the same for the injured hikers below them. It would take every inch of muscle the volunteers had to pull them back up.

The descent was smooth and fast. Stella was on the ledge before John. She was already explaining her plan to the hikers who were waiting to be rescued.

"How long have you been out here?" she asked one of the two young men. He looked like a college student—they all did.

"Since this morning. We thought we could get everyone free and get out. It took longer than we thought, and the weather turned."

"Why didn't you call for help right away?" John asked as he reached them.

The young man shrugged. He was ill equipped for hiking the rugged terrain in the cold weather. He was wearing sandals and shorts with a light jacket.

"We didn't want to bother anyone."

John eyed him suspiciously. "Tell me this isn't one of those stupid drug drops."

"Out *here*?" Stella asked.

"A plane or helicopter drops the drugs and then emails

the coordinates. That leaves big, dumb lawbreakers to go down and pick them up."

John used his flashlight to pick out a plastic-wrapped bundle with sturdy twine around it. "I guess this must be cheese, right?"

The young man in shorts started crying. "We didn't know this was going to happen. It wasn't supposed to be such a long way down."

"Never mind," John grunted. "Let's get out of here and then we'll have a nice talk."

Stella and John got their ropes around the two injured students, both young women. They had injuries to their legs and arms where the rocks had hit them. Stella felt sure one of them had a broken arm.

"She won't be able to hold the rope for them to pull her up," she told John.

"I think we have the same problem with the other one. Her leg is broken."

Stella radioed her team. "Send the basket down. We'll have to pull these two up one at a time. Are the medics here yet?"

Kent answered, "Yeah, Chief. They're here now. Are we going to need another ambulance?"

"I think so. Call Tagger and let him know."

Once the person-sized basket was lowered down to them, John and Stella put the woman with the broken leg into it. They secured her and let Kent know that she was ready to be pulled up.

John went to check on the young man still trapped under the rockslide. He was unconscious. One of his legs was dangling off the side of the ledge while the other was caught under a large rock.

Stella watched the basket go slowly up the side of the mountain.

"I think this other one might be more complicated," John told her. "I don't know if we can get him out by ourselves." He explained the situation.

"What do you have in mind?"

"I was thinking we might need to borrow a helicopter."

Stella wasn't sure about that. "Will they come out with this heavy ice falling?"

"I don't know. It's either that, or this kid is gonna have to spend the night up here. I don't know if he'll make it. His pulse is already thready and weak."

Stella trusted his judgment. "I'll have Tagger make the call."

The second woman was at the top. As soon as the ropes were returned and the team was ready, the other young man not trapped under the rocks would be on his way off the ledge.

"What's the plan?" Stella asked.

"We have to be careful or the slide is going to move again," John cautioned. "Too much effort, and all three of us will be in the ravine."

Stella thought about the problem. "I think we have enough room to use a jack to lift the rock and pull him out."

John nodded. "Sounds doable."

Tagger radioed back that the forest service was sending a helicopter. That part of the plan seemed to be working. The team above was already hauling out the uninjured hiker. Just one more hiker, and the ledge would be clear.

"Heads-up, Chief," Kent warned. "We're sending down the jack."

Stella waited in the freezing rain, her bunker coat protecting her from most of the chill. Her boots were solid and dry. She was still cold, ready to go home and sit by the fire. Once they got the last young man off the ledge, all she had to do was climb out.

"Ready?" John asked as the spotlight they'd set up on the ledge showed the jack coming toward them with another basket.

She pushed her helmet down on her head and ignored the narrow ledge they stood on. "Oh yeah."

The helicopter came before they could free the young man's leg from the rock. It hovered far enough away that the strong wind from the rapidly moving blades didn't affect them.

The pilot added an extra spotlight on the situation. The rockslide was even more devastating than they'd been able to tell earlier, reaching down hundreds of feet below where they were working.

Stella was using the jack to lift the rock. John had his arms around the young man to pull him onto the ledge when he was free. They had the basket waiting to attach to the helicopter, which would transport him to the hospital.

The problem was the edge and the loose rocks. As Stella jacked up the rock, smaller rocks rolled out from under it. One of the rocks, where John was crouching holding the victim, slid down about six inches and stopped.

"Faster," he yelled at Stella. "I don't know how much more this slide will take."

"Believe me, I don't want to be here any more than you do." She kept pumping the jack as she spoke. She could almost see the injured man's entire mangled leg and foot.

"Chief?" Kent called down from above them. "The victims have been transported. Mackie Fossett came by with his truck in case we need to take anyone else out."

Mackie was a pepper farmer who lived nearby. Stella had visited his farm for a day to learn about peppers for the Sweet Pepper Festival.

"Thanks," she answered back.

"Do you and John need some help down there?" Kent asked. "One of us can come down too."

"I think we've almost got it," she said.

The injured man regained consciousness at that moment. "What's going on? I can't *feel* my leg. Who are you people?"

"We're the local fire department," John answered. "You're gonna be all right. We're gonna put you into a safety basket for transport. Just hang on."

John called the helicopter and told the pilot to come in closer. He and Stella lifted the injured man and secured him in the basket.

As the helicopter came close enough to attach the safety harness, the wind from the blades made John and Stella's footing on the ice-covered ledge harder to maintain. Stella lost her balance and dropped to her knees as she was helping John attach the harness to the basket.

"Are you okay?" he shouted above the noise of the whirling blades.

"I'm okay. We're ready."

John radioed again to let the pilot know the basket was secure. The helicopter began pulling away, and the injured man started screaming.

It could have been the shift in moving the injured man's weight from the ledge. Or it could have been the wind generated by the helicopter. They would never know for sure, but at that moment, the rock slide began moving downward again.

John was on the edge at that point as the basket was moving up past him. The rocks dropped away from under his feet leaving him with nothing but open space to cling to.

Stella thought fast and clipped the end of her rope to John's harness. "Grab on tight," she said to her team. "Double weight on this end."

"Don't worry, Chief," Kent yelled back on the radio. "We're ready."

It was like a scene from a movie or a nightmare. The helicopter rose quickly into the dark sky with its burden beneath it. John was left in midair, his arms straight up, as his hands and feet tried to grab on to something that would save him.

As he fell off the ledge, Stella felt the abrupt pull at her rope and prayed that it would hold. It did, possibly too well, as it dragged her off of the side of the mountain with him.

They dangled in the darkness, swinging against the side of the dark mountain. A few tons of rock slid past them, but they were alive and uninjured, held from above by her team.

"It's okay, Chief!" Kent yelled into the radio. "We got you."

"I hope they have me too," John shouted to Stella once the noise from the helicopter was gone.

"You're here," she said breathlessly. "I think they do."

The progress going back up was slow and painful. Once they were on the bottom ledge again, another rope was sent down.

John ignored it. He grabbed Stella and hugged her, kissing her long and hard, even though the spotlight was illuminating them. The team above cheered.

"Thanks," he said. "You saved my life."

Stella tried not to take his actions to heart. He was just glad to be alive and she was the closest one to him. "It's what I do."

It was easier going from ledge to ledge. Stella and John were with the rest of the volunteers in ten minutes. They put their arms around each other as they began hiking off of the trail.

The Smittys, Chief Rogers, and Ben Carson were all waiting in their cars by the fire engine when the fire brigade reached the main road again.

As usual, the Smittys were full of questions and took dozens of pictures. Chief Rogers slapped John on the back when he saw him. He was equally enthusiastic when John told him about the drugs they had confiscated.

Bernard, Ben's longtime driver, held a large black umbrella above his employer's head. Ben hugged his granddaughter. "I heard the news and came right out. Are you trying to give an old man a heart attack?"

"Just doing my job." Stella shrugged, still surprised by the fanfare that frequently accompanied the work done by the fire brigade.

"Could you be a little less heroic?" he requested. "Just kidding. I love you, Stella. I'm proud of you. I'm so glad you're safe."

The Smittys took several pictures of Ben hugging Stella. The volunteers were exhausted and cold. They climbed into the Cherokee and the fire engine and went back to the firehouse.

There was always the afterglow of what they'd done that carried them through changing clothes, cleaning the engine, and getting home again. By the time Stella had reached the cabin, that glow was gone, leaving her exhausted and ready for bed.

Eric and Hero wanted to hear everything. Eric had the TV on with the big headline *Local Fire Department Saves Hikers, Discovers Drugs*.

"That was a close call," Eric said when he heard the story

from her. "Shouldn't you be the one on the top ledge giving orders? You're the chief."

"Like you did that?" She yawned. "You do what's needed. I don't have to tell you that."

She'd finished the brandy-laced hot chocolate that Eric had made for her. The soft leather sofa near the fire made it too comfortable to get up. Stella yawned again, and closed her eyes.

When she opened them again, it was morning. Ice covered everything, making the tree branches hang low and the front door hard to open. The sun was up, sparkling on the frozen wonderland outside her window. It was a good day not to venture outside.

"There's no food," Eric complained. "You have to keep enough supplies around in case of conditions where you can't get to a grocery store."

"I'm sure there's something. I know Hero has food. As long as there's a Pop-Tart left, I'm fine. You don't eat. Problem solved."

Eric opened the kitchen cabinet. "No Pop-Tarts. No bread. No milk. Walt drank the last of the coffee. The best you can hope for is pancakes with mustard on them."

Stella laughed at his worried face and then grimaced. "I think I must've hit that mountain a little harder than I thought. I'm sore all over."

"Take a hot shower. I'll search for more food."

There was a loud, crunching sound outside. They both went to the window to see what was happening. "I hope that isn't Bob again," she muttered.

But it was John's old pickup, chains on the wheels, crunching across the ice on the mountain road.

"What time is it?" Stella panicked.

"A little after nine," Eric replied.

"I was supposed to be at the memorial at nine." She rushed into the bedroom. "No time for food. Problem solved."

Chapter 9

Stella took out her formal dress uniform. It was still in a plastic bag. The uniform was stark black with dozens of shiny brass buttons. The Sweet Pepper Fire Brigade emblem on the front gave it a touch of red and gold.

It was a little snug. She'd been fitted for it a few months before. Either it had shrunk or she'd grown. Darn those biscuits. Who'd have thought she'd like biscuits almost better than pizza?

Her hair was too long to tuck under her uniform hat. She had to tie it back at the nape of her neck. There was no time for makeup. The cold weather would make her face pink anyway. She put on her boots and was ready to go.

As an afterthought, she grabbed the box that held Eric's fire chief badge in it. The town had sent it away to have it cleaned after it had been recovered, and the mystery of Eric's death had been solved. The badge would be kept at the firehouse in his memory after today.

Stella looked at the badge she wore. The two were almost identical. Eric's badge had some dents and wear to it. She thought she could always hold his badge up if words failed her during her speech.

Two speeches in two days. She put on her black wool coat that matched the uniform. That was two speeches too many.

John was anxiously waiting in the kitchen. He looked tall, fit, and handsome in his dress uniform. "What are you doing? The mayor is about to burst a blood vessel. Come on!"

"I slept in. I didn't even think they'd do this today after the storm." She grabbed her gloves and keys with her bag.

"I have my pickup," John said when he saw her keys. "It's warm already. Let's take it."

"I'm not going to the memorial in your old pickup," she said. "That's why we have the Cherokee. I know the town council would take it the wrong way if I don't show up in the vehicle that has my name on the door."

"Are you kidding?" He held up his hands when he saw that she was serious. "Okay. I'll meet you there. Hurry."

John ran outside, and Stella looked back at the room. Eric had reappeared, which had sent Hero into fits of jumping and barking.

"Hero's already been outside, and I fed him," Eric said.

"Thanks. I'm sorry you can't be there."

"How weird would that be anyway?" he asked with a laugh. "I don't think people are supposed to be at their own memorials. Drive carefully."

Stella considered that it made sense for him not to hear people make speeches about what he'd been like when he was alive. She was still sad that he couldn't go. But there was nothing she could do about it.

"I'll see you later."

Hero ran out the open door and started jumping at the door of the Cherokee.

Mayor Erskine Wando had been talking about Eric Gamlyn for almost forty minutes when he gratefully saw Stella drive up in the bright red Cherokee with the fire brigade symbol on the door.

Despite the weather there was a good turnout—including representatives from the state and the investigators who were there to look into Barney Falk's death.

Barney Falk had been scheduled to speak at the memorial. Instead the present state representative for the area, Susan Clark, was on hand. She was waiting impatiently for her turn. It was scheduled after Stella's speech.

Stella and Hero ran from the parking area at the Heavenly Peace Cemetery to the temporary platform that had been set up on the back of the Scooter's Barbecue flatbed trailer. It had been decorated with fire department paraphernalia and colors. There were also large black-and-white pictures of Eric and the original fire brigade from the 1970s.

The last time Stella had seen the trailer was during the Sweet Pepper Festival when a group of people had been clogging on it.

"And here's our brave fire chief now," Mayor Wando said into the microphone. "Stella Griffin, get on up here."

Representative Clark, Chief Rogers, and members of the town council were seated in chairs set in front of the flatbed. They applauded as she went quickly up the stairs. Hero started to follow her, but Kimmie called him to where she was seated in the audience with his mother, Sylvia.

Stella looked out into the faces of the people she'd come to know. She smiled at all of them and adjusted the microphone for herself. "Good morning. Sorry I was late. I'm glad to see so many people out here this morning."

Mayor Wando ducked in close to her. His formal top hat that he wore to all town events was slightly askew on his shaved head. A heavy coat made his tall, bulky body look even larger.

"I just want to say a word about our present fire chief." His breath was visible in the cold air. "Chief Griffin was out with her volunteers a good part of last night when the rest of us were home drinking hot cocoa and staying out of the weather. They rescued a group of young people on Dead Bear Trail. Could I get the fire brigade members to stand where they are so you all can give these heroes a round of applause?"

The members of the fire brigade—all of them as far as Stella could see—got reluctantly to their feet. The rest of the audience gave them a long round of applause.

Stella was surprised the mayor put his arm around her. He smiled so the Smittys could take their picture. Then he shook her hand for another picture.

Mayor Wando finally gave her two thumbs-up and went to sit in a chair off the dais.

Stella knew that was her cue to speak. "We're here today to honor a man who gave everything he had to keep the people of Sweet Pepper safe. Fire Chief Eric Gamlyn."

There was more applause as Stella gestured to one of the pictures of Eric.

"Chief Gamlyn created the fire brigade in the early 1970s after perceiving the need for a local group to fight fires in Sweet Pepper. He recruited his volunteers and built a firehouse. I heard from a reliable source that there was already a group in place before the original fire brigade. I think they were called the garden hose brigade."

People in the audience who remembered those days laughed and applauded. Stella went on to explain how the garden hose brigade worked.

"Wish we had pictures of that," Walt Fenway yelled from the front row.

"No, you don't." Tagger laughed and shook his head, his eyes tearing up at the memories.

"In Chief Gamlyn's time, the fire brigade saved thousands of dollars in property and hundreds of lives," Stella continued. "Today the Sweet Pepper Fire Brigade continues Chief Gamlyn's vision and legacy to the community. We honor those first brave citizens who came forward to make a difference."

She nodded to Kent, who pulled the large gray tarp that had been wrapped around the larger-than-life sculpture of

Eric. The wind helped him, and the tarp flew back from the statue.

It was remarkably lifelike, made of granite and set beside Eric's grave in the cemetery. Already the Daughters of the American Revolution had raised funds to put in a flower garden with a bench beside it.

Everyone applauded again. A few people from the old fire brigade got up and saluted the image of their chief. Tears flowed freely as everyone stood to salute Eric.

Stella thanked everyone again for being there. She felt for the box holding Eric's old badge that was in her coat pocket. She took the badge out and held it up for everyone to see it. She knew she hadn't spoken even close to twenty minutes, but she was late and Representative Clark's assistant was tapping his watch. She knew no one would mind if she left the podium.

There was a bright shaft of sunlight that came down to illuminate the badge. It was as though the clouds had parted to let the sun shine down just at that moment. The badge glinted as it caught the light. Everyone saw it and gasped, holding one another's hands and remarking on it.

Stella put the badge away and stepped aside to let the representative say a few words.

Susan Clark spoke about how important local volunteer firefighters were. Her words fell on unappreciative ears. Sweet Pepper had appealed to her when the county had decided not to continue fire service. They'd hired Stella to start their own group soon after. Most there wouldn't forget that when election day rolled around.

The applause for her wasn't as hearty as it had been for Stella, but people in Sweet Pepper tried to be polite.

Mayor Wando announced the Sweet Pepper VFW memorial group. The men, none of them under eighty, got to their feet, clutching their rifles. Their uniforms were pressed and neat.

Stella admired their military precision—and the fact that they could still fit into their old uniforms. She hoped fifty years from now she'd be able to do the same. She was going to lay off the biscuits, or get some workout equipment in the firehouse. Otherwise, Molly Whitehouse, the town seamstress, was going to have to let out her uniform.

The captain who was the head of the group raised his hand for the twenty-one-gun salute. He called out orders to the seven shooters. They pointed their rifles at the clear blue sky. "The Star-Spangled Banner" started blasting from the speakers on the truck. The shots rang out, echoing off the Smoky Mountains that ringed the town.

When the salute had finished, people applauded, and the cold group began to break up.

"That's enough noise to wake the dead," a voice said very near Stella's ear.

She looked to her left and gasped. "Eric! How did you get here?"

Chapter 10

"**I**s something wrong, sweetie?" Flo asked on the other side of her.

"No." Stella took a deep breath and looked again. Eric was still there.

"*Shh.*" He laughed. "Someone might think you're crazy."

"I know what you mean." Flo wiped tears from her dark blue eyes. She patted her blond hair into place. "It gets me too. Eric was *such* a good man. He should've married me when he had the chance. He'd have lots of grandchildren here to see this memorial."

"I never knew she felt like that about me," Eric whispered.

Stella almost choked as she told Flo she had to leave—important fire brigade business. She went quickly to the Cherokee and got inside, locking the doors after her.

"This is really nice." Eric rubbed his opaque hands appreciatively on the door and seat. "They spent a lot of money on it."

Stella turned to him. "How did you get here? I thought you couldn't leave the cabin."

"I don't know. All of a sudden, there I was—at my own memorial service. Nice statue, huh? It even sort of looks like me."

"How can the rules change? All this time, it was either the firehouse or the cabin. I don't understand."

His eyes were serious as he said, "Did you *want* me to stay at the cabin?"

"No. Of course not. I'm happy for you. I can't imagine what it's been like being trapped somewhere for forty years."

She *was* happy for him. Except this might make her life more complicated.

"Good! I want to see *everything*. The cemetery, not so much. Your speech was nice. Thanks. Now let's drive around Sweet Pepper. I want to go in the café and up to the pepper plant. Then I want to go past all the old houses. Maybe we should stop in at Flo's too."

"Slow down. I have other things I have to do today besides playing tour guide."

"Good." He rubbed his large hands together. "I'll go with you."

There was a knock at the window. Stella opened it. It was Agent Whitman from the Tennessee Bureau of Investigation. She'd met him during the investigation into Eric's death.

"Sorry to bother you, Chief Griffin. I wondered if I could have a word with you in private."

Stella glanced at Eric. Could Agent Whitman see him too? No. Of course *not*.

She unlocked the doors and got out.

"I was wondering why you locked the doors." Eric was instantly at her side. "I know you didn't think that would keep me in. Were you trying to keep me out?"

"I can't talk to you right now," she muttered.

"Sorry." Agent Whitman straightened his blue tie. He was an average-looking man who seemed to like wearing plain gray suits. He reminded Stella of a schoolteacher she'd had in Chicago. "Is there a better time?"

"No." She smiled as she started walking beside him. She liked Agent Whitman, but she was very conscious of Eric walking on the other side of her. Having a ghost follow her everywhere would take some getting used to. "This is fine. What can I do for you?"

"Great. I'm glad to see you decided to stay on as fire chief. I've heard glowing reports about your work."

"Thanks. It's a great job."

"I'd like to take you into my confidence on the fire that killed Representative Barney Falk."

"You're here investigating that matter too?"

"No. I'm actually only here to see *you*, Chief Griffin."

"Look out." Eric shook his head. "Another fan of Stella Griffin. You'd better ask if he's married before you start dating him."

Stella glared at him and had to bite her tongue to keep from answering. She'd have to get used to *that* too.

"There are plenty of TBI agents working this case, but we need someone on the inside track. That would be you, Chief Griffin. Our concern is that someone within the group may be part of a cover-up."

"A cover-up? What kind of cover-up?" she asked.

He stopped walking under a huge cedar tree that had been blown toward the east for so long that it permanently pointed in that direction. "We're not sure yet. We know Mr. Falk was murdered. What we need to know is why and who was involved."

"Who is *we*?" Eric asked.

A valid question, Stella thought. "Who are you working with on this, Agent Whitman?"

"The governor, Chief Griffin. I can't tell you any more than that. I want to ask you to keep your eyes and ears open for anything that sounds wrong." He handed her his business card. "Give me a call or email me if that happens. Please don't say anything to anyone else. We're not sure who we can trust on this."

"Okay." Stella looked at his card. She already had one of his cards from the last time they'd met. She kept the new one anyway.

Agent Whitman held out his hand to her. "Great. I

appreciate your help. Would you like to get some coffee? It's cold out here."

"Sure. That sounds good."

Agent Whitman drove his modest gray Buick to Main Street and parked in front of the Daily Grind Coffee and Tea Shop. Stella drove the bright red Cherokee and parked behind him.

"Can we go to the café instead?" Eric asked.

"You haven't been in the coffeehouse ever," she reminded him.

"All right. I seem to be tethered to you, Stella. I tried to leave the cemetery and look around town by myself. I couldn't do it."

"That doesn't make any sense. I've been here all this time and you haven't been able to leave the cabin with me."

"I guess something changed. It's not like there's a handbook for ghosts, like that cute ghost couple had in that movie with the snakes, *Beetlejuice*."

Stella didn't have time to ponder what movie he was talking about. Eric was a TV junkie, probably because there wasn't much else he could do.

Agent Whitman was looking at her through the window with a questioning expression on his face. She had to ignore Eric and get out.

This is going to be complicated.

"Do you mind if we have coffee in the café?" She got out of the Cherokee and locked the doors with the fob.

"Wow!" Eric looked at the keys she held. "That was *cool*. They didn't have those forty years ago. Do all vehicles have them now?"

Stella ignored him. They were going to have to come up with a protocol if Eric was going to be out of the cabin with other people around. He couldn't talk to her and expect her to answer for one thing. She knew he had to be excited about getting out for the first time in so long. But she couldn't walk around as though she were talking to herself either.

Agent Whitman smiled. "No. That's fine. I could use a little breakfast anyway."

"Me too. I had to run out of the cabin this morning without eating. Not that I'm much of a breakfast person anyway."

"You can say that again," Eric agreed. "But thanks for coming here. I ate breakfast here every morning when I was fire chief. Sometimes Ricky Senior would join me with Tagger and Bobby Trump."

Stella and Agent Whitman sat across the table from each other. The café was crowded with people who'd been at the memorial service.

Eric was able to walk around the entire café, exclaiming at people he knew and talking about how the place looked exactly the same. "I wish I could eat chili cheese fries."

"Bradford." Agent Whitman held out his hand to Stella again. "My name is Bradford."

Stella had been watching Eric. "Sorry. Half asleep from the call last night." She shook his hand. "And please call me Stella."

"Okay." He smiled. "Stella. It was a good rescue."

"So people call you Brad?"

Eric was walking around like a big ghostly kid in a candy store. She had to ignore him.

"Yes. I'm sorry. I realize that we've never used first names. I thought we should. If that's okay with you?"

"That's fine, Brad." She looked at her menu. As always her eyes went right to the biscuits. Well, she was committed to the idea of getting that workout equipment for the firehouse. It would be okay if she ate another biscuit. "I think I'm going to have the egg-and-cheese biscuit with a large Coke."

"Not a coffee drinker." He said it like he was writing it in the notebook she knew he carried in his inside jacket pocket. "How are the biscuits?"

"I love them." She laughed. "A little *too* much." She pulled at her snug-fitting dress uniform. "People feed you a lot around here. Someone always wants me to eat something."

"It's the home of the sweetest, hottest peppers in the world. And the pepper festival. Are you involved in that yet?"

"Have I been here for more than five minutes? Everyone

here lives and breathes the pepper festival. In fact, I'm on the planning board this year. I'm in charge of bringing in new recipe contest entries. Do you have something you'd like to contribute, Brad?"

"I'd be glad to." He took his notebook out and began to jot down a recipe. A waitress came and took their order— Brad had an egg-and-cheese biscuit too, with coffee.

"Chief Griffin." Police chief Don Rogers came to their table. "Agent Whitman. Is there a meeting I didn't know about?"

Agent Whitman got nimbly to his feet and shook Chief Rogers's hand. "We're not meeting officially, Chief. We met at the cemetery after the memorial service and we decided to get out of the cold and have some coffee."

Chief Rogers's eyes narrowed. "You mean this is *personal*?"

Agent Whitman smiled. "I guess you could say that, yes. It's good to see you. Have a nice day."

Chief Rogers stood there for another moment looking like he was digesting a lump of coal before he raised his eyebrows and walked away.

The waitress brought a Coke and a cup of coffee. She promised the biscuits were coming out fresh and would be there soon.

"Are you married, Brad?" Stella asked when they were alone again.

"No. But I'm engaged. Why do you ask?"

Stella took a sip from her Coke. "You're about to have a new girlfriend."

He carefully scanned the restaurant. "Excuse me?"

"Me." She sighed. "Don't look now, but people in Sweet Pepper are probably already planning our wedding."

"Oh." He still sounded confused. "I see."

Stella didn't try to explain. She hadn't understood for a long time either. Life in a small town was different from life in a big city. People liked to speculate on anything a single woman did in public or private.

Their biscuits arrived hot from the oven and they enjoyed

their breakfast in companionable silence. Stella waited for him to mention the investigation again but he never did. She wasn't clear on what she was supposed to be looking for or expecting to find during the course of the arson investigation. She assumed he'd let her know as they moved forward.

When they were done eating, Brad paid for the two meals and said he had to get back to Nashville. "I enjoyed our talk. You have my phone number. Call me if anything seems strange."

Stella mused over the idea of what he'd think of as "strange." Would it be a haunted cabin? At one time, she would've thought that was strange. She studied the neatly printed recipe he'd given her for smoked chili peppers in garlic sauce, and hoped she didn't have to make it for the taste-testing part of the contest.

Obviously a man of many talents.

She walked out of the café, not thinking about Eric until he was at her side.

"Don't do that again." He swore softly, his chest rapidly rising and falling. "It was like a punch in the gut."

"What was?"

"I think it was you leaving the café. There seems to be a certain amount of space we can have between us, but not much. I don't understand it either. As soon as we get back to the cabin, maybe we can run a Google search on it." He laughed. "Does anyone think that name is funny? *Google?* Is it someone's name?"

She laughed at his Google reference. He was a bigger Internet junkie than she was. "I have an hour before I'm supposed to meet the arson investigator from Nashville. We can do whatever you want until then."

Eric was beyond ecstatic. "You know that liquor store wasn't here before." He pointed out dozens of changes on Main Street. "And the town hall used to be in the old furniture store."

They both got in the Cherokee so that he could see as much as possible. Stella drove slowly through Sweet Pepper.

Eric exclaimed over the pepper-shaped water tower and

the traffic light. "I heard you and Agent Whitman are dating now," he teased Stella. "That's what happens to fast women who eat breakfast with gentlemen from Nashville."

"Wow. Maybe no one can hear *you*, but you can certainly hear everything," she muttered as they drove through the historic district. "I have a feeling that as long as I'm single, the people of Sweet Pepper will be matching me up with boyfriends everywhere I go."

"That's what happened to me. They always had me dating someone I'd never met or introducing me to daughters, nieces, cousins, and sisters. The trick is to keep them guessing. If you get married, and have breakfast with someone like Agent Whitman, they'll think you're cheating."

"Life in a small town."

"Exactly. Hey! Can we go up to the pepper factory?"

"Sure. I'm due a report on the progress they've made getting that duct system set up anyway. We'll do that at the same time."

Last year, Stella had made headlines in the *Sweet Pepper Gazette* for shutting down the Sweet Pepper packing plant for fire hazards. It had only been for one day. Everyone had been sure she'd lose her job, even though her grandfather owned the plant.

Ben Carson had thrown a fit, but they'd found a compromise that had kept the plant open. He'd repaired the faulty duct system that had periodically caught on fire.

"Greg Lambert's up there now as manager, right?" Eric stared out the side window.

"Yep. He's not too bad."

"I always thought he was a little oily."

"Oily?" She put her foot down hard on the gas pedal to get up the steep road that led to the packing plant.

"You shouldn't gun it like that," he warned. "There's probably still ice on the road."

"Don't tell me how to drive in ice and snow. Chicago gets more ice than Sweet Pepper will ever see."

The back end of the Cherokee fishtailed as it hit a patch of ice.

"I told you," Eric said.

"Never mind. You were about to describe oily."

He shrugged his broad shoulders that were barely see-through at all. "You know—underhanded. Slippery. Someone who offers you ten dollars as he takes twenty."

"Okay. I get it. And I agree."

"At least we agree on something." He was melodramatic, showing her how far up and back he rocked as she pulled the Cherokee to a quick stop in front of the main office of the pepper factory.

The original brick structure of the first pepper bottling plant was still intact from the 1800s. It was used as the office/administration building. The whole facility and distribution center covered more than ten acres and employed hundreds of workers from Sweet Pepper and the surrounding areas.

"This place has grown." Eric nodded. "The pepper business must be booming for the old man. You too, I guess."

"I don't think about it much." Stella got out of the Cherokee. "It's not like I get a paycheck or shareholder's benefit."

Greg Lambert was in his office when they were shown into the building by his assistant. Greg was in his sixties but still maintained some of his youthful good looks. His chiseled face was smoothly handsome, but his brown eyes were cold. "Chief Griffin." He got to his feet and shook her hand.

It was the oddest feeling knowing that Eric was standing next to her when Greg didn't acknowledge him. "Mr. Lambert. I believe the last report was due on the ductwork overhaul. I thought I'd drop by and pick it up."

He smiled in a stiff manner. "Save me a postage stamp, eh Chief?" He handed her the paperwork. "I'm sure you'll find that everything is in order. Would you like to tour the plant and take a look?"

Stella took the paperwork. "Not today. You've done a good job. Thank you for your cooperation."

"I hear there was an unfortunate accident last night on Dead Bear Trail. I hope no one was seriously injured. It would be too bad if something happened to Barney Falk's grandson the same day the old man died."

Chapter 11

"Barney Falk's grandson was there?" Stella asked. Eric shrugged, not saying anything.

"Barney Falk III." Greg leaned against his desk. "I think they call him Chip—as in chip off the old block. Only he's always been a disappointment to his father and grandfather."

"I don't know the names of the boys. He might've been there. How do *you* know, Mr. Lambert?" Was this the link Brad was looking for?

"You know. It's the grapevine." Greg sat back down. "If that's all, Chief Griffin, I have to get back to work."

That was it, as far as Stella was concerned. She and Eric went back to the Cherokee.

"Same old Greg," Eric remarked. "He's older, but his personality hasn't changed. I don't know what Tory ever saw in him."

Tory Lambert was the first person in Sweet Pepper to make friends with Stella. She'd been instrumental in getting the fire brigade going. She was Greg Lambert's wife and had died in a house fire soon after Stella had arrived in town.

"I wonder why he brought up that little tidbit about

Barney Falk's grandson. I'm sure he wanted us to know about it for some reason."

"*You*," Eric corrected. "He wanted *you* to know about it. He doesn't know I'm here. If you start talking like that people will start gossiping about you."

She rolled her eyes and started the Cherokee back down the steep road. "Thanks for the advice. I'll have to get used to you being around all the time."

"I suppose. Can we go out to the lake?"

Stella glanced at her watch. "Sure. Then we have to head back to town hall."

Eric raised a questioning brow.

"Okay. Then *I* have to head back to town. Stop talking to me. I have to forget you're here."

"That seems a little rude."

"You're a ghost. Rudeness doesn't figure in."

They drove out to Sweet Pepper Lake. It was roughly a three-mile circle of water surrounded by mountains and ringed with expensive houses like Barney Falk's. The scenery was spectacular, with the clear lake reflecting the mountains and the sky.

Stella had taken the tourist boat around the lake when she'd first arrived. The boat captain had talked about how the lake had been created by a nearby dam project. The water had covered the original town of Sweet Pepper. He told stories about a church that couldn't be moved, and hearing its bells tolling during dark nights.

Stella took Eric to the public access area. He vanished from the Cherokee and was at the shoreline before she could even open the door.

"When I was a kid," he said when she'd reached him, "I used to come down here every day. I don't think I could ever get tired of this view. I can't tell you how much I've missed it. Thanks for bringing me here."

Stella sat down on a large rock while Eric ran up and down the shoreline, scaring away lake gulls. The breeze was strong coming down from the mountains, but no wind touched his clothes or hair. She wondered what it was like for him to attend his own memorial and have another chance to see his hometown.

She got an idea as he explored. Maybe he could help her with Barney's death. When he'd finished enjoying the shore-line, he came back and sat beside her.

"Do you think you could talk to other ghosts?" she asked.

"I don't know. I've never tried. Why? Do you have a ghost you need to talk to?"

"I was thinking about Barney Falk. We're right out here. Maybe you could talk to him and find out what happened."

A gust of wind caught at the dress cap she wore and would have blown it to the rocky beach as it was swept from her hair, but Eric caught it—solid when he wanted to be—and handed it back to her. It only took a moment for the wind to blow the strands of her red hair loose around her face.

"I could try." He grinned at her. "You should always wear your hair down, Stella. The sun makes it look like it's on fire."

When she'd been a child, she'd received such remarks on a regular basis. It had been years since anyone had remarked on the deep red of her hair.

To cover her embarrassment at having her hair likened to fire, she laughed. "I guess I shouldn't do it too often. Somebody on the fire brigade might douse it with a hose."

His blue eyes stared off at the lake. "Do you have any regrets about your life so far?"

"Not really."

"Not even that your relationship with Doug got messed up?"

Doug had been the deciding factor in Stella coming to Sweet Pepper. He'd been her longtime boyfriend back in Chicago. They'd discussed getting married from time to time. That had been before she'd found him in bed with one of her good friends.

Stella had slugged him, and the ensuing chaos, along with an injury from a fire, had helped make her decision to leave Chicago for a few months. Doug had apologized later, but their romantic relationship was over.

"I wouldn't say that I regret it. I was angry at the time. Now I see that Doug and I were never right for each other."

"My biggest regret was that I never found anyone to share my life. I never had children." He turned to her. "Don't let that happen to you. I know you think you have all the time in the world. I'm proof that isn't true."

Stella looked away to wipe a tear from her eye. She hated when he talked like this—like a young man who'd had everything taken away from him too soon. There was nothing she could do to help him. His life was in the past. It pained her that he still grieved over it.

"Let's go take a look around Barney Falk's house before I have to go to town hall." She got to her feet and wiped any dust from the rock off her dress pants. "I should've brought something else to wear."

"But you weren't expecting company that was going to run you all over town before your meeting?"

"That's right." She grinned back at him. "Let's go."

"Can we come back again sometime?"

"Of course. We could rent a canoe and paddle around the lake. That way you'd get to see everything up close. Maybe I could even push you in the water."

Eric talked nonstop as they got into the Cherokee and drove up into the Sunset Beach community.

Barney Falk's house was a pile of blackened rubble. A small backhoe was waiting to help in the investigation. Crime scene tape still surrounded the property. Officer Frank Schneider was standing guard at the site.

"Chief." Officer Schneider acknowledged her as she got out of the Cherokee. Frank Schneider was average height and weight with brown hair and eyes. He liked to whistle. Stella had smiled many times when she'd heard him on the job. John said he was very musical. He belonged to several singing groups that appeared regularly in the area.

"Frank. I'm surprised to see you out here." Stella stared at the property. "I thought they'd only have part-time officers out here."

"We've got a few of them out with the flu," he told her. "I can still answer calls if I need to. Personally, I don't see anyone wanting to vandalize this place. You know what I mean?"

"I know. I think Chief Rogers is more worried about people getting hurt in the rubble. You know how everyone wants a picture."

He nodded. "Yeah. I suppose someone crazy might want to climb up on the stuff and fall off. I don't mind being out here anyway. Great view of the lake."

While they were talking, Eric had floated across the land and disappeared into the pile of blackened wood and concrete. He came back toward the end of the driveway where Stella was talking to Officer Schneider.

"I don't see anything," Eric said. "If there's a ghost out here, I don't see him. I didn't sense anyone else there, alive or dead."

Stella smiled at Officer Schneider. "I guess I better go. I'm expecting to meet the state arson investigator in town. I'll see you later."

"Okay, Chief. Hey, would you remind John that he said he'd send lunch out for me? I usually eat at the café. Don't think I'll be doing that today."

"Sure." Stella heard him whistling as she got back in the Cherokee.

"Do you really have ghostly senses?" she asked Eric when she was clear to talk to him without anyone else seeing her.

"Yes. How do you think I know when someone is coming up Firehouse Road?"

"I've noticed that. I guess I thought Hero was alerting you."

"There have to be some perks to being dead."

Stella drove to town hall and managed to find a parking space in front. "If you're coming in with me, we have to set some guidelines."

"Such as you not talking to me when other people are there."

"Yes. It might be better if *you* don't talk to me unless we're alone."

"Unless I have something important to say that pertains to the conversation."

"Yes!" Stella considered it. "Maybe. I'm not sure. Let's see how it goes. Thank you."

"You don't understand how much it means to me to be out in the world again, even if I'm dead. I'm willing to do whatever it takes to see a sunset again, and attend practice sessions with you at the firehouse."

She was glad to hear it, even though she wasn't really sure how it was going to work. "Great. Let's go in."

Sandy Selvy was the town clerk. She greeted Stella at the door with information. "The arson investigator is in Chief Rogers's office. Her name is Gail Hubbard. She seems very nice."

Stella thanked her. Sandy was another good friend— she'd been Stella's mother's friend in school too. Sandy squeezed Stella's shoulder and smiled before she smoothed down her matching pink skirt and sweater.

"I'm sure it's gonna be fine!" Sandy winked, her bee-hive hairdo reminiscent of the 1950s.

"This is nice," Eric remarked as he glided down the hall to Chief Rogers's office. "You should have an office here too. You're the fire chief after all."

"Shh." Stella shushed him.

"What? We're alone."

"In a building full of people."

"I think you and I have interpreted the rules differently. When we get home tonight, we're going to have to sort them out."

Chief Rogers's door was open when Stella reached his office. He got up and greeted her, introducing her to the state arson investigator.

"Chief Griffin." Gail Hubbard shook her hand. She was a tall, large woman, probably in her early fifties, with ultra-short brown hair. She had a plain face, bordering on homely, except for her beautiful hazel eyes. "I've heard many good things about you."

Stella smiled and said the right words as she sat next to Gail. In previous cases, Stella's requests for an arson investigator had been met with icy silence. It seemed the death of a former state representative changed that policy.

"Now that we have the pleasantries over," Chief Rogers began, "I think we should address the issues."

Gail got to her feet. "Is there another room where Chief Griffin and I could meet?"

Don Rogers looked unpleasantly surprised by this request. "I can close the door, if that would help."

"No. You misunderstand. Chief Griffin and I will be investigating this fire. We will report to you on our findings after the investigation is over. No reason to take up your time with our meetings. I don't know much about catching speeders, and you don't understand about fires."

Rapidly put in his place, Chief Rogers took them to the conference room. "If you need anything, ladies, ask our town clerk. Have a good day."

Gail thanked him and closed the door to the conference room. "Whew! I thought his eyes were gonna bug out when I explained that we didn't need him. These small-town cops are all the same."

Stella was amazed at her attitude. She still wasn't sure if she could trust her—especially after her conversation with Brad. But she liked Gail's approach.

"I went over to the site of the Falk fire this morning and took a few pictures." Gail spread the photos out on the large, polished wood table. "Have you been over there since the fire?"

"I was there earlier today. You can tell the fire burned hot after the explosion," Stella said. "There's almost nothing left."

"Explosion?" Gail arched a dark brow. "I haven't heard anything about an explosion. Fill me in, Stella."

Stella went through the entire fire call, including getting

Barney Falk out of the house. She liked the way Gail paid attention to what she had to say. She'd missed that in her dealings with other professionals since she got to Sweet Pepper.

Eric looked at the photos too. "You should start having one of the fire brigade videotape your calls. That way you'll have evidence of everything you do."

It was a good idea, but a clear violation of the guidelines they'd agreed on. Stella pretended she hadn't heard him.

"All right. We'll have to bear that in mind while we tear through this pile of debris." Gail frowned as she put the photos away. "I've heard that your fire brigade had some difficulties reaching Falk's house and others in that community."

"Not since they repaired the road into the area. It was previously rutted gravel. It was hard to get the trucks into. We had no difficulties with that yesterday."

"And what about the water issue?"

"She knows everything, doesn't she?" Eric asked. "I don't trust her."

Strike two. Stella was not only going to write down the guidelines when they got home, she was going to have him read them aloud.

"The only water issue was at the back of the house." Stella showed her on the map. "There are steep drop-offs from the houses along the lake. We got our pumper back there, but we weren't prepared for a fire of that size. We couldn't get the engine in back, so we ran out of water well before the fire was over. I've asked the town to consider purchasing a fireboat. There are hundreds of houses along the edge of the lake. Some of them aren't accessible by decent roads at all. A boat could draw all the water from the lake that we'd need, and could get to these areas."

Gail smiled. "No wonder I've heard such great things about you, Stella. You have a good head on your shoulders. I think it would be an excellent idea for the town to invest in a fireboat. If you need any help convincing them, let me know."

Stella thanked her. If she could get this kind of cooperation going with the police department, things would run a lot more smoothly during emergencies.

"It's already late in the day, and it gets dark early now." Gail took a look at her watch. "Let's get out there first thing tomorrow, shall we? Have you thought about getting some training for arson investigation and becoming certified?"

"I have," Stella admitted. "Right now the fire brigade is shorthanded. I can't make the six-week commitment to be in Nashville every day for the training. I hope to accomplish that later."

"Good enough." Gail got to her feet and shook Stella's hand again. "See you in the morning. It was very nice meeting you."

As Stella was leaving the building after Gail's departure, Chief Rogers stopped her. "Do you have anything to share with me regarding the fire that killed Barney Falk?"

She noticed that he'd waited until Gail was gone. "No. Not really. We'll begin the on-site investigation tomorrow. I'll let you know if we find anything important."

He wasn't happy with that assessment, but there wasn't much he could say. Fire investigations were her purview. It would be like her butting into his investigation of a robbery.

"If nothing else, she put him in his place," Eric remarked as they walked out of town hall.

"Yeah, well, she doesn't have to work with him every day."

"You're right. It was nice working with Walt when I was fire chief. We understood each other."

Stella was about to read him the riot act in regard to their agreement about when and where to speak when councilman Nay Albert stopped her. He had a big grin on his pocked face. His greasy black hair was combed over the bald spot on his head.

"Chief Griffin. Have I got a fireboat for you!"

Chapter 12

~~~~~~~~~~

It was hard not to look at Eric to see how he felt about taking on a boat from Nay Albert. Stella had never had run-ins with this council member as she had with Bob Floyd. But there was something shifty about him that she didn't care for.

Lucky for her, John was on his way into town hall. Still waiting for Stella's response to his offer, Nay dragged him into the discussion.

"You know I've had that old wooden boat in my storage building for years," Nay said to John and Stella. "I had her in dry dock. She was checked out thoroughly before I put her away. She's older, but she's got the strength and weight you're gonna need to hold a water cannon."

John had a bewildered look on his tired face. He'd gone right from the rescue last night to work, to the memorial, and back to work. He was finally done with a double shift and badly in need of sleep.

"What are we talking about?" he asked.

"Councilman Albert has a boat for the fire brigade," Stella explained.

"Sounds like a good idea to me," John said. "Is it free?"

Nay put his hands in his pockets. "Not exactly *free*, but a fair price for the town to pay for a boat. An aluminum boat will never hold up to what you're planning to do. There aren't a lot of boats out on the market like the one I'm offering you."

"I don't know," John said. "Chief? How does our budget look?"

"We're pretty tight until July," Stella explained.

"Hey!" Nay stopped them. "The town council will pay for the boat out of emergency funding. I'll help see to that. I'm not saying you all have to come up with the money right away."

John yawned. "We'll have to take a look at it."

"Okay. I'm free for a couple of hours." Nay smiled at them with expectant eyes.

Stella had absolutely no experience with boats except for having worked as a firefighter on one for a few weeks. She didn't feel qualified to make a decision.

"Maybe later," she said. "John, could you be there?"

"Sure. Just not right now. Sorry."

"That's fine." Nay approved the decision. "How about I meet you two out at my farm about six tonight?"

John nodded. "Sounds good. See you then."

Nay ducked back out of town hall with a wave. Stella was alone with John. "Do you know anything about boats?"

"I know how to drive one, and ski behind one." He smiled. "Don't worry. I have a friend who sells boats. I'll ask him to come out with us. Right now, I've gotta get some sleep."

Stella understood. She was amazed he could keep up with his usual double police shifts and be available so often when they needed him for fire calls.

"Thanks. I'll see you later."

She got into the Cherokee with Eric at her side. "I have to get home and take off this uniform."

"That works for me." He grinned at her.

They'd had a few issues with Eric respecting her personal

space. Mostly he joked about it now, but rarely came into the bedroom when she was dressing. It hadn't been that way at first. She'd worked it out, as she had when she'd been the first woman firefighter at her station in Chicago.

"Ha-ha. What did you think about the boat offer?"

"I don't know much about boats. I know a lot about Nay Albert. I'm betting he's charging the town an arm and a leg for a boat you're going to have to put tons of work into before you can use it."

She started the Cherokee and pulled out into the slow-moving traffic going down Main Street. "That's kind of what I was thinking. I guess we'll take a look at it anyway."

"Firehouse first?"

"Stopping at the firehouse will give you a chance to see the new place." She realized he hadn't been there since the old building he'd built had been destroyed. "After that, I have to find people who don't normally contribute pepper recipes for the festival contest. I'll understand if you want to stay at the cabin."

"Are you kidding me? I don't care if I ever go back to the cabin again right now. I'm sure I'll feel different later. I want to see *everything*. Who knows how long this will last? I want to take advantage of this opportunity to see the world in case it's gone tomorrow."

It made sense to Stella. "That's fine. We'll see as much of the world as we can today."

"What about Bob buying the cabin?" Eric asked.

"I don't know yet."

"I'm thinking that will be the next shoe to drop. Bob tears down the cabin, and I'm in some kind of limbo where I can't go anywhere or do anything." He grimaced. "I'm probably just being paranoid."

She shrugged as she pulled into the firehouse parking lot. "I'm with you. I don't know anything about ghosts—beyond what my dad's family always told us. Believe me, they never covered *any*thing like you driving around in the truck with me."

"More like moaning and clanking chains, right?"

"And the Irish ghosts liked to pull people into moats, and rise up from castle keeps to take vengeance too."

They both laughed at that as Stella turned off the engine and got out of the Cherokee.

"I like the castle keep idea," Eric said. "I probably should have built a castle on the mountain instead of the cabin. I didn't know then that I'd be trapped."

"I'll try to remember that before I die," she said. "Let's end this conversation before we go inside, okay? I'm thinking that talking to ghosts would be a bad thing for a fire chief who wants to keep her job."

"And her team's respect." He did the old mime trick of zipping his mouth closed and throwing away the key. "Although maybe not so much in Sweet Pepper."

Kent was there doing some maintenance on the pumper-tanker.

Banyin was there too, hanging out with the fire brigade. Even though she couldn't go on calls because she was too close to term with her pregnancy, she still manned the communications system when she could. "Hey, Chief! Nice memorial today, huh? The mayor gave me the plaque they had made up for Chief Gamlyn. He said he couldn't find you when the service was over."

Kent, Banyin, Eric, and Stella looked at the large award that the town had made to hang in the firehouse. It commemorated Eric's life and sacrifices to create the first fire brigade.

"It looks good there," Stella said. "Perfect place for it, Kent. Thanks."

Stella studied the old black-and-white image of the original fire brigade with Eric in front of the group. He hadn't changed at all in his incorporeal form. He was even dressed in the same clothes that he was going to wear for as long as he haunted the fire brigade.

"I was a handsome devil." Eric admired the photo.

Stella glanced at him and rolled her eyes.

"Hey, Chief." Tagger greeted her, coming out of the

communications center. "Everything has been super quiet—
whoa!" His eyes opened dramatically wide. "Chief Gamlyn! When did *you* get back?"

Kent and Banyin chuckled. Stella uneasily moved away
from the picture on the wall, motioning to Tagger so he'd
go with her to the small office in the back of the firehouse.

Tagger might be the only one, besides herself, who
could see and hear Eric. He'd told Stella this several times.
She hadn't known whether or not to believe him. Everyone
in Sweet Pepper claimed to have seen a ghost at one time
or another.

Stella closed the door to her office behind them. Eric
walked through it.

"Chief!" Tagger greeted his old friend. "I've missed you.
You stopped coming to the firehouse. I never had a chance
to thank you for saving my life."

Stella watched as Tagger awkwardly tried to put his
arms around Eric. She knew Eric could choose to be solid.
He didn't this time. Tagger's arms flailed in the air.

"Sorry," Eric said to him. "I couldn't get here for a
while. I'm glad you're okay."

Tagger was laughing and crying at the same time. Stella
could only imagine what Kent and Banyin thought.

"That's okay, Chief." Tagger glanced at Stella. "Is it
okay if I still call him Chief?"

"That's fine," Stella said. It was even weirder to stand in
a room with another person who could see and hear Eric
too. "You know a little something about ghosts, Tagger. Do
you have any idea why Chief Gamlyn can suddenly leave
the cabin?"

Tagger thought about it, his red-rimmed eyes unfocused,
as he stroked his grizzled chin. "You know, I heard tell
once of a man who made moonshine hereabouts. Devil Patterson. You remember him, Chief Gamlyn? He was a mean
son of a gun. Beat his kids, his dogs, and his wife too."

Stella had heard so many of these folksy stories she almost
wasn't paying attention. It seemed that the storytelling gene

had been passed liberally throughout the population of Sweet Pepper.

"I remember." Eric grinned as though pleased with himself.

"Well, sir, when Devil Patterson died—an unfortunate set of circumstances that involved him being so drunk that he fell headfirst into a pot of his own 'shine—he didn't stay dead. He followed his wife around everywhere. Of course, he couldn't hurt her anymore, but the widow was smitten with a local blacksmith."

"Black Jack Marshall," Eric added.

"That's right, Chief. The lovers had to think of something to get rid of Devil."

When neither of the two men said anything for a moment, Stella urged them to continue. That was one of the big problems with these stories—it took all day to tell them.

"Oh yeah." Tagger grinned and scratched his thinning gray curls. "The widow and the blacksmith talked to a witch who lived over in Frog Pond. The witch told them that the widow was carrying something that belonged to Devil, and that's why he could show himself to her whenever he wanted."

Eric's blue eyes lit up with the answer. "And the widow threw away the old metal flask full of moonshine that had belonged to Devil. They were never troubled by his ghastly apparition again."

"That's right, Chief." Tagger congratulated him. "Someone must have something that belongs to you."

They both turned and stared at Stella.

"I don't have anything that belongs to him," she protested.

"What about the chief's old badge?" Tagger snapped his fingers. "There was a moment when you held it up at the cemetery. We all remarked on it. It was like a flash of light from heaven came down and blessed it."

Stella took the badge out of her coat pocket. "Let's see if he's right."

"How are we gonna do that, Chief?" Tagger asked.

"I'll leave the badge in here and walk outside. We'll see what happens."

Eric sat on her desk. "Let's do it."

Tagger waited in the office with Eric while Stella went outside.

"Everything okay, Chief?" Banyin asked her as she walked through the firehouse.

"Sure. I'll be right back."

Stella walked around in the parking lot. There was no sign of Eric. Had Tagger been right—even though it took that story to make his point?

She went back inside. Kent stopped her with a worried expression on his face. "Is there anything I can do to help, Chief?"

"No. Everything's fine. Just trying an experiment."

Stella went back into the office. Eric and Tagger were both still there.

"So that's it?" she asked. "As long as I have Eric's badge, he can go where I go?"

"I don't know," Tagger admitted. "Let me try taking it outside, Chief. We'll get to the bottom of this."

Tagger put the badge into his pocket. He walked outside.

Eric disappeared from the middle of Stella's desk.

Tagger came back into the office and shut the door on Banyin's and Kent's puzzled faces.

"I guess that's it," Eric said. "It doesn't matter who has the badge."

"I guess so," Stella agreed.

Before they could continue the experiment, the fire alarm sounded. The radio went off at the same time as Stella's cell phone.

"That's all for now." She jerked open her office door. "What's going on, Banyin?"

"There's a kid stuck on a roof in town, 725 Hill Road."

"Tagger, you stay here with Banyin. Kent, you drive the engine. I'll bring the Cherokee. Banyin, let everyone else know they don't have to come in for this. Monitor our transmissions in case we need paramedics." Stella yanked open her locker door. "I'm not going to a call dressed like this."

Everyone moved quickly to follow her orders. Stella looked at Eric's badge, not sure if that was what had allowed him to be out of the cabin or not. She stuck it in the pocket of her bunker coat and headed to the Cherokee.

Chapter 13

"**D**o we know who lives at that address?" Stella called back to the firehouse as she drove toward Sweet Pepper.

"I looked it up," Banyin said on the radio. "Jerry and Brenda Sue Farmer live there."

"Two-story house?" Stella asked.

"Yes, Chief."

"I can't tell you how much I've missed going on calls," Eric said. "I never got tired of it when I was alive. It's a thrill, as well as an honor, to serve the people of this town."

"You were meant to be a firefighter," Stella said. "Just because your career was cut short in life doesn't mean you can't still do it now."

She reached over to touch his hand as she would have any other person's who seemed to be in distress. He was as solid as the truck they rode in. He definitely made conscious decisions when that was going to happen.

Stella followed Kent in the engine. The lights were flashing and sirens blazing through the streets of town. People who'd been about to cross the street stepped back quickly to the curb. Children pointed and waved. It was the same in Sweet Pepper as it had been in Chicago.

When they reached the Farmer household, two adults and a small child stood in the front yard. They were talking to a teenager on the roof.

"Please," Brenda Sue begged, "you have to get him down."

"I think he went up there for some air," Jerry Farmer said. "He needs some time alone."

"That's rubbish!" Brenda Sue's voice was harsh. "It's that Foster Waxman. She pretended to be interested in Billy. She doesn't give a rat's whisker about him. She was trying to make someone else jealous. She's too old for him anyway. She isn't interested in someone like him."

Kent had already assessed the situation. "Chief, I think I can get up there without the ladder and get him down."

Stella turned away from the worried parents and checked out the problem too.

"He's probably right," Eric agreed with Kent. "The chances are the boy is upset but not suicidal. If he can get him down without the ladder, you won't have to drive the engine up there and tear up the yard."

Stella walked over to stand with Mr. and Mrs. Farmer. "How upset is Billy?"

"He's just being stupid," his father said.

"You know how it is to be a teenager, Chief Griffin," Brenda Sue said. "Everything is a matter of life and death. But I'd rather you not mess up my new grass, if you can help it. It cost us a pretty penny last summer to get it in."

Kent shrugged when Stella looked at him again. It was her decision.

"Let's try it," she decided. "Use some of that winning personality."

He tipped his hat to her, and muttered, "If this doesn't work, just stand by the roof and hold out your arms."

"He's joking, right?" Eric was alarmed at the idea.

"Joking," Stella said under her breath.

They watched as Kent climbed easily up the side of the house using a sturdy trellis anchored to the structure. He swung up onto the roof and ambled over to where the boy was sitting.

"Nice day to be on the roof." He sat next to Billy.

"Go away. I don't want to see anyone." Billy had tears streaming down his young face. "Why can't everyone leave me alone?"

"That's the way life is, kid, when you have people who care about you." Kent removed his helmet. "When I was growing up, my parents could've cared less if I was on the roof or under the house. You don't want that."

"The one thing I *did* want," Billy yelled at him, "I can't have. Why should I care about anything else?"

Stella listened to everything Kent said to the boy. He was persuasive and understanding. He'd missed his true calling; instead of a big rig driver, he should've been a psychologist.

"So, let's get down from here, huh?" Kent stood and offered his hand to Billy.

"Okay. My mom and dad are gonna kill me."

"I don't think so," Kent whispered. "Play on the sympathy card, kid. They're gonna be so happy that you're all right, the other part won't matter."

"He's good," Eric said. "I knew a lot of rescue workers who would've picked that kid up and climbed down with him."

"People are different now." Stella stared at the roof.

"What do you mean?" Brenda Sue asked her.

Stella realized she'd spoken aloud to Eric in front of other people. "I meant that people are more understanding now."

Brenda Sue wiped her tears on a tissue. "I suppose they are."

Kent and Billy were climbing down as Stella shot a dirty look at Eric. When Billy's parents were running toward their son, she said, "Don't talk to me when other people are around."

"Sorry."

Kent had been right—Jerry and Brenda Sue were happy to have their son back. After being reunited, Jerry came back to shake hands with Stella and Kent. "Thanks for your help, Chief Griffin. If there's anything we can ever do for you, please don't hesitate to ask."

Stella raised one delicate red brow. "Have you ever entered the Sweet Pepper Festival recipe contest?"

"That was smooth," Eric said when they were alone in the Cherokee. "What's the recipe for?"

Stella looked at the piece of notebook paper, hastily ripped from a binder. "It's for grilled peppers. I hope I don't have to try making all these recipes."

"I hope not too," Eric teased her. "There wouldn't be any entries in the contest if that happened."

"Never mind that. You made me talk to you again in front of people."

"I didn't *make* you do anything. You chose to answer me. All you have to do is ignore me like you do at the cabin when other people are around."

For some reason, this was different, but she couldn't explain it to him. It was new for one thing. She didn't get that many visitors at the cabin. She spent most of her time there with Eric and Hero. "You could help me out by not talking unless something comes up so that you have to speak."

"How would I know when that was?"

Stella gritted her teeth as she was turning in to the parking lot at the firehouse when she noticed a familiar vehicle.

"Petey!" She parked and jumped out of the Cherokee.

Patricia "Petey" Stanze waved and ran to hug Stella. "Chief! It's *so* good to see you. I hope I haven't missed all the good stuff. I heard about the fire at the lake and the rescue on Dead Bear Trail. Outstanding!"

Petey was a waitress at Scooter's Barbecue. She was short, barely weighed ninety pounds, but was a human dynamo. She was always out in front, tough and determined to get the job done. Stella hadn't believed she'd make it with the fire brigade when she'd joined. Petey had proved that she could do everything the bigger men could do.

"I'm sure there'll be other things," Stella said. "What about you? When did you get out of the hospital?"

Petey had been injured in a fire call. "I've been out for a week. The doctor has me doing some physical therapy, but I'm good. I want to come back to work."

Stella wanted her assistant chief back, but she also wanted to make sure Petey was okay. "You're welcome to do everything but go out on calls, at least until the doctor releases you."

Mousy brown hair flying around her thin face in the breeze, Petey grimaced. "I could come back now full force, Chief. I'd keep doing my physical therapy. I'm going back to work at Scooter's tonight. I'm fine."

"I'm glad to hear it. I need a sign-off from the doctor that agrees with your assessment. I'm sorry. Our insurance requires it for injured firefighters."

"That sucks." Petey put her hands in her jean pockets. "I know you need me, with Ricky gone and everything."

"She don't need you." Kent came out of the garage bay where he'd parked the fire engine. "She's got me. I'm thinking about applying to be assistant chief."

"That's crazy," Petey protested, but her bottom lip trembled.

"Just joking." Kent hugged her. "Glad to see you back. You know no one can take your place. We don't have anyone else to make us feel bad like you do."

Petey laughed at him. "You mean because I'm stronger than all of you put together? Or because I'm younger and prettier?"

"Whoa!" Kent put up his hands. "Don't forget your humble modesty too."

"So that's Petey, huh?" Eric asked.

Stella ignored him. "Petey, we're having an important training exercise tomorrow afternoon, two p.m. You could show up for that and start coming back for practice again until the doctor clears you for active duty."

"Okay. I guess that's better than nothing. What are we doing tomorrow that's so important?"

"You'll have to see," Stella said. "Oh yeah, you can also start taking some communication shifts again."

"All the boring stuff and none of the glory," Petey complained.

"That's the way it is. I'm gonna get the Cherokee cleaned up. Kent, you've got the engine to work on."

JC chose that moment to pull sharply into the parking lot. He quickly got out of his pickup and stalked over to Stella, Petey, and Kent.

"Hey, what's with Kent driving *my* engine?" JC demanded.

"Hi, JC," Petey said with a smile. "I'm coming back to work."

JC turned his scowling, dark face toward her for an instant. "Great." He glared back at Kent. "Someone told me you were driving my fire engine through town."

"It's not *your* engine," Kent said. "And you weren't here. The chief said take it out."

"There was no point in calling everyone in when Kent and I could take care of it," Stella said. "You and Kent are the only two members of the fire brigade who are licensed to drive the pumper and the fire engine. That means either one of you—or both of you—can drive when we need you."

JC's frown showed his displeasure. "Chief, you said when Ricky left that I was the engine driver. This makes me look bad."

Stella had heard many such arguments when she'd worked at the station back in Chicago. Sometimes ego got in the way of getting the job done.

"It doesn't make you look bad," she assured him. "We can't get caught up in who does what. There aren't a lot of us. We have to share responsibilities."

"I still don't like it." JC shook his head. "I gotta go. Late for work. Good to see you, Petey."

"Can I help wash the engine?" Petey asked Kent.

"Sure. You can do the whole thing if you want."

They walked together toward the firehouse.

"You did a good job handling that, Chief." Eric saluted Stella.

"Thanks. It happens from time to time."

Stella spent about thirty minutes cleaning the Cherokee and then headed up to the cabin. Eric let Hero stay outside for a while.

The phone inside the cabin was ringing. It was her grandfather's lawyer, Steven Morrow.

"I wanted to advise you that I've been able to put a stay on the sale of the old Gamlyn cabin," he said after introducing himself. "This buys us some time to take a look at the deed, and Eric Gamlyn's will, to make sure everything is in order. I'll keep you posted, Chief Griffin, and let you know if anything changes."

"That didn't sound much like progress," Eric said after she'd hung up.

"It sounded like lawyer-speak to me." She shrugged. "I'm changing clothes."

Stella put away her dress uniform, wondering if she needed to have it dry cleaned already. She shouldn't have worn it to the lake.

But who could've imagined that she'd suddenly find Eric walking around outside the cabin with her? There was no way to plan for that.

Did the experiment with Tagger mean that Eric could leave the cabin with anyone as long as the person had his badge? This was a whole new set of weird rules. She'd only just gotten used to the first rules of living with a ghost.

She heard the kitchen door open. Eric greeted Hero as the dog ran into the cabin.

Stella didn't mind being tethered to Eric, in theory. She wanted to make his afterlife better. He'd already suffered enough in her estimation. She wasn't sure yet how it was going to work in *practice*, though. There would be times she'd want to leave the badge in the cabin. She had to have some privacy.

Eric had started a fire in the hearth, and Hero ran to say hello to her as she walked out of the bedroom.

"I guess I should run in to Pigeon Forge and get some food." She stroked the Dalmatian's fur and scratched his ears. "I wish I didn't have to go so far for it. We need a grocery store in Sweet Pepper."

"Do you want me to go with you?" Eric asked.

"It's up to you. If you'd like to do a quick trip to Pigeon Forge, that's fine. If not, it's not like you can help carry groceries until I get back here."

"Then I'd like to stay," he said. "Hero needs some playtime, and I was never overly fond of the city."

"Okay. I'll be back."

"Don't forget you're going to look at that boat at six," he reminded her. "I'd like to do that, if you don't mind."

"That's fine. Anything you need from the store other than the usual?"

"Not this time. I've got some ideas for pepper recipes, but they're not ready for the testing stage."

Stella said goodbye, put on her jacket, and grabbed her bag. She purposely left Eric's badge on the table in the kitchen area. Maybe she didn't have to be so worried about finding private time away from him. Maybe he wanted some time away from her too.

It was cold outside, particularly since the wind continued to blow briskly down from the mountains. She'd noticed that most of the Little Pigeon River was frozen solid, with only a small stream moving through the middle of it. The pines and oaks were glistening with ice as she went out to the Cherokee.

There was an odd sound behind her. She thought at first it was just twigs snapping under the weight of the ice. It was quiet on the mountain, especially in the winter.

Then something hard poked her in the back and Bob Floyd's voice said, "You didn't think I was giving up so *easy*, did you?"

Chapter 14

~~~~~~~~~~

Stella realized as she turned around that the thing poking her in the back was a gun—a shotgun, in this case.

Bob's usually florid face was pale. He had dark circles under his eyes, and his hands were shaking.

"Bob, you have to stop this." She tried to stay calm. "I know there are other pieces of property around here that you could buy. You should get one of them."

"I bought this piece. At least I thought I did. Then your grandfather's hired gun stopped that, didn't he? I'm not giving up. One way or another, this cabin is coming down, and the ghost of Chief Eric Gamlyn is going away forever."

Stella was in a bad position. She could see Eric and Hero watching her from the front window in the cabin. She and Bob were too far away from Eric's proximity to get any help from him. She hoped Eric wouldn't let Hero out—she didn't want Bob to shoot him.

Bob was sweating, despite the cold. His dark eyes were glassy. Clearly, he wasn't in control of himself. She had to keep him talking until she could figure out what to do.

"What makes you think getting rid of the cabin will get rid of Eric's ghost?" she asked him.

"Madam Emery told me so."

"You mean the psychic reader who has that sign up in front of her house?" Stella had noticed it right away. The house was small, and not particularly eye-catching, except for the big sign in the front yard—"Madam Emery, Psychic Reader, Tarot, Palm Reading."

"That's right. I asked her what I should do when you threatened to send Eric after me."

Stella sighed. She knew she'd been wrong to do that last year. She'd lost her temper. "I'm sorry about that, Bob. I shouldn't have said that. I really can't make Eric come after you. I don't know what Madam Emery told you, but there's really no ghost here."

"We all know this place is haunted. And we all know Chief Gamlyn haunts it. Madam Emery told me all about the spirits. She told me Eric can't live here without the cabin. I believe her."

Eric was standing outside now. There was still nothing he could do to help Stella. Hero was inside, barking and jumping up and down at the door, trying to get out.

"Shooting me isn't going to change that," she reminded Bob. "Eric will still be here."

"Maybe. But if you're gone, your grandfather's lawyer won't care if I buy the property and destroy the cabin. He only cares because *you* do. I don't see any other way now. I'm sorry. I wish I did."

Me too. Stella glanced around, trying to figure out what she could do. The shotgun wasn't steady, but it was in her face. She couldn't risk it going off while she tried to take it from him. On the other hand, she wasn't going stand there and let him shoot her either.

"He's got a trick right knee," Eric told her. "When he tried out for the fire brigade, he couldn't get up the stairs with the hose."

Stella considered her target. She'd have to get out of the

line of fire when she made her move. But at least she'd have a fighting chance.

It helped that Bob had started crying and asking God to forgive him. Stella took a deep breath and kicked him hard in the right knee, shifting away from the business end of the shotgun.

When the weapon went off, the buckshot flew harmlessly into the trees. A flurry of ice and snow fell from the branches as the sound echoed up and down the mountain.

She took the gun away from him and put it in the back of the Cherokee. Bob was writhing on the cold, wet blacktop. "You broke my knee," he screamed at her.

"I'm going in to call an ambulance and the police." Her voice was shaking. "Don't get up. I wouldn't want anything else to happen to you."

She didn't say what could happen to him. She left that to his imagination. Stella walked inside and dialed 911 on the phone. "I can't believe this guy. He's ruining his whole life over this."

"He's an idiot," Eric said as she got off the phone with the 911 operator. "Sounds like Madam Emery might know a thing or two about ghosts, though."

"We could pay her a visit and find out."

That sign has been in the yard since I was a kid. My dad always said I shouldn't look at it as we drove by. He said it had something to do with the devil."

Stella whistled. "That's *really* old if you remember it as a kid."

"You're good with the sass."

"Is that the same 'Devil' that Tagger was talking about at the firehouse?"

"I was too afraid to ask."

Stella went back outside to see how Bob was doing and wait for the ambulance and police. He was gone.

She checked around. There was no sign of him. She heard a faint buzzing noise off in the woods. That's why she hadn't seen a car or truck. He'd come up on a snowmobile.

"Where is he?" Eric asked from the porch.

"I guess he got away. Maybe his knee wasn't that bad."

"He's slippery. I guess you should've waited out here with him. Did he take his shotgun?"

She looked in the back of the Cherokee. "Yep. I guess that means it will be my word against his that he was even here."

Eric frowned as they heard a siren coming up Firehouse Road. "I'm sure they'll take your word. He's already been brought in by the police because of his obsession with the cabin. There won't be any question. You're the fire chief."

Officer Frank Schneider drove the police car near the Cherokee and parked. He got out of the car, searching the area with his eyes as he came toward Stella.

"Chief Griffin." He scratched his head as he surveyed the empty driveway. "I got a call from 911 that you needed help. What's up?"

Stella explained what had happened. "He was gone when I came back out after calling it in. I think he left on a snowmobile. Maybe we can look around and find the tracks."

She and Frank spent about twenty minutes shuffling through the snow. They finally found some snowmobile tracks.

"These look fresh," he said. "Sounds like the ambulance. I hope they don't charge the town for a false alarm."

"Can they do that?"

He shrugged as they approached the ambulance drivers before they could leave their vehicle.

"Where's the victim?" the driver asked.

"He got away," Frank said. "Sorry you had to make the trip. We'll take him to the hospital ourselves after he's in custody."

The paramedic on the passenger side wrote in his logbook. "Okay. We're saying there was no victim when we arrived. Would you like to sign off on that?"

Frank signed his name and apologized again. "Next time you're off duty, let me buy you a drink at Beau's."

The offer didn't make the paramedics seem any less irritated by their fruitless effort and a long trip back home.

Stella and Frank watched them pull in a circle around the Cherokee and go back down the road.

"Think that helped?" she asked Frank.

"Probably not. I can at least say I offered when Chief Rogers is screaming in my face."

"What now?"

"You file a complaint against Bob Floyd. I write it down and call it in. Then I go pick him up. The chief is going to love *that* too."

"I'm sorry. I hope this is settled soon."

Frank smiled at her. "It's not your fault, Chief. Bob has gone off the deep end. Watch your back."

I It was starting to get dark. An owl hooted as it flew from a one large pine tree to another closer to the house.

"We'd better get going if we're meeting John to look at the boat," Eric reminded her. "Take my badge with you until all of this is over with Bob. It was terrible not being able to help while you were standing out here with him."

"This is crazy. I hope Ben's lawyer finds an answer soon."

Stella went inside and pocketed Eric's badge. She opened the door to the backseat of the Cherokee, and Hero happily jumped in.

"I guess we'll buy supplies at the convenience store," she said as she started the Cherokee. "Pigeon Forge will have to wait."

In Chicago, sometimes it was hard to tell that it was night because of the orange glow from the streetlights. There was no doubt in the mountains. The night came down like a sledgehammer. There were no streetlights except in the heart of Sweet Pepper. Stella had a large mercury vapor light put in at the cabin, and two similar outside lights at the firehouse. It was still really dark. She'd begun to appreciate how important the moon had been to people two hundred years ago.

She drove off the main road toward Nay Albert's farm,

the only lights she could see at his house and barn. The edges of the road, and the land that rolled away from it, were cloaked in complete blackness. It made the headlights on the Cherokee seem very bright.

"I think John is here," Eric said.

"I can't see his pickup." She carefully glanced at him. He looked luminous in the light from the dashboard. "You can use your ghostly powers to sense that?"

"I guess so. I can feel he's here."

"Good thing he can't see you," she quipped. "You look *really* scary right now."

He looked down at his torso, arms, and legs. "It's this light. This light would've made it so much easier to scare people away years ago."

"I think you did a good job keeping people away." She turned the Cherokee in to the area where John's pickup was parked. "Were you moaning and clanking things or just throwing things?"

"A little of both. Elvita Quick fainted once when she came inside the cabin with the town council." He grinned as he remembered.

Stella laughed as she got out of the Cherokee. Eric was immediately beside her. Hero barked a little and then whined and sat down on the seat when he realized he wasn't getting out.

"No wonder Elvita doesn't like you."

"I guess not many people do anymore."

Stella didn't have a chance to remark on the huge number of people who'd been at his memorial that day. Plenty of people loved him, or at least his legend. Bob, Elvita, and her sister, Theodora, weren't in that group.

"Chief." John walked out of an old garage to meet her. He had another man with him. "This is my friend, Rufus Palcomb. I told you about him. He and his family own a boat company."

Rufus appeared to be in his late thirties. Like John, he was tall, maybe six-foot-two with a large body structure—

broad shoulders and chest. It was hard to tell for sure in the dim light, but his hair might have been as red as Stella's.

"Chief Griffin." Rufus shook her hand. His voice was loud and hearty. "It's good to meet you. I've heard a lot about you from John."

"Only the good stuff," John promised with a slightly self-conscious smile. "Rufus and I went to school together. He was the captain of the Sweet Pepper Cougars during a year when we never lost a game."

Rufus grinned. "It was a good year. Everything since pales in comparison."

Stella smiled. Eric snorted but didn't comment.

"So I hear you're looking for a fireboat," Rufus said. "I've taken a peek at what Nay has to offer. It's not too bad. It'll need a lot of work though."

"Let's check it out," Stella replied.

They walked inside. Rufus pointed out the strengths and weaknesses of the old boat. "I'm sure she'd work for you," he said as they walked around the *Geraldine*. "Someone did a good job putting her in dry dock."

"That's right," Nay joined them. "Me and my son took care of her. She'll float for sure. She's strong too. I think she'll make a fine fireboat."

"I agree with Nay," Rufus said. "The only thing I'm not sure about is her size. She's kind of small for what you need. When John told me you were looking for a fireboat, I looked it up online. Most fireboats start at twenty-two feet. *Geraldine* is barely nineteen feet, not exactly standard size. Probably because she was homemade. I'm not sure about her holding a water cannon."

"I suppose you have the *perfect* boat," Nay said sarcastically. "Why am I not surprised?"

Rufus grinned at him. "Maybe because three generations of my family have built and sold boats? Your family has always been farmers. I don't know anything about farming—just the food that I buy at the store. Makes sense, doesn't it?"

John looked at Stella with almost the same expression that was on Eric's face at that moment. It made her smile.

"I'm sure whatever boat Rufus wants to sell you will cost a lot more than I'm selling this one for," Nay added.

"How much?" John asked.

Nay gave them his price.

Rufus whistled and shook his head. "This boat was *never* worth that much money. I can get the fire brigade into something better for less than that."

"Do what you want." Nay turned his back on them. "I can't guarantee the council will approve the purchase."

Stella nodded. She didn't want to get into a fight about this too. "I'll take a look at Rufus's boat and get back with you. Thanks for taking the time to show me yours."

Nay's remark was something like "*Bah.*"

John was already heading out of the garage with Rufus. Stella thanked Nay again and followed them. Her cell phone went off in the quiet of the evening.

"Chief Griffin? This is Officer Frank Schneider. We've located Bob Floyd. It seems there may have been some mistake about what happened earlier at the cabin."

Chapter 15

~~~~~~~~

Stella stopped walking. She could tell by Frank's voice that something was seriously wrong. "What do you mean? Have you arrested him?"

"No, ma'am. Can you come to the station? We need to clear up a few things."

John and Rufus had waited for her to get off the phone.

"What's wrong?" John asked.

She briefly sketched out what had happened at the cabin. "Now Frank says there may have been some mistake. He wants me to come to the station."

"Darn little weasel." John took out his truck keys. "I can't see how he can get out of this after that little stunt he pulled yesterday at the cabin."

"I don't know either, but I'll have to take a look at that boat another time, Rufus." She shook his hand and thanked him for his help. His warm grasp lingered slightly longer than a friendly handshake.

John didn't notice, but Eric did. "Not *another* admirer."

"That's okay." Rufus gave her his card. "Call me when you can. We'll go over everything."

"I'll follow you to town hall," John said. "I've gotta hear this."

Stella and Eric got back in the Cherokee. Hero was glad to see them, snuffling them and wagging his tail.

"Now John and his friend will be fighting over you," Eric said as they pulled down the long driveway to the main road.

"Stop it. He shook my hand."

"And you felt all *tingly*, right? I could tell."

"Ghostly powers?"

"I don't need to be dead to see something like that. Besides, I know you pretty well by now. You better slow down before you run out of eligible men. This is a small town."

She laughed at his words. His point of view was odd since she could never keep up with her girlfriends in Chicago. They were always joking about her being a late bloomer.

In the time she'd been in Sweet Pepper, she and John had kissed a few times and argued a lot more. She'd dated Zane Mullis, who was a helicopter pilot for the forest service. He'd been fun to go out with but had moved to Colorado.

"You make me sound like one of the loose women Molly Whitehouse is always talking about."

"If the floozy fits—"

"I'm not sure exactly what a 'floozy' is, but if it's what I think it is, you're lucky I can't turn one of the hoses on you. I guess I'd have to content myself with dropping your badge into someone's outhouse."

Eric laughed at her. "Kidding. You get hot really easy. Must be that red hair. I can only imagine the conflagration you and Rufus could create. The fire brigade would need bigger hoses to put it out."

"Yeah. Whatever. You're jealous."

"You're right. I wish I'd met someone like you when I was alive."

Stella stopped at the traffic light as she reached Sweet Pepper. Main Street was empty of cars and pedestrians. The only light she could see was at town hall.

"You think we would've gotten along?" she asked. "I mean, we're both bossy types. We both like to have our way."

Eric's hand was solid when he touched her cheek. "I think we could've been a major fire together."

Stella's heart raced for a moment. *He's a dead guy, stupid!* She kept her eyes glued on the road.

"I'd like to go with you inside," he said. "I can't wait to see Chief Rogers up close."

It felt normal between them again after that. Stella's mind still conjured a few images of her and Eric together. It was impossible. He'd been dead since before she was born. No matter how solid and lifelike he could appear sometimes, he was still a ghost.

"Looks like the gang's all here." Stella parked the Cherokee. "They must've decided to call a town council meeting at the same time."

"I'm sure Bob has a good story cooked up. Like Officer Schneider said, you better watch your back. I could do it, but you told me to shut my mouth when we're around other people."

Stella got out of the Cherokee and locked it. "Like you've paid any attention to me asking you not to speak around anyone else."

Eric passed through the doors into town hall as Stella opened one. Sandy Selvy was there to take her jacket and offer her a cup of coffee. John came in after her.

"They're in the conference room," Sandy whispered with a nervous eye on the group of men waiting in the hall. "Bob Floyd is there with his lawyer. Officer Schneider arrested him earlier. Mayor Wando is here too, along with Chief Rogers. Good luck, Stella."

"Maybe you could get some pepper recipes from this group," Eric said.

"I called Frank on the way here." John took her arm as they walked to the conference room. It was odd because he was almost exactly where Eric was beside her.

After a minute, Eric shook himself and moved to the other side of her. "That's kind of creepy."

"He gave me a heads-up," John continued, having no idea that he'd walked through a ghost. "Bob is claiming he was never at the cabin. Mayor Wando is backing him up. Chief Rogers is threatening to take Frank's badge for arresting Bob."

"I wish you wouldn't have told me," Stella muttered before they reached the group of men.

"Happy to do my job as police/fire department liaison."

"Ms. Griffin." Don Rogers greeted her with a big grin and a hearty handshake. "I'm glad you could make it. As you can see, everyone else is already here. Let's step inside the conference room."

The terrible part was that he was always at his most pleasant when he thought she'd done something wrong. She wondered, as she took her seat, if he'd ever accept her.

Everyone around the table was introduced. Bob was there with his lawyer. John sat beside Chief Rogers. Mayor Wando was biting his fingernails. Hugh Morton, the town attorney, was there with him.

Stella was the only one there alone—at least as far as anyone could tell. Eric was there beside her. It didn't make her feel much better.

"Let's get started," Don Rogers said.

The door to the conference room opened, and Stella's grandfather walked in. He sat next to her, as though he knew Eric was in the chair on her other side.

"Sorry I'm late," Ben Carson said. "I almost didn't find out about this meeting. Has something happened to the town notification system?"

Everyone around the table drew a deep breath. Ben Carson didn't look like much—tall and thin, his shoulders stooped with age—yet they all knew this man held a great deal of power and influence.

"Sorry about that, Ben." Chief Rogers cleared his throat and glanced away. "I guess I didn't think to call you because I didn't think you'd be interested."

Ben folded his long hands on the table before him. He was seventy-five and his gray hair was thinning, but his brown eyes were as sharp as ever.

"You mean you didn't *think* I'd be interested in you calling *my* granddaughter—the fire chief for this town that her great-great-grandfather built—a liar?"

There was more foot shuffling and throat clearing. Both lawyers took that moment to peruse the contents of their folders with more interest than they probably warranted.

"Come on." Mayor Wando smiled and tried to smooth things over. "No one is here to call Chief Griffin a liar."

"Then suppose you tell me, Erskine, exactly *why* we're here." Ben cast his steely gaze in his direction.

Stella didn't like the way this was headed. While she appreciated her grandfather trying to run interference for her, she could take care of herself.

"If we could allow Chief Rogers to continue," Stella said to the group. "I think he was about to explain why we're all here."

With Ben's angry glare directed at his face, Chief Rogers thanked her for giving him the floor again. "As I was saying, we have a situation here that requires immediate attention. My officer, Frank Schneider, has a complaint against councilman Bob Floyd that he received from our fire chief. Councilman Floyd has told me that this is a misunderstanding. He wasn't at Chief Griffin's cabin at the specified time that she is charging him with assault."

Ben tapped his fingers impatiently on the highly polished wood table. "So? Is that a reason to drag all of us out here tonight?"

Bob's lawyer cleared his throat and organized his papers. "Because this charge would do terrible harm to my client's reputation, Chief Rogers offered us the opportunity to present the facts here before the charges are permanently filed."

"You mean the charges against Bob haven't been *filed* yet?" Ben's voice sounded like the knell of doom. "I think I should call my attorney. It might be worth his while to fly in tonight and correct this problem."

Again, Stella stepped in. "I didn't want to file charges against Mr. Floyd for what happened yesterday at the cabin. He left me no choice when he came to my home again today, this time waving a shotgun at me."

"I think I sense a pattern developing," Ben drawled. "He's obsessed with the cabin."

"Hey, for once, I agree with the old man," Eric said.

Stella ignored him and focused on the living group around her.

"I was with Erskine the whole time Chief Griffin says I was at the cabin." Bob was sweating profusely, despite the coolness of the room. He kept fiddling with his tie and glancing at Ben. "Ask him. He'll tell you."

"I was with Bob at my house during that time." Mayor Wando's voice was stiff and rehearsed.

"Was there anyone else with you?" Ben asked.

"You don't have to answer that." Bob's lawyer scowled at Mayor Wando. "I'm sure the town attorney would tell you the same thing if he weren't scared of Ben Carson."

"You can tell he's not from around here," Eric added.

Stella frowned at him.

"What? You know it's true."

"I'm not afraid of Ben," Hugh Morton said. "There hasn't been an arrest as yet. You can say whatever you want."

"Look," Stella said. "I was there. So was Bob. Officer Schneider and I found the snowmobile tracks that were left behind. I don't want to press charges, but I will if that's my only recourse. We can let a jury figure out where the truth lies."

"I want to caution Chief Griffin," Bob's lawyer threatened. "There could be a forthcoming lawsuit from this accusation."

Eric and Ben shouted, "*What?*" at the same time. Ben stood up and pounded his fist on the table. Eric hovered above it.

"I'll make sure you never practice law again in Tennessee," Ben promised.

Bob's lawyer began to appear unsure too. The two lawyers exchanged glances. They bent their heads close together and whispered a few words.

"My client would be willing to guarantee that nothing

of this sort will ever happen again, if you don't press charges, Chief Griffin," Bob's lawyer said carefully. "Not that he's *admitting* to any wrongdoing in this matter. We simply want to make sure that his reputation in the community is not tarnished."

Everyone looked at Stella.

It was a club—a boy's club. She'd never be part of it. While it was appealing to try to fit in with them, Stella couldn't let it go.

"Ms. Griffin?" Chief Rogers verbally nudged her.

She stood next to her grandfather. "I'm willing to give a little on this, gentlemen."

"Stella!" Ben tried to stop her.

"But Mr. Floyd will have to meet my terms for me to drop the charges."

Bob's lawyer raised his head, pencil in hand. "Yes?"

"Mr. Floyd admits that he came to the cabin with the shotgun. He promises not to come to the cabin again, *ever*, for any reason, and he apologizes right now, in front of all of you. Afterward, you will all be my witnesses that this happened should the need arise."

"Go get 'em." Eric soundlessly applauded.

"My client will *not* admit to guilt in this matter," Bob's lawyer began.

Bob tugged on the man's jacket and whispered something to him.

"My client has agreed to these terms." The lawyer changed his tone quickly.

Stella sat down and waited.

"I apologize for losing my temper and coming up there today." Bob sniffled as he spoke, tears running down his cheeks. "I was scared. I wanted to get rid of the cabin right away. Madam Emery said Chief Gamlyn will haunt me until I do. That's why I bought the land."

Mayor Wando patted Bob's arm and convinced him to stop speaking.

"My client's last words are not to be spoken outside this room," Bob's lawyer said.

"My granddaughter isn't interested in your mewling apologies," Ben countered.

"That was the deal." Stella looked into each man's face. "You're my witnesses. You're legally bound by his confession. I won't press charges this time. If anything even remotely like this happens again, I'll call on each of you to testify against Bob Floyd in court."

Chief Rogers nodded as Bob broke down into anguished sobs. "I think that concludes our business tonight. Thank you all for coming out so late."

As everyone began leaving, Stella thanked her grandfather. "I hope we can do something about the cabin. Bob's not in his right mind. I don't know if he'll remember what happened if he starts thinking about coming up there again to get rid of the ghost."

Ben took her hand as they walked out of the conference room. Outside, in the empty room of makeshift walls and telephones used by the Sweet Pepper police, he said, "You shouldn't have let him off so easy."

"Why? Now they owe me. Isn't that the way it works?"

He smiled, a devil lurking in his dark eyes. "I believe it is."

Chapter 16

~~~~~~~~~~~

They watched Bob Floyd limping through the building to the front door with his lawyer.

Ben chuckled. "How'd you know to pick his bad knee?"

Stella put her hands into her pockets. Eric grinned at her.

"Lucky guess." She yawned. "I'm going home. I have to be up early tomorrow."

"That's right. You're starting the arson investigation." He took her elbow as they walked out together. "If it's any perspective for you, Stella, I don't think that fire was an accident. Like me, Barney was reviled and feared—unless people needed him to take care of their problems."

She studied his face as they went outside, the cold air biting into them. "Are you afraid you might end up the same way?"

He laughed. "No. That's why I have security. Barney believed all that blather about people around here loving him. He didn't understand."

Stella shook her head, too tired for any more politics. Bernard, her grandfather's driver, waited in his big black Lincoln. "Thanks for coming, Ben. It was nice to have someone on my side."

He hugged her carefully, as though she might break. "Get some rest. I love you. Watch your back."

She got in the Cherokee. Eric was already in the passenger seat. Hero whined and barked at them, glad it was time to go home.

"Well? I know you have plenty to say about this. Thanks for keeping most of it to yourself during the meeting."

"I hope you don't trust him any more than you do the rest of those good old boys in there."

Stella started the engine and pulled out into the empty street. "I try not to trust anyone too much. You never know where that will get you."

"The only people I ever trusted were the men on the fire brigade when I was chief."

"And look where that got you." The words were out. She couldn't call them back.

For years, everyone had thought that Eric was killed in the line of duty. Now they knew the truth. A man he'd trusted had been partially responsible for his death.

Eric was silent the rest of the way home. When they reached the cabin, he let Hero out for a while. Stella brought in a few pieces of junk mail and made sure the bear-proof trash cans were closed and locked down.

"I'm going to bed," she said. "Make sure you turn the sound down on whatever electrical device you're planning to use tonight, please."

"Goodnight." He didn't look up from the fire he was lighting in the hearth. The firelight played through him as though he were only made of colorful mist.

"Okay. I'm sorry. I didn't mean for you to take that the wrong way about trusting people."

He smiled sadly at her. "Goodnight, Stella."

The next morning dawned bright and clear. Stella had slept badly. *Probably a guilty conscience for reminding Eric about his death.*

She stared bleary-eyed out the bedroom window. Hero was outside again, chasing birds and squirrels.

After getting dressed in warm clothes, Stella pulled on her black work coveralls with the Sweet Pepper Fire Brigade insignia. The town had purchased twenty pairs of them at discount from a retailer in Nashville. All of the members of the group wouldn't go out to an arson investigation at the same time, so there were plenty for now.

This morning none of the group was going with her. Working with a real arson investigator would be challenging enough for Stella. She didn't want to make it a training exercise for her volunteers. The fire brigade went out with her on smaller fires to help discover their causes.

"Eric?" she called when she'd finished putting her hair up and walked out into the living area. She didn't see him until she checked out on the deck in back. He was standing at the rail, staring down at the half-frozen Little Pigeon River.

"Did you sleep well?"

"Not really," she admitted, standing next to him. The cold wind blasted the high deck, sprinkling snow and ice from the trees above them. "Go ahead. Say it. I didn't sleep because I said that to you last night."

"Feeling guilty?"

"I guess."

He turned to her. "Don't. You're right. I trusted unwisely. You should keep your distance. People can hurt you if you let them."

"But what about the fire brigade?"

"No one was there when I needed them, Stella. I'm dead because of it. Don't let that happen to you."

She folded her arms across her chest and stomped her feet. "Yeah, well, I'm going to freeze to death if I don't get inside. I'm going to make some hot tea. I know I'm out of Cokes and coffee. I wish you could go to the store for us. You could probably figure out what food to buy better than me."

"You mean something besides Coke, popcorn, and breakfast pastry?" He smiled at her efforts to get warm.

"Not everyone cooks, you know. When it was my turn to cook in Chicago, the guys knew they were always getting takeout. Chief Henry told me once that I'd never get married because I couldn't cook a meat loaf."

"Was that his criteria?" Eric followed her back into the cabin. "Do you regret that you gave up your job there?"

Stella foraged for something edible still left in the cabinets or the refrigerator as the water warmed for her tea. "No. Sometimes I miss the discipline, and people on my own level to talk to."

"People on your own level will always be hard if you're the one in charge."

She found a piece of cheese in a plastic bag and sniffed it before she ate it. "You're very wise. It must be because you're so *old*."

He laughed at that, looking more solid and alive than he had on the deck. "I think if you don't get married, it will be more because of your smart mouth than your meat loaf. Are we heading out to the arson scene or what?"

"Yes." She sipped some hot tea, frowned, and left most of it at the cabin. "And we're stopping later for supplies. Don't let me come home without food again. I think that cheese was bad."

They got in the Cherokee and called Hero into the vehicle. It didn't take much. He was always ready to go. Stella was worried that she might miss the beginning of practice that afternoon, so she dropped Hero off at the firehouse.

Petey was there with Allen Wise. They were talking about the latest Sweet Pepper gossip.

Allen worked for Bob Floyd at the barber shop. "The police found him on the floor this morning. He called to ask me if I could open for him. I've never known the like."

"Who are you talking about?" Stella quickly checking her messages.

"Bob Floyd," Petey supplied. "Someone beat him up and robbed the barber shop early this morning."

"What?" Stella looked up at him. "How is he?

"I don't know. They transported him to the hospital." He

shook his head, always mindful of his thick, wavy hair. Not a strand moved out of place. "I haven't heard anything else."

"Were we called on that?" Stella asked.

"Nope. Just the police and ambulance." He slurped his coffee and ate another cheese cracker. "Bob has a hard head. He'll get through it. Maybe next time he'll be careful who he crosses."

Stella was puzzled by his words. She didn't have time to ask him to explain. She reminded both of them that John would be there to oversee practice that afternoon if she was still working on the arson investigation.

Petey frowned. "It's not bad enough that I'm assistant chief and can't lead the practice; I have to miss an arson investigation."

Stella smiled and urged her to get well soon. "I'll see you later."

When she got in the Cherokee with Eric, he didn't hint around or mince words on what he thought had happened to Bob.

"I guess Ben showed that little man what line he shouldn't cross."

"What are you talking about?"

"Your grandfather. Did you think he was going to let Bob threaten you and *not* do anything about it?"

She shook her head. "He wouldn't do something like that. He's too smart. He'd know everyone would be expecting it." Stella didn't believe it was true, but she knew it would be the talk of the town by noon.

"He doesn't care," Eric responded. "And I think it's amazing he didn't kill Bob for what he did."

She didn't mention it again as she drove to the Sunset Beach community and parked the Cherokee beside Gail Hubbard's SUV with the state arson investigator seal on the driver's side door.

"Good morning, Chief," Officer Skeet Richardson greeted her. "Mrs. Hubbard is already back there. I heard about the trouble up at your place yesterday. Sorry that happened to you."

Stella put on her gloves as he was speaking and took out her tool kit of items she'd collected to help with investigating arson. She always carried extra gloves and face masks in case her volunteers forgot theirs. She also had a small digital camera, duct tape, and plastic containers for samples.

"Yeah. It wasn't any fun. I'm sorry Officer Schneider had to get involved. I hope he'll be okay."

"I'm sure he'll be fine. I suppose you heard about Bob Floyd?" He shook his head. "He was a mess."

"That was unfortunate." Stella was careful what she said. Her words would be out there like other news, floating through the streets of Sweet Pepper.

"Yeah. No ID on the perp yet." He hitched up his belt. "I guess we'll probably never know *for sure* what happened."

Stella smiled at him. "There's a lot of that going around. Excuse me."

Gail looked up and waved as Stella walked around the back of the burned house. "Good to see you. At least we have nice weather for this. It's the only part we'll think of as pleasant today, I'm sure."

She had already collected some samples from the rubble and had moved some pieces of charred wood and metal into separate piles on what was left of the grass.

"I see you've created a kit for yourself, Stella. Good work. I'd heard you'd done a few arsons by yourself. Your work on Victoria Lambert's house was impressive."

Stella put on her face mask, wondering how that information made it all the way to Nashville. It seemed like no one there would be interested or impressed by what went on in Sweet Pepper.

"I wasn't prepared for it, but I got by with help from my volunteers."

"It must be odd for you, given your background, working with a bunch of amateurs," Gail commented. "What do you make of this?"

Stella studied the broken shard of pottery Gail showed her. "I don't know a lot about pottery. It looks like some of the stuff we saw in here when we answered the call."

"This isn't any ordinary pottery." Gail turned it over again in her gloved hand. "I'm pretty sure this is Seagrove pottery. I have some myself. Beautiful stuff."

"I'm sure Barney Falk had a lot of antiques and other expensive items in the house." Stella picked up a melted computer. "There won't be much left."

Gail and Stella continued moving and cataloguing items they found. Some, like the computer, were easy to recognize. Others—it was anybody's guess.

"Now you said Mr. Falk was found on the kitchen floor," Gail said. "But you think he was upstairs in the bedroom, and the fire had burned through the floor, dropping him down."

"Yes. But not the fire. It was the explosion."

"Oh. Right. Any idea what caused that?"

"No. Not right offhand. Obviously not C-4 or even dynamite. This was smaller, not as powerful."

Gail squinted up at her as she asked for help moving a large piece of furniture. It looked like what was left of a sofa. There were still some springs that were recognizable.

"What's that white powder in there?" Eric asked.

Stella peered into the bottom of the sofa. There was some white powder that was left behind after the fire. She took out two small containers and labeled them before she scraped some of the powder into them. She also took a picture of the place where'd she found it.

"What's that you've got there?" Gail looked over Stella's shoulder with inquisitive eyes.

"I'm not sure. It doesn't look like residue from the fire. I don't think it's ash. I thought I'd send it in to be analyzed."

"I'll be glad to have that done for you." Gail took one of the containers from her. "We can get it analyzed more quickly if I take it to the lab."

"Thanks." Stella was surprised and pleased by her partner's enthusiasm. She pocketed the other container.

"Are you gonna trust her with that?" Eric asked.

Stella couldn't answer, but she saw no reason not to trust Gail with it. Eric was too used to working by himself when he was fire chief. Stella was used to working with a team that handled various parts of fires and investigations.

By lunchtime, the two women had moved a sizable part of the debris, separating and cataloguing as they went. They sat down together in the front yard, eating lunches that Officer Richardson had brought them from the diner.

"Are you married, Stella?" Gail asked as she picked up the large pickle that went with her chips and roast beef sandwich.

"No." Stella munched on her chips. "You?"

"Yep. Twenty-five years. He's a paramedic. We both love what we do, but we get too wrapped up in it sometimes. We have two kids, a boy and a girl. They don't mind telling us when we've forgotten something we promised to do."

"I had my parents for that in Chicago." Stella laughed. "Here, I'm on my own. It's not always a good thing. I can't remember to buy groceries."

"That's the nature of the job. I was a fire chief for a few years in Nashville before I was offered this position. Your job is a lot more hectic than mine."

"That's because she doesn't come out this way unless someone rich and famous dies," Eric said.

"You must be tough to reach your position." Stella saw a large, dark sedan pull up behind her Cherokee. "I was the first woman at my station back in Chicago. It wasn't easy."

Gail agreed as she cleaned her hands on a napkin and got to her feet. "It wasn't easy for me either. It never is when you're a woman. Who have we got here?"

Chapter 17

～～～～～

Two men climbed out of the car as Stella got to her feet. It was easy to tell who worked for whom. The first man wore an expensive suit and shoes. He was dark haired and grinning before he reached them. The other man was thick and broad shouldered. He carefully surveyed the area as he followed his boss.

"Ladies. I'm Barney Falk Jr. I wanted to come by and tell you how much I appreciate your efforts on behalf of my family." He shook both their hands with eagerness before pressing a campaign button into their palms.

Stella had seen his election signs around the area. At first, she'd thought it was the older man running for election again. John had enlightened her that this was Barney Falk's son. He was running for his father's old seat in the House of Representatives against Susan Clark.

"Mr. Falk." Gail smiled at him as she accepted his political button. "I'm so sorry for your loss."

"Yes. It's been a hard time for us all."

"He could at least stop smiling while he's saying it," Eric observed. "It would take some of the fake emotion out of it."

Falk turned to Stella. "I believe I owe you another debt of gratitude, Chief Griffin. You helped save my son when he was trapped on that mountain trail."

"So I heard." Stella put his political button in the pocket of her coveralls. "I'm glad he was all right."

"Yes. He was fortunate to have you and your volunteers on hand to help him and his friends."

There was something shifty about his eyes that Stella didn't like. He didn't speak his mind as his father had. Even though the older man was obnoxious, she would've trusted him more to tell the truth.

"So you're going through everything?" He gave the burned house a quick once-over and then turned away. "I can hardly stand to look at it. My father was from this area, you know. We moved to Nashville after he became state representative. I was raised on our estate there. But my heart has always been here in Sweet Pepper. We vacationed here when I was growing up. My roots run deep."

"Oh brother." Eric walked away to look through more of the rubble.

"My heart goes out to you and your family," Gail assured him as two local TV trucks pulled up to join the group.

Both women were interviewed—Stella more on her miraculous rescue of the college students on Dead Bear Trail than on fighting the fire that had destroyed the house.

Gail spoke about the complexities of figuring out what had caused the fire that had taken the life of Barney Falk. She had to tell the camera crews that they couldn't go any closer to the house.

This made the TV news personality focus on Barney Falk Jr. and his political campaign to defeat the incumbent. The news crew even talked to Officer Richardson.

The media left about twenty minutes before Chief Rogers arrived at the scene.

Gail snickered. "A little too late, isn't he?"

She and Stella were back behind the house again by that time. Chief Rogers bypassed Officer Richardson and joined them there.

"Ms. Griffin. Mrs. Hubbard." He nodded to them.

Stella noticed that he was wearing a new uniform. There were no coffee stains, and the crease in the pants was sharp.

"Something we can do for you, Chief Rogers?" Gail's voice was muffled by the face mask she wore.

"Just wondering how things are going. When we can stop furnishing a deputy up here."

"I'm not sure about that yet. Chief Griffin and I will make that call." Gail looked up at him with a container in her hands. "Anything else?"

He smiled and adjusted his pants. "Have you all seen a TV news crew here from Nashville?"

"You missed them," Stella said. "You missed the candidate too."

"That's too bad. I went to school with Barney at East Tennessee. He's a good man."

"Not if he's a friend of yours," Eric remarked.

"Okay." Chief Rogers rocked back on his heels. "You two let me know when you learn something about all this. Or if you need anything. Have a nice day."

Gail watched him walk away. "Is he always so pompous?"

"Yes." Stella grinned. "Though I have it on good authority that he's a very fine human being."

"It must be under that uniform somewhere." Gail snorted at her own joke and went back to work.

The sun was warm as the afternoon got started. There were sounds of boats on the lake and the strong, fishy smell of the water. Officer Richardson fell asleep in his police car. Gail and Stella worked side by side, identifying what they could as they progressed through the rubble.

Stella had to quit at two p.m. This was going to be a long, slow process. She wanted to be at the practice session that afternoon. Her volunteers were going through a new drill none of them had ever tried before. She knew John could handle it—he had the training. She just wanted to be there.

"Okay," Gail said when Stella told her. "I'll see you again tomorrow morning. I'm quitting too. I need to catch a shower and talk to my husband for a while. It's his birthday tomorrow, and he's a little pissy about me being in the field on important days."

"Wish him a happy birthday for me," Stella said.

"Leaving for the day?" Officer Richardson said as she reached him.

"Yep. I'll be back tomorrow. Thanks for all your help."

"Why are you going?" Eric asked when she was taking off her coveralls and putting away her gear. "Trump can handle the drill."

She got in the Cherokee with a last wave at Officer Richardson. "I know John can handle it. I want to be there. It's not like we're going to be done here within another couple of hours. Besides, this is Hero's chance to show off his training. I know you want to see that."

"I thought you'd want to get the investigation done first."

"We have to get the drills in where we can. I know *you* know that. Are you worried about the investigation?"

"The longer it sits, the colder the trail is going to be."

She pulled the Cherokee into the road. "We'll have to agree to disagree on this, Chief. Keeping my people going, getting them ready for calls—that's what's important to me."

"You coddle your people, you know."

"Yeah, well, they're mine to coddle."

Eric talked about similar fires he'd investigated as they drove back through town. He'd had to work with barebones knowledge too. He'd had no formal training as either a firefighter or an arson investigator.

"I thought by this time we'd have our own paramedic unit and ambulance too," he said. "Nothing ever happens as fast as you think it should."

"That might be true in some cases." She nodded toward the firehouse parking lot. "It looks like this one may have moved a little *too* fast."

"Nice boat. I guess Rufus decided not to wait for you to come to him." There seemed to be an extra large group of people at the firehouse. Stella's regulars were there, examining the boat, along with Frank Schneider. She recognized two other part-time police officers, though she didn't know their names.

"It looks like Don Rogers made good on his promise to send some volunteers our way." She pulled into the parking lot.

"I hate to always be the conspiracy theorist," Eric said, "but why his sudden generosity? All this time he's fought you tooth and nail. Why is he suddenly sharing troops with you?"

"I don't know. I guess we'll find out."

Stella wasn't sure if she cared that Don Rogers had an ulterior motive. Her ranks were depleted. Every call made her nervous, wondering if there would be enough people to handle it. Taking in these new volunteers, and getting Petey back, would make her feel better. She welcomed the new people with a handshake and a greeting. Tagger was in charge of having them sign up.

"I thought I was coming to *your* place to see the boat." She smiled up at Rufus after dealing with the new recruits.

"Chief Griffin. Good to see you! I had the boat on the trailer already. I thought I might as well bring it out here."

"Nice sales pitch."

"Can we keep the boat, Chief?" Tagger asked excitedly. "I love it. Could I drive it once in a while?"

Tagger waved and smiled at the ghost of his former chief.

"Yeah, Chief." Kent ran his hand along the side of the boat. "Maybe we could take turns taking it out on weekends. It could be kind of a perk for being a volunteer."

"I call dibs on that!" Bert yelled out as he jumped into the driver's seat.

"It's exciting," Petey said. "What will it cost to outfit the boat for use at fires?"

Stella smiled. That was why Petey was second-in-command. She was always in tune with what was important.

"Rufus?" Stella hailed him as he gave tours of the boat. "Any idea on a price for the boat and what it will cost to get it set up to fight fires?"

He jumped down on the pavement next to her. He was a

strong-looking man, with big arms and a powerful chest. He seemed to be light on his feet too. Stella wondered how she could get him to commit to being a volunteer.

"I have everything worked up for you, Chief. I left the paperwork in your office."

John clapped him on the shoulder. "Tell her the best part. *That's* what will get her motivated to clinch the deal with the town council."

Stella focused on Rufus. "Don't keep me guessing."

"I'm thinking about becoming a volunteer," he said. "I could get the boat set up, no charge, and you could make me captain of the fireboat team."

"That's a good idea. John knows I never say no to a volunteer. Suit up with us for practice today. Let's see what you've got." Everyone, including Stella, put on their turnout gear.

The volunteers ran through their usual practice routines. Rufus had no trouble running up and down the stairs with the sixty-pound hose around him or pulling a one-hundred-fifty-pound dummy across the parking lot without its feet touching the ground. He didn't break a sweat when he ran up and down the ladder with Allen across his shoulders.

"Does that get it?" he asked Stella with a grin.

"As far as being a volunteer, it does. I'll have to take a look at the contract for the boat and get the approval of the town council."

"Good enough. Consider me a new recruit."

All of the fire brigade members were happy to welcome Rufus into the group. It wasn't only Stella that had been aware of their shortage of manpower. The new police crossover recruits, Clyde Hampton, Nancy Bradford, and Frank Schneider, only observed this time around. Stella was hoping to have them sign up next time.

"I know you've been waiting for our last exercise." Stella pointed to the old car at the far end of the parking lot. "Kent was good enough to donate this old clunker for our practice."

"For a hefty tax write-off," John called out.

"My wife jumped at the chance to get it out of the yard," Kent said. "I feel bad getting rid of her. She was our first car."

"1972 Plymouth Barracuda." Eric eyed the car with great respect. "Sweet."

"I know, right, Chief?" Tagger laughed. "Remember when you wanted one of those?"

Stella was the only one who noticed the exchange between Tagger and Eric. She gave Tagger a warning look, and he apologized.

"Thank you, Kent." She returned to the introduction of the new drill, breaking up the razzing Kent was getting about the car and his wife.

"What are we gonna do with the car, Chief?" JC asked.

"We're gonna light it on fire and rescue Clara and her family from it." Clara and her family were the group's training dummies.

Everyone gathered around the car.

"Light it on fire?" David Spratt asked with Hero and Sylvia at his feet. "Isn't that counterintuitive to being a firefighter?"

"Sometimes being able to experience the real thing with no lives at peril is good." Stella told him about the first fire the team had responded to at Nay Albert's old chicken house. It was before he'd joined the group. "I'm always looking for a house where we can do a controlled burn. No luck so far, but the day will come."

Stella sent Kent with Rufus to hook up a hose to the hydrant at the edge of the parking lot. That killed two birds with one stone—Rufus got to see how to hook up a hose at the same time.

"Is the town okay about using the water for practice?" Kimmie asked.

"More than okay," Stella replied. "It helps them flush out the system."

She could see some trepidation on the faces of her volunteers. No one who had ever fought a fire was happy with the idea of starting one. There were always variables, always the chance it could get out of hand.

"I can't believe I have to miss this," Petey complained.

"Me either," Banyin sighed. "At least we get to be here."

"I don't think you're gonna be here much after your baby is born." Allen shrugged. "That's what Jake said last time I cut his hair."

Banyin's mouth thinned mutinously. "Jake's got a big mouth."

Royce and Tagger brought out large fire extinguishers. It seemed that they were ready to get started.

Stella let Tagger have the privilege of lighting the Barracuda on fire after Clara and her family were in the car. He lit a fire under the hood and stepped back.

"Okay. This is going to be easier because there are no seat belts. We want to get Clara, her husband, and her two kids out of the car first," Stella instructed them. "We have a mock first-aid station over there where you'll take the family until the paramedics get here. Remember to work together. As the family is rescued, put out the fire under the hood."

They had to reignite the fire several times so that everyone had a chance to rescue the family as well as put out the fire under the hood. It went very smoothly. Each volunteer did exactly what needed to be done.

Rufus took his turn when everyone else had showed him what to do. He was fast and efficient, taking the two children to first aid and returning for the two adults in record time. Stella clicked the stopwatch and commended him.

"Now we'll start again," Stella said. "This time, we'll be evaluating Hero and Sylvia."

Chapter 18

~~~~~~~~~~~~~~~

"**A**re you sure they're up for this, Chief?" Kimmie's face was flushed and smudged with soot.

"We're going to find out," Stella said. "They've both been in training to learn how to deal with this type situation. They need practice too."

Kimmie and David whispered together for a moment. David picked up one of the fire extinguishers and went close to the car. "Ready," he said.

Stella had to evaluate the dogs too. The state was paying for their training and wanted to know the results. It was also the only way the dogs could be certified to go into emergency situations with the fire brigade.

Sylvia was up first. John and Kent put the dummies back in the car, and Tagger set the fire.

Stella gave the command for Sylvia to rescue one of the dummies. Sylvia whined and looked at Kimmie. She still sat obediently at the side of the car.

"Sylvia," Stella said again. "Go."

Sylvia ran into the car and pulled one of the children out. She went in again with no prompting and pulled the other child out before she went back for the adults. Then she went back and sat at Kimmie's feet, her tail hitting the pavement as she waited to be praised for her work.

Stella wrote down her hesitation and her time rescuing the family, which was still within the parameters set by the state for rescue dogs. She gave Kimmie a nod, and Kimmie praised Sylvia and gave her a treat.

The fire was put out again. The dummies of the family were put back in place.

Stella cued Hero, who'd been waiting at the side of the car.

There was no hesitation on Hero's part. He barked as he leapt into the backseat and dragged out the children. He went back immediately and got the two adults out as well, in less time than Sylvia had taken for rescuing the children.

Everyone applauded and praised the young dog. There was a curious moment when Hero ran to Eric to get his praise. The dog stood there—appearing to lick and snuffle the air as Eric told him how smart and good he was.

"Hey." Royce pointed to Hero. "What's he doing over there?"

Kimmie called Hero to her. He came after jumping up and barking at Eric. Kimmie gave him his treat, and the rest of the fire brigade patted his head.

"He shouldn't have done that." David frowned. "I don't know why Hero ran over there, Chief. He broke his training. It doesn't make any sense."

Tagger snickered and Eric shrugged, both of them leaving Stella to explain without telling the truth.

"I'm sure he was just excited." She put away her stopwatch. "Look at these times! We have two great fire rescue dogs coming up in the ranks."

Everyone was diverted by that, and the moment was forgotten as they took the equipment back inside, cleaned up, and changed clothes.

Stella put Rufus's name, along with Frank Schneider's, Clyde Hampton's, and Nancy Bradford's, on lockers with a pieces of masking tape. The police officers had decided to join up after they'd seen what would be required of them.

"I'm buying drinks for all the new recruits at Beau's when we're done. I'm glad to welcome all of you."

Most of the fire brigade members went to Beau's when they left the firehouse. Many had to go back to their jobs. Being a volunteer required hundreds of hours away from jobs and families at inconvenient times of the day and night. It was essential, but Stella knew it was hard on them.

Willy Jenkins, the owner of Beau's Bar and Grill, was there when the fire brigade members came in for Stella's free drink. Beau's was a dark place with two pool tables, a few older video games, and sometimes a band playing on Friday night.

"It's the Sweet Pepper Fire Brigade," Willy called out. He looked like a nightclub bouncer with powerful arms and a wide chest. Stella had never seen him without his red suspenders and a Beau's T-shirt. "First drink is on the house for all volunteers."

Stella said she'd still spring for the second drink. Willy was a good friend of the fire brigade and a town council member. He'd voted repeatedly for money the fire brigade had needed.

"Thanks, Uncle Willy." Rufus shook his hand.

"Don't tell me you finally did something useful and joined up?" Willy was obviously pleased.

John shrugged when Stella glanced at him. "Didn't I tell you? Rufus and Willy are family. I think it might make it a little easier to get council approval on that boat."

"You're a sneak," she said, but she meant it in a good way.

"That's so sweet," Eric said. "Can we find out what my radius is so I can go home?"

"Chief Griffin!" Willy bellowed her name. "What's your poison?"

Stella ordered a Coke. It was too early for her to start drinking.

"What's this I hear about the fire brigade buying a boat from my no-account nephew?"

"I've got the plans and the contract. I haven't looked at them yet." Stella smiled. "I'll have to get council approval too."

"Bring 'em down here to me. I'll take care of it. I have to keep my brother and this sweet young thing in work." He pinched Rufus's cheek.

"Should I tell him about Nay's boat?" Stella asked John.

"He probably already knows, but you can if it would make you feel better."

Stella told Willy about going to look at Nay's boat.

He acted like it was nothing. "That old piece of junk? He's been trying to get rid of that for the last twenty years. Whatever Rufus offered you is a better deal, I guarantee it."

She thanked him and told him she'd bring the papers by.

"No reason to trouble yourself, Chief." Rufus pulled another set of documents from his jacket pocket. "I'm always prepared."

He winked at her as he gave his uncle the papers. Stella wasn't happy with the bypass. She was the head of the fire brigade. It would be wrong for her not to present the project to the council after she'd had a chance to look at it herself.

"I appreciate your help, both of you," she said to Willy and Rufus. "I don't want to do it this way. I'll let you know after I look at everything. Then we can present the project to the council."

Rufus and Willy shrugged.

"Whatever you like, Chief. Just trying to expedite the project," Rufus said.

"Thanks." She studied the two men. They were only similar in height. Willy's hair had thinned and turned gray. He was probably well over three hundred pounds. She wondered if Rufus would look like his uncle in twenty years.

"No hard feelings, Chief." Willy shook her hand. "I've been meaning to talk to you about a fund-raiser barbecue I'd like to put on for the fire brigade. I know you need more members. You could have a sign-up here too. The money we raise could be for the boat or whatever you all need. What do you think?"

Stella was glad he wasn't annoyed with her preferring to present her choice of boat to the council. "Thank you. What do you need me to do?"

He laughed. "Come on by and eat some barbecue, dar-lin'. Wear that sexy dress uniform you were wearing at the memorial."

Stella agreed, though she wouldn't wear the dress uni-form. It would be a great opportunity to raise money and awareness for the group.

"I think the uncle and nephew might have to fight it out over you." Eric seemed amused. "I'm surprised John isn't knocking them both out of the way."

"You of all people know there's nothing solid between me and John." Stella walked away from the bar with her Coke. Country music was blaring from the jukebox, and Kent was beating David at pool.

"Good call." John joined her, beer in his hand. "I'm curious though. Why work with the establishment drop-ping charges against Bob Floyd but not let Willy take care of the whole fireboat ordeal?"

"One is different than the other," she explained. "With Bob, it's personal. It's my decision. With the fireboat, that's the town's business. I'm the fire chief. I'm expected to work within the guidelines."

John laughed and put an arm lightly around her shoul-ders. "You are *so* green. Wait until you're here another couple of years. You'll be glad someone like Willy is will-ing to take over."

Stella stepped away from the casual arm across her shoulders. She didn't want anyone getting the wrong idea about her and John. She sipped her Coke and didn't reply. She understood the boundaries she had created for herself. John didn't have to understand.

"So how is old Bob Floyd?" JC asked with a laugh as he chalked up a pool cue. "I hear the old man roughed him up a little."

"What did you expect?" Royce replied. "He held a shot-gun on the chief. I wanted to rough him up when he was at the cabin with the bulldozer. The man needs to learn some respect."

Stella pretended not to hear their conversation. It was

exactly as she'd thought it would be. There didn't have to be any proof to blame her grandfather for what had happened to Bob. It looked like revenge—so that's what it was.

"I warned you." John took another sip of beer as he squinted at her. "Everyone knows."

"If everyone knew, I'm sure Chief Rogers would arrest Ben. But there's no proof. Just another story about the old man protecting his own."

She walked away from him toward the door to leave. John started to follow her, but his foot seemed to encounter a slick spot on the floor. No one could find it later. His foot flew out from under him and he ended up on his rear, covered in beer.

"*Oops.*" Eric smiled. "I guess he'd better watch where he's going."

"Really?" Stella asked around clenched teeth as she walked out the door. "It's not bad enough everyone thinks Ben had Bob beaten up. Now my dead housemate, the Paul Bunyan of Sweet Pepper, wants to play frat boy tricks because he's *jealous.*"

Stella continued walking, ignoring the laughter behind her as everyone made fun of John. She climbed into the Cherokee and drove toward town.

"Frat boy?" Eric asked from beside her in an indignant tone. "I never went to college."

"That's funny. You seem to have the humor of a kid in college."

"And I wasn't jealous. John was being an idiot. Anyone could see that. They saw it better when he was on the floor."

"Never mind. Let's figure out how far apart we can be when I have your shield."

"All right. How do we do that?"

Stella sharply pulled the Cherokee into the gravel driveway beside the "Madam Emery, Psychic Reader" sign. "Maybe she knows."

"I don't like this plan."

"We can find out what she's been telling Bob about ghosts and how to get rid of them." Her brown eyes narrowed.

"I don't like that look on your face, Stella."

"Too bad." She got out of the Cherokee and went toward the older house.

The house and yard had seen better days. At one time, it seemed as though it had been a quaint and cozy cottage. There were old climbing roses, withered and brown now with the cold, growing everywhere with no sign of pruning. The house needed painting and a new roof. The sidewalk leading to the purple front door was cracked and overgrown with weeds.

The sign, suspended from a two-by-four with metal rings, flapped in the mountain breeze. Beside the house was an older Buick that looked as sad as the rest of the property.

"I guess there's no money in being a psychic reader," Stella remarked.

"The amazing thing is that this place looks exactly like when I was a kid, seventy-plus years ago." Eric stared at the broken window frame the same way as he had going by as a child.

Stella knocked at the door. There was no response. "This must be a different Madam Emery. She couldn't still be practicing that long."

There were dozens of cats. They peered down at them from the roof and slunk by on the ground, rubbing against Stella's leg. One sat on the broken window ledge and put out a delicate white paw. Stella scratched its head, and the cat started purring.

"I don't think anyone's here." Stella glanced around. She wasn't sure if anyone even lived there anymore.

"I'll check." Eric tried to walk through the wall. He bounced off it as though he were solid. "I guess I'm not going to check. I've never had that happen before."

Stella knocked again. "Performance issues, huh? I guess it even happens to ghosts."

"Performance issues?" Eric was puzzled by the phrase.

"Never mind. I guess she's not home. We'll try again next time."

She turned away to go back to the Cherokee. The faintest

scraping sound caught her attention as the purple door slid open.

The old woman didn't look as ancient as Stella had expected. She had to be in her eighties, at least, but her long, thick black hair made her face appear more youthful. Or she wasn't the same Madam Emery that Eric recollected from his childhood.

She smiled at Stella and then glanced to her right where Eric stood. "Well, well. I've been expecting *you*."

Chapter 19

~~~~~~~~~~

Stella walked into the tiny house. Inside was a hodge-podge of trinkets, books, and cats. The furniture was worn to the point of exhaustion. Plants were at every available window. There was an odd aroma of tobacco and herbs that teased her nose.

She'd expected the old woman to follow her. Instead, she stood at the doorway. "Shoo!" The woman waved her arms at Eric. "Go away. You'll have to wait outside."

Eric tried again to walk inside, this time through the open doorway. He bounced off it the same way. "Stella?"

Madam Emery slammed the door in his face. "Now that's better. If there's one thing I don't need, it's some pesky poltergeist hanging around my house." She smiled at Stella, her thin brown face becoming a mass of wrinkles. "Would you like some tea?"

"Sure." Stella glanced at the closed door again. "How did you do that? And how did you know he was there?"

"When you've been around ghosts as long as I have you can always see them." Madam Emery led the way into her tiny kitchen. "Mind you, some are pathetic, not like that big, strapping one that came with you. Most are slighter wraiths of their former selves."

Stella, awestruck, sat down at the small table. Madam Emery shooed away the three cats that were sitting on it. There were even more plants, books, and trinkets in there, including a large black bear head on a cake plate.

"What makes Eric different?"

Madam Emery put on a copper kettle and lit the gas pilot under it. "Usually it's the ones who think so much of themselves in life. In his case, I'd say *you* make him different."

"Me? What did I do?"

"He was probably fading away until you came into his life. You could see him and hear him. That's enough to make a ghost real again. Jasmine or honeysuckle?"

"Jasmine." This was going to be a much more interesting conversation than she'd imagined. "Is that good or bad? Shouldn't he move on or something?"

Madam Emery cackled. "That's the veriest nonsense. You hear that kind of stuff on the TV. Don't make it true. Most people die and wander. It's our nature."

"So he'll always be in the cabin?"

"No. Not if Mr. Bob Floyd has his way. If he destroys the cabin, Eric will fade. He's not the wandering kind. He's seen what he wanted to see. He wants to stay home . . . with *you*."

Stella fingered Eric's badge in her pocket.

"That token won't help," Madam Emery said before Stella could ask. "It gives him some purpose, and he can walk with you. But if his home, his *center*, is laid to waste, he'll fade. No doubt about it."

"Which is what you told Bob," Stella said.

Madam Emery swung her waist-length, black hair off her shoulders, displaying the one white streak in it. She wore a long gown and a heavy shawl. Both were deep purple, the color of the door, and most of the inside of the house.

"He asked me. I told him. You shouldn't have used your ghost to threaten him. It violates all good codes of conduct."

Stella took her chipped cup full of fragrant jasmine tea

from the old woman. It was too hot to sip, so she put it down on the table.

"I understand that now. I was trying to keep Bob in line."

"Guess you didn't need a ghost for that, did you?" The wrinkled face grinned at her. "You've got the devil backing you up."

"You mean Ben Carson." Was there anyone, besides people who wanted something from her grandfather, who didn't think he was evil?

The psychic/tarot reader sat beside Stella with her cup of tea. "He's not evil, or if he is, he's a *necessary* evil. He loves you. He also covets you. He could live again through you, if you let him. That makes you precious to him."

Stella didn't want to talk about Ben. Madam Emery made her skin crawl when she spoke about him. She started to change the subject.

"More important, you have your own wraith following you. She's perched on your shoulder like a guardian angel." Madam Emery's unnaturally bright blue eyes stared at Stella's right shoulder. "She needs your help. You're kin to this woman. She came to you when you were with *him*."

Stella had no idea what she was talking about. As far as she knew, Eric was the only ghost in her life. She didn't want another one, even if it was only this woman's drama pretending that there was one.

"Abigail," Madam Emery whispered.

"You'll have to do better than that," Stella scoffed. "You obviously know who I am. We both know my grandmother, Abigail Carson, died in my grandfather's house and my mother left home because of it. I know how these scams work. My ex-boyfriend was a cop."

"Find your own way then." Madam Emery dismissed her with a wave of her small hand. "She might get stronger and be able to tell you why she's attached herself to you. You don't need my help. Maybe your big protector out there can talk to her for you."

"I didn't come to talk about Abigail or my family." Stella wanted to end that conversation. It wasn't only because she felt like she was being taken in. There was a weird, tingling feeling, and almost a sigh from somewhere near her right shoulder. She knew nothing was there. It was just her imagination.

She was as susceptible as the next person. It gave her chills down her spine. She wanted to get out of there and into the fresh air again.

"I know. I know. It's all about your problems with Eric." Madam Emery nodded her head at Stella's pocket where the badge was hidden. "You want to know how to get rid of him now that he's attached to you."

"No. I want to know how far this goes. How far apart can we be with him out of the cabin?"

"We aren't talking about physical realities. You won't *ever* be without him as long as you hold the token. Should you want to keep him in the cabin permanently, destroy the token. That will take care of it."

Stella took a hasty sip of her tea, trying not to be rude. "Thanks for that information. How much do I owe you?"

"At some time, I'll need a favor from you. You won't refuse me, even though you'll want to. Not everything can be bought with the King's currency."

That was about all the weird Stella could handle. She had no idea what the King's currency was. She thanked her hostess, praised the tea that had tasted like dirt, and started walking toward the front door.

"One more thing." Madam Emery was somehow immediately in front of Stella blocking the door. "Be careful not to get caught up in the spirit world. You have no training. You've already crossed the line in many places. You could find yourself unable to turn back."

"Thanks. I'll watch out for that."

Stella looked again, and the woman was gone. It only took two quick steps to get to the door and out of the house. She took a deep breath of frosty air when she was outside.

"What happened? What did she say?" Eric demanded.

"Let's get out of here," Stella growled. "I'll tell you as we go."

She brought him up to speed after backing down the driveway. She didn't want to take any chance that Madam Emery might rush out to say anything else.

"Does any of that make sense to you?" she asked him.

"If you're asking me if I see a guardian angel who looks like Abigail Carson on your shoulder, the answer is no. Maybe a little dandruff. Why'd you let her get to you like that?"

"Why didn't she get to *you*? She was able to keep a ghost out of her house. That seems kind of amazing to me. I should've asked her if I could borrow that charm to keep you out of the bedroom and bathroom."

Eric ignored her remarks. "So it's true. I'll disappear if the cabin is destroyed."

"If she knows what she's talking about. These people are scammers, Eric. She was all dramatic and everything, but what did she say that we can quantify?"

"What about the part with the badge? She might be right about that. Maybe it doesn't really matter if you have it or not."

Stella took a deep breath and steadied her shaking hands on the steering wheel. "I don't know. And I don't know why she got to me. It was so *odd* being in that little house. You weren't in there so you don't know."

"Rub it in," he said.

"Let's try something." Stella drove into Sweet Pepper and parked the Cherokee on the street in front of the hardware store. "I'm going into Flo's to ask her if she knows anyone else I can get pepper recipes from. You stay here."

"Hang around on the sidewalk?"

"Yes. We'll see what happens."

Stella started walking after locking the Cherokee. Tommy Potter, who owned the hardware store, stopped and spoke with her about what had happened to Bob. Valery, from the Daily Grind, called out a greeting as she crossed the street.

When she got to the curb at the colorful bed-and-breakfast that Flo owned, Eric was right there at her side. "I thought you were staying by the Cherokee."

He shrugged and spread his large hands before him. "I didn't move. When you put your foot on the sidewalk, I was suddenly pulled here. It's like being attached to a rubber band. So we're joined no matter what as long as you have my badge."

"It looks like it." Stella was conscious that she was standing on the street corner talking to herself—at least that was what it would look like. She quickly went up the stairs and knocked on Flo's front door.

Flo popped her head out, her teased-high blond hair not moving in the strong breeze that swept down Main Street. Her curious, blueberry-colored eyes opened wide. "My goodness! Stella. I'm *so* glad to see you!"

"I hope you don't mind me stopping by. I thought maybe I could get some pointers from you about finding recipe donors. I don't have many recipes so far. I think almost everyone in town has already donated."

"Come in." Flo held the door wide. "I took some cupcakes out of the oven a minute ago. Matilda is here too. I'll put on a pot of coffee. I have some fresh-squeezed lemonade too."

"Thanks." Stella went inside and looked around. Flo had created a wonderful, welcoming atmosphere for her guests. There were always fresh-baked snacks on the sideboard and wonderful aromas coming from the kitchen. Her rooms were cozy and as close to home as anyone could get.

"Chief Griffin," Matilda Storch greeted her. She already had two empty cupcake wrappers on the table before her. In all fairness though, they were *very* small cupcakes.

"Matilda," Flo chastised her. "Call her Stella. Everyone does. Except for Don Rogers—we don't want to talk about him right now."

Matilda and Flo both giggled.

Matilda was the town's hatmaker. Because of the Sweet Pepper Festival, which required hats to be worn by certain participants and sponsors, she was busy all year. She was a large woman with white hair, her sturdy German stock evident in her strong frame, pink and white complexion, and bright blue eyes.

"You've been the talk of the town, Stella." Matilda used her name easily. "Between that fire up by the lake and Bob Floyd taking a beating, I swear everyone has something to say about you."

Stella took a cupcake from Flo as she sat at the table. Eric hovered beside her, eyeing the confection. "I hope everyone is saying good things about the fire brigade."

Flo laughed. "Well, you *weren't* able to save Barney Falk, but most people understand that. Any ideas yet on who murdered him?"

"Really, we have no *proof* that he was murdered." Stella unwrapped her red velvet cupcake. "It was a terrible fire. He was in the thick of it."

Matilda and Flo exchanged looks.

"Barney was a good man," Matilda continued, "but he had his enemies."

"Like your grandfather," Flo said. "Barney and Ben were never exactly friends. And Barney had that run-in with you earlier. Maybe Ben didn't like it."

Matilda nodded knowingly as she unwrapped another vanilla cupcake. "Like what happened to Bob. I heard he's coming home from the hospital tomorrow. Someone said he may never walk again. His knees were smashed or some such."

"Not that it was *your* fault," Flo assured Stella. "You were protecting Chief Gamlyn's property. We all understand that."

"Of course!" Matilda echoed her sentiments.

Stella knew she had to change the subject. "I was wondering about getting recipes. Any ideas on that? I have a few from people who haven't donated yet. Do you think there's anyone in town that hasn't entered a recipe in the contest?"

"If there is, they must be someone living under a rock." Flo laughed. "Most of us give something every year. Are you signed up as a judge this year, Stella? What do you think of my red velvet pepper cupcakes?"

There was no outright cheating or bribing of contest judges, but there was plenty of room for suggestions and taste-testing of new recipes. Since it all benefited the town, Stella didn't feel like it mattered much. The rules on such things were stringent, but not enforced.

"The cupcake is great," Stella praised as Flo put another one on her sunflower plate. "I'm not judging this year."

"Well, not *yet* anyway." Matilda laughed heartily at her joke.

"As far as recipes from people who haven't been involved . . ." Flo tapped her chin. "I'd start with people who aren't from here. You have that young couple with the Dalmatians volunteering at the fire brigade. You should ask them."

"And what about old Tagger?" Matilda asked. "If he's ever donated a recipe, I don't know it."

"You're friends with Walt Fenway too," Flo reminded her. "What about asking him?"

All of those were good suggestions. Stella thanked them for their help and got to her feet before Flo could press another cupcake on her.

"Too bad you can't talk to Eric," Flo said. "He always had *wonderful* recipes."

Stella could hardly tell her that she had relied on Eric's recipes since they'd asked her to donate one during the first pepper festival she'd attended.

Eric laughed. "They'd be surprised if they knew the truth, huh?"

"Well, I have to run. Thanks for the cupcakes and the suggestions."

"Don't forget to get your hat fitting well before the festival," Matilda said. "As a member of the planning committee, you'll need it. And don't forget the dance and the picnic, not to mention the crowning of the Sweet Pepper queen and her court. You know the theme this year is 'Our Golden Years.'"

Stella knew there was a theme every year. She tried to

keep up with it but wasn't sure what golden years they were talking about. Would everyone dress in gold?

"It's all about the first people who settled here in Sweet Pepper," Flo explained. "Since your family was one of the very first maybe you can get some help from Ben. He probably has some old things sitting around in his attic that Matilda and Molly can copy."

Molly Whitehouse was the local seamstress, who'd created the costumes for the participants in the last festival.

"I'll talk to him," Stella promised, although she couldn't imagine her grandfather being sentimental enough to keep old clothes and hats in an attic.

Even though both women tried to convince Stella to stay longer, she finally left the bed-and-breakfast. Eric was with her when a young man wearing a red hoodie walked up to her as she was crossing the street.

"Chief Griffin?" he asked. "I'm Barney Falk III. My friends call me Chip. Do you have a minute to talk?"

Chapter 20

~~~~~~~~~~

S tella and Chip sat down in the coffee shop together.
Chip had offered to buy her a coffee. Stella opted for a
Vanilla Coke. He did the same.

The coffee shop was empty. Valery was in the back cleaning after the evening rush of commuters who drove from
Sweet Pepper to one of the bigger towns to work each day.

"Thanks for meeting with me." Chip was an attractive
young man with golden brown hair and big blue eyes. Stella
could see the family resemblance after meeting his father
and having known his grandfather.

"Sure. How are you feeling?" Stella had noticed that his
arm was in a sling under his brown leather jacket.

"I'm fine." A little red came into his cheeks. "I've been
hurt worse playing lacrosse. I appreciate the rescue, Chief
Griffin. So do my friends. We had no idea how to get out of
that mess."

She stirred her Coke with her straw. "I'm glad we could
be there. You guys shouldn't have been down there at this
time of year—even to pick up drugs."

Chip looked even more embarrassed. "I swear we didn't know what was in those packages. There were some other hikers on the trail. I think my friends and I must've picked up their packages by mistake."

Eric sneered. "Yeah. Right. Good thing you're not a cop."

"It's not my problem," Stella said. "But I'd hate to see a young man with such a promising future go to jail."

"The district attorney already dropped charges against us for possession. He understood what I was talking about. Apparently, there's a problem with people dropping off drugs for hikers to pick up. We weren't involved."

"That's a good thing." Stella kept her opinion to herself.

"Money and power can still buy justice," Eric said.

"I'm sure you've met my father." Chip grinned. "His picture is plastered all over the highway. You can't miss him on TV."

"That's true," she agreed. "In fact I had a little run-in with some people who wanted to put his election posters on the outside of the firehouse."

"I'm so sorry. I'll speak to my dad about it."

"It's okay. I know how to say what's needed." She smiled at him. "Why did you invite me out for coffee, Chip?"

"I wanted to thank you, of course. You probably saved my life—mine and my other stupid friends'." He sipped nervously at his drink. "There was something else, Chief Griffin. How did my granddad die?"

"We haven't received word from the coroner, but it looks like he died in the fire."

"And what about your investigation into the fire?" He leaned closer and whispered, "How did the fire *start*?"

"We only started working on that this morning. It's hard to say right now. I think there was something that caused the fire, possibly something unusual that shouldn't have been in the house. Or it might have been something as simple as a can of deodorant."

"You mean an accelerant?"

She nodded. "Something that caused a small explosion."

"Not like a gas can or something, right?"

"Probably not like that, although I can't tell you what it was right now."

"Do you think my granddad was murdered?"

"I really can't speak to that yet." Stella sipped her Vanilla Coke. "Why are you asking me these questions? Did the family receive a threat? Had your grandfather spoken of someone who might want to see him dead?"

Chip backed off quickly. "No. Of course not. Everyone loved my grandfather. He did a lot for the people of Sweet Pepper and the rest of his district. I was just curious. It seemed odd to me, his death. I was wondering. That's all."

"Something's up with that," Eric said. "Take him to the police station. I'll bet if someone gets tough with him, he'll spill the beans."

Stella wished Eric was telepathic so she could tell him to shut up and stop being so annoying. Instead she concentrated on Chip, who looked incredibly guilty about something.

"I'm sure your father will get a complete report from the coroner and the state arson investigator. I'm really only helping her."

"Okay. I see." Chip was still collecting himself. "Thanks for your time, Chief Griffin. I appreciate all your hard work."

"If you need any help . . ." She handed him one of the hundreds of business cards the town had had made for her. "Give me a call."

"I will. Thanks." He stood up a little painfully. His shoulder seemed to hurt him more than he let on. "It was very nice meeting you."

He reminded Stella of a young boy trying to mimic his father and grandfather in speech and demeanor. No doubt he was being groomed to succeed his father one day in state government.

There was only one thing Stella was curious about. "Why did your father wait until so late to run for your grandfather's seat in the statehouse?"

"He was in the military. He served three tours in

Afghanistan and another two in Iraq. My granddad thought it would be good for him. I plan to join the military too at some point. My granddad retired unexpectedly, before my dad got back. Susan Clark stepped in and beat the man who was appointed to that seat."

Stella nodded. "Politics, huh?"

"Best game in town." Chip grinned, revealing how he felt about the job he'd be expected to do in about twenty years.

They parted company. Stella said goodbye to Valery and walked back out on the street.

"You know—"

"I know. You don't trust him. You think he's lying. You think I should talk to Chief Rogers about him."

"Actually, I was going to remind you that you have to shop before you go home."

"Thanks. You're worse than a reminder on my cell phone." She got in the Cherokee and headed out of town.

"But for the record," Eric continued, "I think he's lying. He's got some idea about what happened to his grandfather, and he was on the trail after picking up his drugs."

"And you think I should tell Chief Rogers."

"It would probably be a good idea—at least about the part that doesn't pertain to the fire. Obviously, that's up to you and Gail Hubbard. Just remember that *you're* the fire chief. You don't investigate police matters."

Stella smiled at him and pointed her cell phone in his direction, tapping her finger on it a few times. "Where's your off button?"

"Excuse me?"

"Oh. That's *right*. Madam Emery said to leave your badge at home or out in the truck while I'm shopping if you get too annoying."

"You wouldn't leave me outside."

"I thought you didn't want to shop."

"I realized that I haven't been in a grocery store for forty years. I haven't asked you for a lot, Stella. You have to take me inside with you. No telling what kinds of foods are out now that weren't available before."

"Well then let's not talk about Chip or Chief Rogers anymore."

He agreed, and they made good time to the Save and Shop in Pigeon Forge.

Stella walked into the large grocery store with Eric beside her. She grabbed a big blue shopping cart. "Let's pick up as much as we can. That makes for fewer shopping excursions."

She glanced to her left in what she hoped was an unobtrusive manner. Eric was gone. She saw his back disappearing down the first aisle. *Dairy.*

He was literally like a kid in a candy store. He exclaimed over every type of product he hadn't seen before. Some of the items he begged Stella to put in the cart. Others mysteriously found their way into the cart without her help.

"I only make so much money," she complained through gritted teeth.

"Maybe you need another job," said a woman standing behind her.

Stella laughed it off and followed Eric. "Seriously, not only will we run out of money, we'll run out of places to put everything. We've only gone down one aisle and you've got as much food as the refrigerator will hold."

"We need a bigger refrigerator," he informed her. "As for finances, I've seen you use that card to pay for things. I guess people don't run out of money anymore because there's no money."

"It doesn't work like that." A box of Frosted Flakes sailed into the cart. Stella put it back on the shelf. "You can't eat any of this."

"No. But I could watch you or Walt eat it. You should have friends over for dinner."

"We've had this conversation before. Everyone is afraid to come to the cabin. You've managed to scare them all away through the years."

"I'm sure Tagger would come over. John and that new

recruit, what's his name? The one who's already mooning over you?"

Stella put three cans of green beans back on the shelf. "Are you talking about Rufus?"

"That's him. He'd come to be near you. Walt would come over. Flo might come."

"Rufus isn't mooning over me." She followed him quickly around a corner. "And I'm not sure where all these people would sit and eat."

"There's plenty of room in the cabin," Eric disagreed.

Stella looked at two cans of boiled peanuts that he'd pushed into the cart. "Boiled peanuts? Really? What are you supposed to do with them?"

"You eat them," a familiar voice responded.

"Rufus." Stella glared at Eric for leading her into this ambush. "Imagine seeing you here."

"Not too much of a surprise since this is the closest grocery store to Sweet Pepper." Rufus laughed. "If you don't like boiled peanuts, why buy them?"

"For our guests," Eric said. "One of whom may be you if you're lucky."

"They kind of fell into the cart."

"You must only shop once a week." Rufus scanned her rapidly filling cart.

"No. I try to come down once a month. I'm not much of a shopper. I wish they had more food at the convenience store. That way I'd never have to come here."

"Why?" Eric demanded. "This place is like heaven, Stella. If I'd died and woken up here you wouldn't get any complaint from me."

"I know what you mean," Rufus said. "I only come when I have to, but that little bit of chicken scratch wouldn't last me a month."

"It won't last *us* a month either," Eric quipped. "Not anymore. *Woo-hoo!* They've got bratwurst. I haven't seen that since I worked in Minnesota."

"I don't cook much," Stella told Rufus, wishing Eric would pipe down. She let him run around the corner of the next aisle without trying to follow him. She hoped he wouldn't levitate any food into the cart from that far away. It would be difficult to cover up.

"Enough said." Rufus smiled. "Come and eat dinner with me. I'll cook. All you have to do is eat and keep me company."

Stella wasn't sure about that. It wasn't her mixed-up relationship with John, or that she'd just met Rufus. She didn't know if she wanted the reputation that Eric had talked about. Sweet Pepper *was* a very small community. She didn't want to date every single man before she was there two years.

"Just say yes." Eric waited until Rufus had looked away before he dumped a few more canned goods into the cart with several packages of bratwurst. "I want to see what he's got."

"Even if I go you're not coming," Stella promised Eric without thinking.

Rufus stared back at her. "Were you talking to me?"

"No." She grinned. "It was that other shopper. Didn't you see him?"

"I didn't see anyone else." He looked down at the bratwurst and then back at her. "So what do you say? Dinner. My place. Friday night, sevenish."

"Okay. Where do you live?"

"The marina at Sunset Beach. Slip forty."

"You live on a boat?"

"Where else? See you then."

Rufus walked past her and up the next aisle. Stella told herself that it was okay. She'd never been a heavy dater. Most of her life had been taken up by her ex-boyfriend, Doug. But this was good. She couldn't wait around forever for John to forget that she was part of the Carson family and ask her out again. She wasn't even sure that she wanted him to.

By the time she'd reached the produce aisle, Stella could hardly find room in her cart for a few bananas. This wasn't going to work. She was going to have to figure out something different if Eric was going to shop with her.

"What in the world are these?" he asked with a big grin on his handsome, ghostly face.

"I think they call them star fruit. I've never eaten one."

"Good. Let's get a few. You can describe them to me."

He was having such a good time. Stella hated to tell him it was over, and that half of what he'd gotten was going back on the shelves.

"This is too much food," she whispered as she pretended to closely examine some sweet potatoes. "I'm not joking about the money. Food is expensive. Not to mention that most of this would spoil before it could be eaten. And I don't like bratwurst. Isn't it enough to look at it here?"

Eric heaved a large sigh. "I guess that will have to do. If you're going to date I can go with you and see all kinds of new food in restaurants."

"You can't go with me on a date. That's not open for discussion."

"Then I'll put back the bratwurst and we'll get some other canned goods."

She finally agreed, and they walked back through the store getting rid of some of the extras without taking on too many replacements.

It was still an expensive buying spree. She was glad that she hadn't needed dog food for Hero at the same time. They took the food out to the Cherokee, packed up, and headed back for Sweet Pepper.

"So you like Rufus," Eric said as they turned off the main road.

"He's okay considering I haven't known him that long. Why are you so excited about me dating? Have you considered that I might get married and move away with my new husband?"

"Not as long as you're dating someone from Sweet Pepper."

"Rufus lives on a boat. He probably wouldn't want to live in the cabin."

"A boat? Why would anyone live on a boat when they could live in the cabin that I built with my own two hands?

I cut every tree and set every log in place. I know where every nail is."

"I don't know." She shrugged. "But you might not be too happy with the outcome of me dating."

Eric seemed to think about that for a minute. "I guess you're right. Don't date the man with the boat. Let's find someone who appreciates the cabin."

Stella laughed. She'd started to respond when she noticed a car in a ditch on the side of the road. She couldn't tell if there was a driver inside. She slowed down and pulled behind the car.

"I'm going to check this out. Someone could be hurt."

"Don't take too long. We have frozen food in the back."

Stella got out with her flashlight and approached the car. The hood was all the way down in the deep ditch that the county maintained for runoff from snow and heavy rain that flooded the Little Pigeon River and its tributaries.

"Anyone out here?" she called, still not able to see into the car in the darkness.

No one answered. She inched closer into the ditch to get beside the car. Her foot slid on some wet grass, but she remained upright. She called out again. There was still no reply. It looked like a problem for the county sheriff. She was too far out of Sweet Pepper to expect town police to answer.

Stella glanced back toward the Cherokee. Eric was in the front seat. He glowed and shimmered softly in the dark with the streetlight above him. She took out her cell phone to call the sheriff.

Something hard hit the back of her head. The last thing she heard was Eric calling her name.

Chapter 21

Stella woke up suddenly. She was tied upright in a ladder-back chair. The floor was concrete under her booted feet. It was dark. There was some residual light, possibly from a streetlight outside the dirty windows around her.

If she had to guess, it appeared to be an old factory—possibly one of those on the main road between Sevierville and Sweet Pepper. She wasn't sure how long those old buildings had been there. Windows and doors were broken in. She'd spoken to the highway patrol and other state agencies about tearing them down. They were nothing but firetraps.

"And good places to drop someone off," she muttered to herself.

Her head hurt. What had happened? She didn't call out for help, fearful that whoever had attacked her was still there. She wondered why Eric hadn't exerted some of his "ghostly powers" on her behalf.

"You're awake," Eric said as in answer to her unspoken thoughts. "It's been at least an hour since they transported you here."

"Are we alone?"

"There are two men outside smoking."

"Why didn't you stop them? You could've done something to keep them from bringing me here. I can understand that you couldn't stop me from getting hit in the head—that happened too quickly. I don't understand why you just followed me here."

"Don't you want to know who's responsible?"

"*What?*" The fierceness behind her question made her head hurt. "Of course I want to know who's responsible. It didn't have to be up close and personal."

"I thought this was the best strategy, what you'd want me to do. I could've scared them off once you were down. I thought you'd want things to unfold. I could see you weren't seriously hurt."

Stella wiggled her hands in the rope that held them behind her. "Okay. Fine. Let's have a strategy meeting before something like this happens again. I need to teach you how to use the cell phone. Untie my hands."

She could feel his strange, tingly touch on her wrists. It was like static electricity harnessed to a specific purpose. He could use it to move things and, hopefully, manipulate the ropes.

"We're not alone." He lowered his voice even though he knew she was the only one who could hear him.

Strange how habit could affect even a ghost.

Her hands were free, but she didn't move. Footsteps from the two men Eric had told her about echoed across the empty building as they came near. One of them shined a flashlight in her eyes. She blinked and turned her head away.

"Chief Griffin," a gruff voice addressed her. "Sorry we had to do it this way. We have a request."

"More a demand," the second voice said.

"Are you crazy dragging me here this way?" she demanded angrily. "How did you know where I'd be or that I'd stop to check out that car?"

"We followed you," one of them snickered. "And once a do-gooder, always a do-gooder."

"You're involved in an investigation at Representative

Falk's house. There may be some things you find there that aren't for public knowledge. Keep your mouth shut and we'll make it worthwhile. Say anything and you'll be sorry."

"What kind of things?" She tried to see the faces behind the flashlight, but it was too bright. She thought she recognized one of their voices.

"You'll know when you see them," the distinctive voice of the second man responded.

"Are you talking about the white powder I found inside the sofa? I'm assuming it's cocaine. Am I right?"

"If I were you I wouldn't be in such a hurry to show off what you know," the first man said. "Keep this to yourself, if you know what's good for you."

"Are you visiting with Gail Hubbard at the same time?" Stella asked. "I'm not the *only* one who knows about this. She's already turned in what we found today. The lab has probably made a determination on what it is. That means lab techs are involved too. I don't think you can keep everyone from talking. You two aren't the best planners in the world are you?"

"You worry about yourself, Chief. We'll take care of the rest."

Stella knew their friendly talk was winding down. It was time to play the ace up her sleeve.

"I don't think they plan to hurt you." Eric's voice was a whisper near her ear. "What do you want me to do?"

Being unfamiliar with what ghosts could and couldn't do, she fell back on the tricks she'd seen him use since she'd become his housemate.

"Is there power we can play with?" she whispered to him.

"I'll check."

"Does she have a cell phone?" the first man asked the second.

"No. We left it in the ditch with the car."

"Is she wired or something? She's talking to someone."

Lights began flickering on and off through the building. At first it was the old emergency lighting system. Orange lights came on along the walls and then went off. Before the men who held Stella captive could react, the large shop lights started blinking. A few lights came on and stayed on.

"What's going on?" The first man's face was unknown to Stella. He was short and thin, wearing a Smoky Mountains ball cap and a black hoodie that had seen better days. He looked around the empty building with fear on his narrow face.

The second man was Barney Falk Jr.'s driver. She remembered him from the investigation site that day. He pulled out a snub-nosed revolver and leveled it at her face. "I don't know what's going on, but she's seen us now. We don't have any choice."

"Hold your head down!" Eric yelled at her.

Strong gusts of wind began buffeting the building from the *inside*. The lights above them rocked with it. Windowpanes blew out. Sparks flew from electric lines that hadn't been used in years.

She closed her eyes and forced her head down.

A terrible keening began. It sounded as though it came from the concrete beneath them, like something was trying to crawl out of the ground. It was terrifying.

Stella knew it was Eric, but still felt dread as she fell to the dusty floor. It was a good call—the driver's gun went off, ricocheting around the rusted metal walls.

The first man ran screaming out of the building. When he got in his truck he found that his vehicle wouldn't start and that he was trapped inside it.

The second man, Falk's driver, shot three more times before he followed his associate's path out of the building. His vehicle wouldn't start either, and the doors were locked tight once he was inside.

"Are you okay?" Eric showed himself.

Stella looked up at him. "That was awful. Good, but *awful*. If you'd done that when I first came to live in the cabin, I would've left that night and never come back."

He laughed. "It was pretty scary, huh? I used it a few times when other people tried to move in with me. No one lasted through it."

She got to her feet and tried to get most of the dust off of her. "Why didn't you do it to me?"

"I was just playing with you when I did those first tricks. You were there to save my fire brigade. I didn't want you to leave. It's not complicated."

"Did they get away?" She nodded toward the door.

"No. They're waiting in their cars. I accessed 911 from one of their phones. Someone should be here soon."

"I didn't know you could access 911. You could've done that instead of letting them bring me here at all," she complained.

"I didn't think about it. I thought you'd want answers."

"I'm grateful for your help anyway. It took you a while to get going, but it was worth it. Next time, don't be so helpful. I never want to wake up in a place like this again."

"Good to know. I guess that takes care of leaving my badge at the cabin, right?"

"We'll talk later." She stretched her neck and felt the bump on the back of her head.

"You should have that looked at. Safety code requires all injuries to be reported and identified by medical personnel."

"Lucky I'm not working."

Sirens and flashing lights let them know help had arrived. Eric released the two men from their vehicles only after Stella had made it clear to the Tennessee Highway Patrol that they had assaulted and kidnapped her.

"You got lucky, Chief Griffin," one of the officers told her. "They could've dragged you out here and we would've found your bones in a few years."

"Not on my watch," Eric said.

An officer gave Stella a ride back to the Cherokee. He helped her fish around in the dark ditch until she found her cell phone.

"You should follow me to the county jail if you want to press charges," he said with a tip of his flat-brimmed hat.

"I will. Thanks for your help."

Once Eric and Stella were on the road heading back

toward Sevierville, Eric asked what had made her think the white powder in Falk's house was cocaine.

"It looked like it to me. I've seen it in fires before. All firefighters in Chicago are trained to notice possible drug connections."

"I've never seen any drug besides marijuana. How did cocaine come to be in Barney Falk's house?"

She shrugged. "I'm beginning to think there's a connection between Falk's grandson, Chip, and what happened at the house. Even though he claims to be innocent of going to pick up that stash we found them with on the trail, it seems a little coincidental to me."

"So you think he planted it there and then burned the house?"

"No. I think he was probably helping his grandfather distribute it."

Eric didn't believe it. "There's no way Barney Falk was a cocaine dealer. I *knew* him. He liked his power, but he wouldn't have done something like that."

"You've been dead a long time. I know you've watched TV, but that's not the same as living in the real world. People like Falk sell cocaine to keep up a standard of living they've become accustomed to. You heard his son talking about the estate in Nashville. Where would the money come from to maintain something like that *and* an expensive house out here?"

Stella reached the county courthouse and sat down with an assistant district attorney to tell him what had happened. She agreed to press charges against Barney Falk's driver and his unknown accomplice. She told him that the men had threatened her unless she agreed to look the other way during the investigation of the Falk fire.

She also told them about the cocaine, even though she was breaching protocol by telling him anything about the arson investigation before it was over. She believed it was too important to wait.

She also told the ADA that she recognized the driver as someone working for Barney Falk Jr. The young man, who appeared as though someone had woken him up and dragged him here to take her statement, wasn't happy with her ID.

"Are you sure about this, Chief Griffin? The Falk family is well-known in these parts. I realize you're new to this area of the world. You might want to reconsider until you've done a lineup."

"I don't need to do a lineup. I just saw him this morning. He drove the candidate to Sweet Pepper where I was working. It's the same man."

The ADA was visibly shaken as he rifled through his paperwork.

"Is there a problem with pressing charges against these men?"

"No, ma'am." He had her sign some documents and said she was free to go. "You'll receive a call from the DA's office when—or *if*—we need to talk to you again. Thank you for your help."

Stella shook his hand and got ready to leave. She saw the driver she'd identified across the empty office. He frowned at her and turned his head.

"I don't think anyone is going to be happy with your assessment of the situation," Eric said as they were leaving.

"I don't care. I know who that man is. The police will have to figure it out."

Stella felt fortunate that no fire emergencies had come up while she'd been trying to get home from the grocery store. It had been a long trip. All of the frozen items Eric had thrown into the cart were defrosted. They put as many things as they could into the refrigerator. There was no ice cream, thank goodness.

Once the groceries were put away, Stella said goodnight and left Eric looking through all the food treasures they'd brought home. She smiled as he exclaimed over artichoke dip and Oreos.

The story broke early the next morning.

Several TV news outlets had picked it up. Stella watched

the news anchors talk about the peculiar incident as she ate Pop-Tarts and drank a Coke for breakfast. Eric let Hero out for his morning run inside the fifty-foot perimeter he maintained around the cabin.

The phone had already started ringing. Everyone wanted to make sure that she was unhurt. The Smittys called about an interview. Mayor Wando called to be sure that he'd understood her accusation against the driver. He couldn't believe that Barney Falk's son would be involved in anything of that sort.

"You're famous." Eric watched TV with her. "You might be fire chief of the year."

"If that's a Sweet Pepper title, I think it might be possible."

She was still in her pajamas when John and Walt reached the cabin at the same time. Walt knocked, and Eric opened the door for him.

"That's a lot of hoopla for one night." Walt took off his hat and put on a pot of coffee. "How do you manage to get into these situations, Stella?"

"Make some of that for me too." John came in behind him, taking off his jacket. "This is a PR nightmare for you, Chief."

"I don't see why." She wished Eric would ask her before he opened the door every time someone came up. Her pajamas weren't provocative, but they did have yellow bunnies on them. They were a gift from her mother, who was worried about her being cold during the winter.

"Barney Falk is denying that the man you claimed was his driver has ever worked for him." John grabbed the Oreos from the top of the refrigerator. "The man was released on bail last night."

"That doesn't surprise me, and it doesn't make it untrue," Stella said. "Gail was there. She saw him too."

"Guess they didn't talk to her yet," Walt said. "I heard this morning that candidate Falk is demanding an apology from you for implicating him in this mess. He'll be in Sweet Pepper today, no doubt. No one likes to have their name linked with drug trafficking."

"I don't have time for this." Stella went to her bedroom. "I have to get dressed and meet Gail at the site again this morning. I don't know what's going on with the Falk family. Between finding Chip and his friends with drugs, and being kidnapped and threatened by his father's driver, I'd say there's a problem. Excuse me."

Stella took her time showering and getting dressed. As usual, the hot water tank ran out before her shower was finished. She shivered and dried off quickly, pulling on jeans and a sweater before she found a clean pair of coveralls.

It wasn't her problem that no one wanted to hear the truth about what she'd experienced. Her head was still sore that morning. She knew she was lucky to be alive. If Eric hadn't been there—even though he'd held off on doing anything useful until the last minute—she might've been hanging out with her ghostly friend as a ghost herself, waiting to see if the cabin was going to be destroyed.

She was righteously angry at the supposed PR nightmare John had labeled her misadventure from last night. She wanted to circle her wagons and get Gail on board with what they'd seen yesterday, from the cocaine to the driver. With both of them on the same page, Stella knew she'd be less likely to be the butt end of the problem.

She brushed her hair and pulled it back from her face before she made sure her cell phone was in her pocket and her radio was clipped to her belt.

"Stella?"

She jumped and dropped her jacket on the floor. "I thought we had an agreement about coming in my room while I was dressing."

"I have my eyes closed." His blue eyes *were* shut, although that didn't make her feel any better.

"What do you want that couldn't wait a minute?"

"You have another visitor. Chief Rogers is pouring himself a cup of coffee in the kitchen."

"Great," she angrily muttered. "What does *he* want?"

Chapter 22

~~~~~~~~

Chief Rogers had also helped himself to some donuts too. His police uniform was tightly creased. Not a graying blond hair was out of place. His tanned face showed some wrinkles as he smiled, his pale blue eyes fastened on her face.

"Good morning, sleepyhead." He sat at the table. "Quite an adventure you had last night."

She looked around the room. "Where's John?"

Walt grimaced. "*Somebody* sent him away."

"He had other duties," Chief Rogers said. "He couldn't hang around here all day consoling you."

"I'm running late, Chief." Stella put on her jacket and grabbed her bag. "I should be out at the investigation site. If you'll excuse me . . ."

He didn't look fazed by her words. He lazily bit into a donut. "Fresh. Mine are usually stale."

"I was coming back from the grocery store last night when everything went down. Would you like some defrosted mini-meals to take home with you?"

"I'll take some," Walt chimed in.

"I heard what happened." Chief Rogers took a gulp of his coffee. "I think everyone in the county knows by now."

"Chief, I *really* have to go. I can meet you somewhere when we take a break, if you like."

"This won't take a minute. Please sit down, Ms. Griffin."

Annoyed, but not wanting to make their relationship worse, she sat. "What is it, Chief Rogers?"

"I know you don't owe me any explanation about what happened last night. Still, I'd appreciate hashing out the details with you."

Stella sighed and ran through what had happened *again*. She did it with a quick glance at her watch and hasty words. There were no details, just the facts.

"Sounds bad." Walt whistled through his teeth and glanced around the room. "Did you have any *help* with that?"

"You're lucky to be here," Chief Rogers said. "How'd you manage to get away?"

"They didn't tie me up securely. I got my hands free. They weren't great fighters."

"I understand you identified one of the men as Barney Falk's driver. You know he's also Mr. Falk's bodyguard."

"If I were him, I'd hire someone else." Hero had been barking outside the door, probably wanting his breakfast. She let him in. The dog took one look at Chief Rogers and began growling at him.

Walt patted him on the head. "It's okay. I won't let him do anything to Stella. If he does, you can bite him."

Chief Rogers barely noticed Hero. "And he and his accomplice were warning you off giving the state your actual findings at the site of the fire. Is that correct?"

"Yes. Is this an interrogation?"

"No. This is one Sweet Pepper officer to another. What do you think he was talking about?"

"I'm fairly sure I found cocaine yesterday in the sofa. It might go along with the cocaine drop that trapped those boys on Dead Bear Trail."

"Did someone tell you we have a drug problem in Sweet Pepper?"

"No one had to tell her, Don," Walt quipped. "It's obvious."

Stella could see anger and hostility taking form in Chief Rogers's tough face. The cold blue eyes were much less friendly and his tone had grown aggressive.

"I don't want to fight about this," she told him. "I'm not with the police. I don't know any more than what I told you. You'll have to put in the rest of the puzzle pieces."

"I don't like people thinking or saying I don't do a good job. It gets me riled up. People get the wrong idea sometimes. For instance—someone could speculate that *you're* involved in this, Ms. Griffin. You were at the drop site on the trail and you allegedly found the cocaine in Representative Falk's house."

Walt let go of Hero. "Maybe you should bite him now, boy."

Hero sat at Stella's feet but had stopped growling.

"That's the most ridiculous thing I've ever heard." She reacted without thinking, all her wishes to work peacefully with Rogers out the window. "I was doing my job. You *know* that."

Chief Rogers shrugged and got up from the table. "It's how people could spin this whole thing that I'm worried about. I'm not saying you're involved—beyond doing your job, of course. I'm only telling you what the *perception* could be."

"Thanks for the warning." The words came out of her mouth like she'd been chewing on rocks. "I'll watch my back."

She wanted to say more—a *lot* more. She had to bite her tongue and remind herself that she had to work with this egotistical, annoying man.

"I'll be going now." Chief Rogers put on his hat. "I think the cocaine is part of this too, but there may be something more. You take care, Ms. Griffin. I wouldn't want anything untoward to happen to you again."

Eric had sat silently on the stairs leading to the attic until Chief Rogers left. "You better watch that man. He's got it in for you."

"Really? You think?" She snatched up her keys. "You don't listen to me at all, do you? I've been telling you about my relationship with him since I got here."

"I thought it wasn't as bad as you painted it." He shrugged. "I'm glad you didn't have to depend on him coming to your rescue."

"I can kind of get the gist of what Eric is saying," Walt added. "I'm telling you, Don Rogers is a good man. I think you scare him, Stella. That's all."

"John says he's a good man too." Stella shook her head. "I don't know, Walt. He doesn't like me because I'm a woman and not his pick for fire chief."

"He'll get over it. You'll see. I chose him to succeed me," Walt reminded her. "He'll come out right in the end."

Stella looked at her watch again. "I hate to kick you out, Walt, but I really have to go. Thanks for hanging around after John left."

"Glad to do it." He squinted, peering around the room. "Eric, take care, buddy. We won't let you lose your cabin."

Stella walked out on Walt's heels with Hero following her to the Cherokee.

Eric also followed her without a second's hesitation. "I know Chief Rogers wants John in your place. That's not gonna happen now. He'll accept it eventually."

Hero jumped into the backseat an instant before she slammed the door to the Cherokee shut behind her. "I guess you *were* listening, at least part of the time."

"We both know what happened last night," Eric reminded her. "Your police chief might be involved."

"I don't know." She started the engine and began driving down Firehouse Road. "He always talks like that. I don't think he actually suspects me of anything. He's probably just looking after his own butt. He might not be police chief much longer if people don't trust him."

"Looking after his own butt." Eric smiled and shook his head. "I like that. You've brought some colorful language into my life, Stella."

They let Hero out at the firehouse. Kimmie and David

were taking him and Sylvia for their fire dog training in Knoxville. The two volunteers hugged Stella and told her how happy they were that she was safe. The dogs barked as they played in the parking lot.

"You let us know if there is anything we can do for you, Chief," David said.

"I will. Thanks." Stella thought about it. "As a matter of fact, I'm looking for recipes for the Sweet Pepper Festival."

The two exchanged glances. "How many recipes do you want, Chief?" Kimmie asked.

"As many as you want to give me. They should be recipes with hot peppers in them."

"Can we get them to you tomorrow?" David asked.

"Sure. That would be great." Stella smiled. "Thanks."

She left Hero with them and headed for Sweet Pepper. Maybe Kimmie and David would have enough recipes that she wouldn't have to ask anyone else.

"Hero is really progressing in his training," Eric said. "I'm not sure about Sylvia. She might be too timid."

"You could be right." Stella glanced at the dozens of election signs tacked up along the road. However this came out, she wasn't voting for Barney Falk Jr.

The Cherokee took the high hill going into the Sunset Beach community like a champ. The Falk house had been the first on the right. Gail's truck wasn't there. Dozens of children and adults were standing around watching the backhoe pick up debris and load it into the bed of a large dump truck.

"What's going on?" Eric asked.

"I don't know." Stella parked the Cherokee and jumped out. "Hey! What are you doing?"

The truck driver shrugged. "Picking up this burned stuff. Is there a problem?"

"Wait right there." Stella ran to the backhoe and flagged down the operator. "What's going on? You shouldn't be taking this away yet. The arson investigation isn't finished."

The young man operating the backhoe stopped. "I'm

only doing my job, ma'am. They tell me where to go and what to do."

"Well they told you wrong. Let me see your work orders."

He handed her the documents. Stella opened the packet and read the papers. The address was correct. The work orders involved total cleanup and dumping the debris from the house.

"Who gave you this?" She kept reading.

"My boss, Phil Roth. He owns and develops this community. He built it all. He says go get the stuff, I go get the stuff."

At the end of the work order was what Stella had been waiting to see. The signature at the bottom was Gail Hubbard's. She had signed off, saying the investigation was over.

"I don't care what your boss says," Stella told him. "Don't move this equipment again until I get back. Got it?" She showed him her badge.

He shrugged and turned off the backhoe. "Okay. It's your skin if Mr. Roth gets mad."

"I can take it." Stella jumped back into the Cherokee and revved the engine before she took off down the road toward town.

"I can't believe Gail would sign off on this." She hit her hand on the steering wheel out of pure frustration. "We barely scratched the surface of what was in there. We have no idea what made that small explosion. How could she do that?"

"Maybe she was coerced. Maybe one of Falk's men paid her a visit too."

"Maybe so." Stella stopped at the traffic light in Sweet Pepper on Main Street. "I guess I'll drive to Nashville and pay her a call. I was scared too. We can't let Falk Jr. get away with this because we're scared."

Stella's cell phone rang. It was Brad Whitman. He wanted her to meet him at the coffee shop. She hesitated, almost too angry to talk to him before she had a good explanation of what had happened at the site.

She finally decided to see him right away since she was still in town. Maybe he should know what was going on. Stella made a U-turn into a parking lot to go back to the coffee shop she'd just passed. As soon as the tires hit Main Street again a flashing light came on from a Sweet Pepper police vehicle behind her.

"What now?" She pulled over into a parking space.

"Intimidation," Eric said. "The oldest game around."

Stella got out of the Cherokee even though she knew she was supposed to stay put.

It was Officer Richardson. He looked nervous. He scratched his fringe of black hair and pulled on his hat. "Chief Griffin."

"Officer Richardson."

"I observed you attempting to avoid the traffic light by making an illegal U-turn into the parking lot over there."

"I wasn't trying to avoid anything." Even though she knew it was Chief Rogers reaching out to make her life miserable, she couldn't let it go. "I sat at the red light until I got an emergency call. I could've put on my lights and siren and gone through it. You know that. What's *really* up?"

Skeet Richardson's chubby fingers scrawled a warning citation on his pad of paper. "Next time use your lights, Chief Griffin. I won't ticket you this time. We have to abide by our laws, don't we?"

Stella was mad enough to throw his warning citation back at him. She bit her tongue and held on to the warning, managing to keep her cool and even smile when it was over. "Thanks, Officer. I hope it's not your home that's on fire the next time someone stops me for something this stupid on the way to an emergency."

Officer Richardson swallowed hard and tipped his hat to her. "Only doing my job, ma'am. I have to follow orders like everyone else."

Stella stalked into the coffee shop after locking the Cherokee at the curb.

"It wasn't his fault." Eric stood up for Richardson. "He was only doing what his boss told him."

"I'm a little tired of that excuse right now," she muttered.

Brad Whitman stood at his table when he saw her. "Coffee?" he asked.

"I don't think so." She slammed the warning citation on the table. "I think Chief Rogers is trying to send me a message."

He sat down again. "You cut him up, Stella. No one likes to look like a fool."

"That wasn't my priority after being hit in the head and kidnapped last night. I made a connection between the drugs that were confiscated off the trail and the cocaine I believe I found in Falk's house. I wasn't passing judgment on his ability as police chief."

"I'll talk to him, if you like."

"No, thanks. I'll handle it."

"I hear the arson investigation has gone so well that the state investigator has signed off on it." He sipped his coffee.

Stella took a seat opposite him. "Right. Because one day is enough to figure everything out. I think someone tried to coerce her like they did me."

"She may have had a similar experience to yours last night," Brad said. "Have you spoken with her today?"

"No. Not yet. Lucky we sent in some debris samples yesterday," Stella said. "At least we have that."

He shook his head. "Sorry. I checked. No samples were logged by the state arson investigator."

"Come on!" Stella sat back in her seat. "That's too much. How are we ever going to prove what happened out there?"

"I don't know yet," he admitted. "This all ties together. We have to figure out how. And I mean *we* as in the TBI. Don't assume because the investigation has been called off that you're safe, Stella. Stay out of this now. Work with your volunteers, and don't worry about Falk's death."

"Has the coroner ruled if his death was caused by something fire related?"

"The coroner has ruled that the death was attributable

to the fire. He won't say anything more yet. I'm afraid there's no help there."

"And no evidence of what caused the explosion I heard?" She sighed. "I think I'll have that coffee after all. Make mine mocha. I need the chocolate to get through the rest of the day."

"Like I said, we'll figure it out. We usually do. I have a few theories right now. Your part is over. Don't take any chances."

"All right. I'd like to have a few words with Gail."

"Please don't. The two of you getting together could expose you both to further violence. You're a fire chief. She's an arson investigator. Neither of you are equipped to do police work."

"I hear you, Brad. I won't get in the middle of it."

He paid for both their coffees and left the coffee shop.

Stella saw him head into town hall. "I hope he doesn't say anything to Chief Rogers."

"He said he wouldn't," Eric reminded her.

"People have a way of following their own directions sometimes."

"Speaking of which, you're not going to get further involved in this, right?"

"Absolutely not." She sipped her coffee and stared out the window at the people going by on the sidewalk. "Whatever happens, the police and the TBI can handle it."

Eric sighed, a sound like a breeze going through the coffee shop. "Why don't I believe you?"

Chapter 23

~~~~~~~~~~~~~~~

Stella drove back out to the site. She argued with Eric the whole way.

"I'm only going to see what's happening out here. I know the investigation is over."

Eric knew better. He knew Stella well enough to understand that she didn't like loose ends. She was stubborn that way. He was afraid for her. "You can wait and read about it in the paper," he said. "You're going out there because you don't want to give up."

"Maybe. But I promised Brad that I wouldn't interfere. I'm not going to say anything to anyone. Okay?"

"Outside of keeping you in the truck for the rest of your life there's not much I can do about it, but it's against my better judgment."

"Seriously?" She turned off the Cherokee when they had reached the site again.

"You knew that I locked those men in their trucks last night. No big deal. I'm discovering new things I can do all the time. I think it might be because I'm getting out of the cabin. My horizons have expanded."

The site was empty. Even the spectators had left the property once the dump truck and backhoe had shut down. Stella didn't know where the drivers were, but she doubted that they'd be gone for long.

"This is our last chance to find a detonator or something else that could have led to an explosion," she told Eric. "Let's look around. You can get in and out of what's left of the debris. I'll search the area around it."

"Is this your idea of not being involved?"

"Humor me. Help me prove what's going on. I know you're interested too."

"But they can't kill me again."

"We'll only stay until the drivers come back. Okay?"

"Okay."

Eric disappeared. Stella began slowly walking around the site. As she'd thought, there were bits of debris everywhere that had been dropped by the backhoe. She found a blackened cell phone and a charred shoe. There were some plates and glasses that were black with soot but had survived the fire intact to be carted off to the dump.

She believed she was a minimalist sort of person—not many personal possessions—because she'd seen so many spots like this after fires. It made her cringe to think of all the small bits and pieces that made up life. It felt to her as though nothing, including fire, could take much from her.

Stella had never discussed this philosophy, although many of her friends in Chicago had remarked on the absence of "stuff" in her apartment. There were no pictures, no bric-a-brac. Eric had more things in his cabin than she'd brought with her from Chicago even though he'd been dead for decades.

All of Barney Falk's possessions were colored with smoke and laid out for the world to see. No sign of a detonator or anything else that could've caused an explosion.

She'd never be able to prove what had happened. Without evidence, it meant nothing that she and her crew had heard the loud *pop* before the fire had started. Whoever had shut down this investigation knew that. He or she had played their hand and protected themselves from any prosecution.

Sighing, she looked out at the beautiful lake at the back of the property. The fireboat idea could work on these lots. There wasn't enough room on a few of them to even get a truck behind the house. She hoped the town council would agree to fund the project.

A brown Jeep pulled up behind the Cherokee. A tall, tanned man, probably in his early fifties, got out. He wore a blue down vest over a blue plaid shirt. The wind blew at his thick white hair as he buried his hands in the pockets of his jeans.

"Who's that?" Eric was instantly beside her.

"I don't know. Did you find anything?" She tried her best to talk without moving her lips. If she spent much more time with Eric she might want to take up ventriloquism.

"Good morning, Chief Griffin." The stranger held his hand out to her. "I'm Phil Roth. I developed this property. Shame about losing Barney. He was a great guy."

Stella shook his hand but frowned as her eyes met his. "It's a tragedy when anyone dies in a fire."

"Yes it is." He stared at the rubble. "I understand you have a plan to keep this from happening again."

She wasn't surprised that he knew. "Yes. The fire brigade is going to approach the town council about the purchase of a fireboat. If we'd had one the day of this fire we might have been able to save more of the house."

"But not Barney's life, huh?"

"We'll never know. This fire wasn't an accident, Mr. Roth. I don't know if someone set out to kill Mr. Falk or if there was something else involved. We may never know."

"That's odd. I received an email report from the state arson investigator." He frowned. "That report didn't mention any of this. I can show you on my phone, if you like."

"I believe you, Mr. Roth. I think some mistakes have been made in the investigation. I can't prove much now." She didn't want to say anything more to him.

"I see. Call me Phil. I hope we'll get to know each other well enough that I can call you Stella."

"Of course."

"So you think a fireboat is the answer?" he asked.

"To lakeside fires, yes." She pointed out the limited area behind most of the houses and the steep drop-offs to the lake. "It would give us a better vantage point to fight the fires and probably save your residents money on their home insurance."

"I can see you've thought this out, Stella. I think you're on the right track."

"Thanks."

"Maybe we could have lunch and talk about this. You eat, right?"

She laughed, her creamy, freckled complexion turning red as she considered what Eric would make of his invitation. "I definitely eat. Lunch would be great."

"Good." He had a nice smile. "How about today? Say noon at the café?"

"Sure. I'll be there."

They shook hands, their fingers lingering before they parted. She waved to Phil as he pulled out from behind the Cherokee.

"Oh for goodness' sake," Eric complained. "I said you should find *someone*—not dozens of suitors."

"I don't know what you're talking about. He was a nice man who offered to buy me lunch. Maybe I can convince him to help push the town council into funding the fireboat."

"And that's why your face got all red and your pulse was zooming. Typical."

"My face got red from the cold wind—I have delicate skin and freckles. It happens. As for my pulse, don't even go there. I don't want to hear anything about you monitoring my vital functions."

"It's your life." He shrugged. "If you'd rather play the field than settle down with one nice man, that's up to you."

"Did you find anything in the pile or not?" That was enough about her personal life.

"No. Not what you were looking for. I checked through everything on the truck too. It's possible Gail removed a detonator when you weren't here."

Stella couldn't argue with that. "I don't know what else to do right now."

She opened her investigation kit and found the container of white powder—the one she hadn't given to Gail. She'd forgotten all about it.

"I still have this powder. I could have it checked to see if it's cocaine. And I have the pictures I took of where I found it. It won't prove anything except that cocaine was here. Barney Falk's death will still be unresolved, at least as far as I'm concerned. But it's better than nothing. They must have gotten to Gail if she didn't send in the samples she had."

"Are you going to give it to John to be tested?"

"I don't know. John won't be able to send it to the lab without Chief Rogers knowing about it. I don't want to cause any more trouble between them."

"Maybe you should test him." Eric appeared in the Cherokee next to her.

"Maybe. Are you talking about John or Chief Rogers?"

"Chief Rogers. Keep some of the sample and give him some. See what he does with it. He may be obnoxious, but John and Walt could be right about him being a good man. Don't forget, he *was* Walt's choice to succeed him as chief."

"I know. I know." She started the engine. "Even if Rogers runs with it, I won't like him any better."

"You don't have to. All you have to do is be able to trust him."

Stella drove back into town. She was looking forward to having lunch with Phil. She wouldn't admit it to Eric. He'd only make fun of her.

"If you don't mind, I'm going to walk as far away from you having lunch with that rich developer as I can. I don't want to sit through all those smiles and winks."

Stella was trying to fit the Cherokee between two other cars in front of the café.

"That's fine. But I don't wink."

"Okay. All that blushing and giggling."

"I definitely don't giggle."

Eric grinned at her. "Whatever you say. *Tee-hee*."

Before she could protest he was gone. She promised to get him back later and locked the Cherokee before she walked toward the café door.

Stella enjoyed her lunch with Phil. He was fun to talk to and had a way of saying things that made her laugh. He confessed to being a former businessman and an NFL team owner from Louisiana. They talked about their past lives and how they'd ended up in Sweet Pepper.

"I was raised in a town smaller than this, if you can imagine." Phil worked on his sirloin steak. "We didn't have a stoplight because that would've interfered with the gators crossing the road."

"I really can't imagine that," she confessed over her pimento cheese sandwich. "When I came down here from Chicago, I couldn't believe people could get by with real stores being thirty miles away. I never had a car at home. I found out right away that you need some type of vehicle here if you want to eat and have toilet paper."

Stella was constantly looking over her shoulder. Maybe Eric wasn't *officially* there, but his badge was in her pocket. He could be anywhere. She was definitely leaving the badge home when she went to eat dinner with Rufus on Friday night.

"Chief!" Ricky Hutchins Jr. stopped to talk as he held a gray tub full of dirty dishes. "I heard you put Clara and her family into a burning car. I wish I could've been there."

"Me too. Clara and her family came out fine." She introduced Ricky to Phil. "You would've been proud of Sylvia and Hero too. Hero jumped in the burning car without even thinking about it."

"That's great." Ricky laughed. "I hope my dad gets out soon. I miss the fire brigade. Hell, I miss working on the trucks. I spend my whole life washing dishes and busing tables. My mom is a wreck without him. This has to end."

Stella sympathized. "I know he'll be back soon. You'll have to fight JC to drive the engine again. He's taken your spot, and he's possessive."

"Chief! I can't believe you let him drive. What about me?"

"Someone with big rig experience had to drive. You know that. When you get back, we'll work it out."

"*He'll* have to work it out," Ricky promised. "I was there first."

Lucille, Ricky's mother, called from the kitchen. Ricky left their table reluctantly to ask what he needed to do.

"I'm afraid to ask why you put Clara and her family into a burning car." Phil sipped his sweet tea and smiled at her.

Stella's heart beat a little faster, and she thought about Eric talking about her pulse. *Could he really do that or was he faking?* She never knew with him. She wished Madam Emery had been a little more forthcoming—and a lot less creepy. Maybe there was a book she could get that would tell her the limits of Eric's ghostly superpowers.

"Clara and her family have served us well at the firehouse." She explained about the family of dummies Molly Whitehouse had made for them. "They've escaped every emergency without a scratch."

"No doubt due to the excellent supervision of the Sweet Pepper Fire Brigade's chief."

Stella laughed and surreptitiously glanced around. She *wasn't* giggling. Eric had made her self-conscious.

"Mind if I ask a question?" Phil pushed his plate away. "Are you expecting someone? You're not married, are you?"

"No. I'm not expecting anyone. I'm not married."

"The last woman I went out with that acted as nervous as you are right now had a husband looking for her. He was a six-foot-four, three-hundred-pound former Marine. That night didn't end well for me."

Stella tried to explain her nervousness without mentioning Eric. "I still can't get used to everyone knowing who I am, I guess. I'm always expecting someone to come up and speak to me. It goes with being fire chief in a small town."

Phil smiled and said he understood. They finished lunch

and were getting ready to leave when town clerk Sandy Selvy ran into the café. She zeroed in on Stella with frantic eyes, her teased-high hair hidden beneath a bright green scarf.

"Thank goodness I found you," Sandy said. "Willy Jenkins sent me to warn you."

"What's wrong?" Stella asked.

"There's a special called meeting of the finance committee in about five minutes. Nay Albert is going to push for the council to go ahead and buy his boat for the fire brigade."

Chapter 24

"**C**an they do that?" Stella wasn't sure what committee was responsible for things that the town council did.

"It's preliminary," Sandy explained. "Nay will get the committee's okay to take it to a vote at the next council meeting. They won't hear from anyone else at that point. With Bob and the mayor behind him, it's kind of a done deal. Willy thought you should know."

Stella didn't even bother asking how they knew she was in the café. "I'm on my way."

"What's the problem?" Phil overheard their conversation as he'd finished paying their bill for lunch. "I thought a fireboat was a good idea."

"Not this fireboat. I had planned to ask the council to buy a boat from Rufus Palcomb. He's got a good boat at a fair price, and he's a member of the fire brigade. I have to go."

"Let me go with you. Maybe I can help."

Stella dialed Rufus's cell phone number as she and Phil hurried to town hall. She couldn't believe Nay would stoop so low to get a few thousand dollars from the town.

Rufus didn't answer. She was going to have to deal with

the problem using her limited boat knowledge and hope the finance committee would see things her way.

The Sweet Pepper finance committee normally met once a month in council chambers. Bob Floyd and Nay Albert were members, representing the council. Baker Lockwood, who owned the town pharmacy, was also on the committee, along with Tommy Potter, who ran the hardware store. Myra Strickland, whose family had started the Sweet Pepper Festival, was also a member.

Stella and Phil burst in through the closed doors of the chamber to unappreciative stares from the committee members. The group had already started the meeting. Stella wasn't sure if they'd had time to vote on the fireboat issue yet.

"I don't see your name on the agenda to speak, Chief Griffin." Nay glanced at the paper on the clipboard.

"This is an emergency." Stella was going to have to make up what she wanted to say as she went along. Sandy Selvy relieved her assistant town clerk to take notes of the meeting, giving Stella a few precious seconds to organize her thoughts.

"And Mr. Roth." Nay inclined his head toward the developer. "Always a pleasure to see you here at town hall, sir. Did you need to address the finance committee?"

Phil glanced at Stella. "Yes. I think I do need to address the committee. That's why I brought Chief Griffin with me."

Stella thanked him with a nod of her head. "We're both here to address the issue of the town purchasing a fireboat."

"We aren't to that matter yet, Chief Griffin," Myra Strickland said. "You're welcome to sign up to speak when we come to that measure. Good day, Mr. Roth. How are you?"

There was a decided warmth in the way the committee members spoke to Phil. Stella supposed it was greased by the money he'd put into infrastructure and other town necessities since he'd come to Sweet Pepper.

The committee droned through several requests for funding from the town. There were road improvements and sewer pumps that needed to be replaced.

Stella glanced at her watch hoping Rufus might still

make the meeting. She wasn't sure what Phil's knowledge of boats was—she hoped it was better than hers.

There was a back-and-forth between Baker Lockwood and Bob Floyd about the particulars of replacing incandescent lights in the town's decorative streetlights with bulbs powered by small solar panels. Stella found herself nodding off while they spoke of the savings to the town versus the cost of installing the new panels.

"Hey!" Eric's voice penetrated her sleepy subconscious. "You're up next."

Stella was startled. She sat up straight and peered around herself.

"I think we're next," Phil said.

Eric was sitting next to her in the chair on the other side.

"Were you trying to ditch me?" Eric demanded. "If so—you should've left the badge at the café."

She couldn't answer him. The conversation had turned to the fireboat purchase. Nay was speaking about his boat.

Stella waited politely for him to finish his presentation, which included pictures of his boat as it was and drawings of what it would be like set up as the town's fireboat.

When he was finished, Myra nodded to Phil and Stella. "I believe you have something you want to say about this matter, Chief Griffin."

She got to her feet with Phil and cleared her throat, not sure what she was going to say that would be as impressive as Nay's presentation.

Rufus burst into the meeting room with large poster boards under his arm. His red hair was standing on end. He hadn't shaved and appeared as though he'd spent the night in his clothes.

"I'm sorry. I got the message late, but I'm here." He bowed to the finance committee as though they were royalty. "I hope there's still time."

"There's plenty of time," Stella muttered to him as she helped with his visual aids.

Rufus was even better prepared than Nay. He actually had videos of fireboats, including the one Stella remembered from Chicago. He had a PowerPoint presentation and renderings on the poster boards that were before-and-after representations of what the boat would look like.

"Mr. Albert's boat is *capable* of doing the job," Rufus addressed the committee. "It's small for what's needed, and in my opinion, that will make it difficult to mount the hoses and other equipment the fire brigade will need if they want to save the houses at Sunset Beach."

"That's very impressive." Tommy Potter ventured an opinion. "Do you have figures to back up your plans?"

"I certainly do, Your Honor." Rufus passed out his documents.

Tommy Potter chuckled as he took the paperwork. "We're not judges. You can call us by our names."

"Oh, sorry." Rufus looked embarrassed but finished passing out the paperwork. "As you can see, because of the extensive work that would have to be done to Mr. Albert's boat, the estimates for my boat are much lower. My boat is ready right now and has years of my family's boat-building knowledge backing it. It only needs the modifications you see on the list."

While they were reading Rufus's figures, Stella added, "I should also point out that Rufus has joined the fire brigade and has offered, at no cost to the town, to work with the fireboat and help us get it set up."

Baker Lockwood glanced up and nodded at her.

"I would also like to put a few good words in about Chief Griffin's recommendation to accept this bid on creating the fireboat for my community." Phil had a practiced speaker's voice. All the committee members looked up.

"Yes, Mr. Roth?" Myra smiled invitingly at him.

"I believe Chief Griffin has given a great deal of thought to this project. I think she's our best resource for making this decision."

"This wouldn't have anything to do with you two having lunch together, would it?" Nay demanded in a sour voice. "We don't want to make a hasty decision that will affect the town based on some *flirtation* between our fire chief and Mr. Roth."

"Jerk," Eric said.

Stella was shocked that Nay would say that.

She was even more surprised when Bob Floyd agreed with him. "I suspect our best effort right now might be to table this decision until later this year."

Stella was furious. "Are you going to let a decision as important as protecting the Sunset Beach community stay on the table so Bob and Nay can make a few extra bucks? If you like you can take anything extra for Rufus's boat out of my salary."

"You can't accuse me of wanting to make extra money," Nay argued. "I'm practically *giving* my boat to the town."

Phil took him up on it. "In that case why not be a Good Samaritan and *donate* the boat to the town. Chief Griffin is willing to give up part of her salary. Surely you must be as dedicated to the project as she is."

Myra looked at her fellow members of the committee. "Well, I've heard enough. I think we should take a vote on this."

Nay and Bob tried again to stall, but Baker Lockwood and Tommy Potter were ready to vote too.

"All in favor," Myra began, "say aye. All opposed, you know the drill. Although I can't imagine for one minute why anyone would vote against our fire chief, Mr. Roth, and the Palcomb family, who has been building boats right here in Sweet Pepper for a hundred years."

There were three ayes to two nos—Bob's and Nay's.

"That settles it. Chief Griffin, we'll make the recommendation to the council that they fund this project for you. Thank you all for being here today." Myra brought down her gavel to end the conversation.

There was still more to be discussed by the committee. Stella was glad she didn't have to sit through it. She, Rufus, and Phil left the meeting room with Eric trailing behind them.

"Yes!" Rufus high-fived Stella. "I'll get started on everything right away. Thanks for giving me a shot at this, Chief."

"Thanks for putting all of it together. I thought Nay's presentation was impressive—until you walked in like you'd been thinking about it for weeks. Good job, Rufus. I'm looking forward to working with you."

Phil shook hands with Rufus. "Thank you. If you need anything from me, let me know. Nothing is more important than the safety of my community."

Stella and Phil helped Rufus take all his presentation materials to his pickup.

Rufus waved as he pulled away from the curb. "Are we still on for dinner Friday night?"

"Yes. I'll see you then if not before."

After Rufus was gone, Phil turned to Stella. "Is that a date type of dinner? Are you two a thing? I don't want to step on anyone's toes."

"We aren't a thing. He invited me to dinner because I told him I hate to cook. I just met Rufus when we started thinking about the boat project."

"That's good to know." Phil smiled at her. "Would it be all right if I asked you out to dinner too? Not on Friday night, but some other time."

"Oh brother." Eric was perched on the hood of Phil's Jeep.

"That would be nice." Stella ignored her ghostly roommate. "Give me a call."

"Good. I'll talk to you later."

Stella was flushed with her victory—and knowing that she had two excellent dinners coming up with two attractive, interesting men. She got in the Cherokee and started the engine.

"You're supposed to take part of your cocaine sample to Chief Rogers," Eric reminded her. "Unless you're too busy gathering boyfriends to find out who killed Barney Falk."

She turned off the engine. "I know. You probably don't realize this, but I can't give him a sample. I'd have to give him the whole thing without breaking the seal I put on it. It's part of the chain of evidence."

"Whatever."

"That means if he throws it away all I have is photos. Are you seriously advocating that I trust him that much?"

"Yes. If he throws it away we'll find another way around the problem. You'll know for sure that you can't trust him. If he does his job, he's an ally."

She opened the driver's side door. "An irritating, misogynistic ally."

"Obviously."

"Okay." She took a deep breath. "Let's go."

Stella went back into town hall. She asked Sandy if she could speak to Chief Rogers.

"He's in with someone right now. It shouldn't be long."

"That's fine. I can wait a few minutes."

"Congrats on your win," Sandy said. "I thought Nay was going to *pop*. He's still in there arguing with Myra even though the meeting's over. I'm sure that won't be the last of it."

"I'm sure you're right."

A moment later, John and Chief Rogers came out of Rogers's office. They were still conversing in low tones that didn't sound particularly friendly. When the two men saw Stella they stopped in their tracks.

"We were just talking about you, Ms. Griffin," Chief Rogers said. "Is there something I can do for you?"

"As a matter of fact, I think there's something you can do for both of us." Stella held out the container she'd filled with what she thought was cocaine.

"All right then." Chief Rogers stepped to the side. "Come on in."

Chapter 25

Stella wished John were going into the office with them. Instead he gave her an inquisitive look, put on his uniform hat, and headed out the front door.

She knew Eric was right about finding out the truth about Chief Rogers. She hoped this was the right time to do it. Giving him her only evidence of possibly finding cocaine at the Falk house was a risky move. If John had been there, at least he would've been a witness to what had transpired.

She sat in one of the chairs facing Chief Rogers's desk. He lounged back in his chair behind it. He waited patiently, but with no encouragement. It was hard to find a way to tell him.

Eric gave her a nudge that felt like a strong electric shock.

"I collected this evidence yesterday when I was working on Barney Falk's house," she blurted out, a little angry at the shock Eric had given her. "I'm not sure what it is. It looks like cocaine. I have corroborating photos of where and when I found it."

She handed the sealed container to Chief Rogers. He looked at it against the background of the lamp on his cluttered desk.

"What makes you think it's cocaine?"

"I've seen cocaine before. It was sprinkled everywhere, possibly blown out of a package by the blast that caused the fire."

"Blast?" His gaze moved from the cocaine to her. "I saw the report on the fire. I didn't read a thing about a blast—or cocaine."

"I know. I saw it too. Like I told you this morning, those men that picked me up last night wanted me to keep my mouth shut about what we'd found. It seems to me that someone bigger than them took care of the problem. Gail Hubbard signed off on the case. The evidence we gathered has been lost. This is all that's left."

"And you're giving it to *me*?"

"You're the law in Sweet Pepper. No matter what the state says about the fire, you can still investigate to find out if this is cocaine, and if there is a connection to the drugs found with the college kids on the trail."

He nodded and swiveled in his chair. "You and me have never hit it off, Ms. Griffin. I don't trust you. I'm sure the feeling is mutual. Why are you doing this?"

Stella leaned forward. "Because this is *my* home too now. Because you uphold the law here. I try to keep people safe from fires. We should be working together. At least that's what a friend of mine told me."

He laughed. "Walt, right?"

She glanced at Eric. "Not exactly."

Chief Rogers considered her words as he contemplated the container she'd given him. "I was just discussing this very thing with John. I don't want my town to get a reputation as being a good place to get or hide drugs. I think you're right. I think something is going down here. I don't like it."

Something inside her relaxed and she took a deep breath. "I'm glad. I don't like it either. Can you have that sample checked?"

"I can, and I will. Send me those photos. I may need you to testify to back this up if we find something."

"All right. Whatever I can do to help."

He got to his feet and held out his hand to her. "*Chief* Griffin. Welcome to Sweet Pepper."

Stella shook his hand. She hoped they'd come to a new place in their relationship. She wanted to believe he'd pursue the problem.

Words are easy, she reminded herself as she left his office. *Will he follow up?*

"So?" Eric asked as Stella waved goodbye to Sandy, who was on two phone lines.

"I don't know. We'll see."

"You're a hard woman to convince of anything, Stella Griffin. You held on longer in the cabin than anyone else ever had. Your father was right. You're plain stubborn."

"You mean that in a good way, right?" She started out of town hall but veered away from the Cherokee.

"I don't know," he teased. "We'll see. Where are you going?"

"I'm glad you stopped me before I went back to the cabin. I need to get my dress for the pepper queen's coronation dance tonight. I'll walk up to Molly Whitehouse's place and get it."

"The coronation of the pepper queen and her court?"

"I know. I can hardly express how excited and thrilled I am."

"You don't want to see the queen and her court crowned?" Eric couldn't believe it. "I never missed it when I was fire chief. It's actually the beginning of next year's Sweet Pepper Festival. The queen reigns for a whole year. Who's in the running for queen this year?"

She shrugged. "I have no idea. I'll ask Molly if you want me to."

"You mean you're on the planning committee for the festival and you don't know?"

"Don't push me, Eric. And what was with that electric nudge inside? Don't do that again. And if you *can* monitor my pulse rate, don't do that either. The idea of it creeps me out."

Eric's voice deepened as he whispered, "Stella, you don't know *all* the things I can do."

A small flurry of leaves danced in a circle to an unseen breeze around her feet even though the rest of the street was quiet.

"And I don't want to know. Let's keep that your little secret, okay?" But she *shivered* and walked faster on the sidewalk.

Molly Whitehouse's dress shop was busy, as always. With the event that night, everyone was coming in for last-minute alterations and add-ons. Stella waited for her turn, thinking of all the other things she could be doing—like taking a nap in front of the fireplace.

"Chief Griffin," Molly greeted her at last. "Your dress turned out beautifully. Do you want to try it on one last time before you take it home?"

"No. I'm sure it's fine. I have practice in a few minutes. If I could pick it up now that would be great. Thanks, Molly."

"All right. I hope it's okay." Molly handed her what seemed to be a very large brown dress swathed in plastic.

"It looks wonderful already." Stella smiled. "Who's running for festival queen this year?"

Molly giggled. "Foster Waxman is running for her last court. She's a senior, you know. We'll miss her when she goes off to college next year. She's the favorite, of course. But she *has* been queen before."

Molly went on to describe all three girls who might be crowned as queen that night. She launched into the seven girls who might be picked for the queen's court too.

Stella waited for her to finish with a patient smile on her face. "Thanks. I'll see you tonight."

"Yes. And if you have any problems with the dress give me a call." Molly patted her arm. "I hear we're having a barbecue at Beau's to benefit the fire brigade on Saturday. I'm looking forward to it. What kind of tricks are the firefighters going to do?"

"*Tricks?*" Stella perked up when she heard that. She'd known about the barbecue in a sketchy kind of way. This was the first time she'd heard a date mentioned. Or tricks.

"I read it on the poster. I think I have one over here. You know we're very proud of our volunteers."

Stella glanced at the bright red and orange poster that offered food, music, and entertainment by the fire brigade on Saturday at noon. She had no idea what that was supposed to mean. There was also supposed to be an official look at the new fireboat. Who'd printed these things?

Eric was excited about the coronation dance and the fund-raiser at Beau's. He talked nonstop about the old days, when he'd been putting the fire brigade together.

She got her answer about the posters when she stopped by the firehouse on the way home. The posters were all over the building. Tagger and Allen were viewing them with pride as they drank their coffee.

"I guess you know where they came from." Eric peered down at a poster on the top of a stack.

"Did you two print these?" Stella asked.

"Hi, Chief!" Tagger beamed. His toothy smile was more pronounced than usual. "I did it with help from Willy and Walt. Having the fire brigade go through some of their routines was Walt's idea. He's hoping the Sweet Pepper Festival will want to add firefighter routines to their program. Neat, huh?"

"Not really all that neat," Stella told Tagger. "I wish you'd said something to me about this first."

Tagger did his best to ignore his former chief who was standing beside Stella. He stared at him but didn't speak.

Allen laughed. "I had the same look on my face, Chief, when Tagger showed me the posters."

Walt and Bert pulled into the parking lot. Bert could hardly hold back his excitement. Walt's hands were full of posters.

"It's great, huh, Chief?" Bert asked. "We've been putting them up all over town. Just imagine getting to show off our skills. It doesn't get better than that—and barbecue too."

Walt took one look at Stella's expression and slapped the rest of his posters on the table. "Why do I get the feeling you aren't excited about this, Chief?"

"I don't know where to start with that one." She took a deep breath and tried to figure out what to say. Obviously this had gone far beyond the planning stages. She didn't want to condemn everyone's hard work and initiative.

"You don't like them, Chief?" Bert could hardly believe it.

"She really does," Tagger assured them. "She's amazed that we got so much done while she was investigating the fire."

It was as good an excuse as any. What could it hurt showing off a little, like Bert said? The volunteers had worked hard to learn their skills. People didn't get to appreciate what they did unless they were the recipients of their services.

"It's a good idea." She gave it her blessing. When the applause and screeches died down she added, "It might help us find a few new volunteers and raise some money for the fireboat too."

David and Kimmie walked in on the celebration. Sylvia and Hero ran barking and jumping through the firehouse.

"Hero got his third certification today!" David announced with tears in his eyes, his voice trembling. "Sylvia is still behind him, but she aced her second certification."

There were calls for more celebration, and the possibility of going to Beau's for beer. David and Kimmie didn't drink. Bert was too young. Allen and Tagger were on duty.

"I guess that leaves me and you, Stella." Walt grinned at her. "Don't say no. You need one after going through what you did last night. How's that head doing?"

That meant going back through the story of the botched kidnapping one more time. Everyone listened intently as though they hadn't heard it a dozen times already today. Stella ended it by telling them the good news about the fireboat.

"I can't go for that beer, Walt. I have to get ready for the festival queen's dance this evening."

"That's not until six." Walt looked at his watch. "What are you gonna do till then?"

"That's none of your business." She grinned. "I'm headed home. Keep it down out here. We don't want people calling the police and complaining."

Hero barked and started running up Firehouse Road. Stella noticed that Eric was gone. David and Kimmie were disappointed. They'd hoped to take both dogs out for a treat to celebrate their certifications.

"Do you think it's safe to let Hero run up the road by himself that way?" Kimmie asked Stella.

"I'm sure it is. It's a private road. Not many people go up that way."

"Of course not." Walt snickered. "They all know Eric is up at the cabin. You should've seen the way he stopped that dozer. I thought Bob Floyd would lose his teeth."

They all believed what Walt was saying. Stella didn't have to confirm his words. Kimmie still looked a little doubtful—she wasn't from Sweet Pepper and wasn't sure she believed in ghosts.

Stella went out to the Cherokee, with a stop to check on her Harley. She'd be glad when the weather was nice enough to ride again. The Cherokee was nice, but it would never beat the Harley.

A new white pickup pulled in to the back of the firehouse as Stella was about to leave. She didn't recognize the vehicle but waited in case it was someone she needed to talk to.

To her surprise, Gail got out of the pickup, scanning the area carefully as she finally saw Stella with the Cherokee. "Thank God you're here."

Stella wasn't feeling exceptionally friendly toward Gail. She felt like she'd been betrayed by the other woman. She tried to remember what Eric had said about Gail backing down from the same people who'd kidnapped her.

Gail was wearing a pair of large, dark sunglasses, the kind you get from the eye doctor after you've been for a visit. She removed them when she got close to Stella. Her cheek was bruised and she had a black eye.

"Are you okay?" Instantly Stella felt terrible that she'd been less than charitable toward Gail. Obviously her experience had been much worse. She didn't have a friendly ghost to help her out of a jam.

"I'm fine. I know I look bad." Gail's eyes welled with tears. She bit hard on her lip to keep from shedding them. "I heard you went through the same thing. I'm sorry I had to let you down. I didn't know what else to do."

"Come back with me to the cabin." Stella saw her jump when Petey drove into the parking lot. "We can talk privately there."

They left Gail's pickup at the firehouse. She put on her dark glasses again when she got in the Cherokee.

"I've never been so scared in my life. I was sure they were going to kill me."

"I know what you mean," Stella commiserated. "What do you think tipped them off?"

"I don't know. It may have been the samples I sent to the lab. I had to sneak in there and wipe them off the computer where they'd been logged. Thank goodness no one had time to examine them yet. I don't want to think what would've happened then."

They reached the cabin where Hero was running in the woods.

"How did you get away? What did you do? You must have had much better training than I had not to fall apart like a wet cupcake."

The door was open to the cabin as Stella got out of the Cherokee. There was no way to explain. "I lived in Chicago all my life. I guess I grew up scrapping with my friends. Come on. I'll make you some coffee. I think I have some food, if you're hungry."

Eric had already put on a pot of coffee. The cabin smelled strongly of it. There were also a few packages of cinnamon rolls that he'd thrown into the cart at the store. They were displayed on a plate in the middle of the table.

Stella, sensitive to seeming too prepared for her guest, smiled. "Lucky I had these ready, huh? We-uh-are planning to meet here later."

"Oh. I don't want to ruin your meeting."

"It's fine." Stella smiled. "I have more."

"Those look yummy." Gail finally sat down and took

off her glasses. "I'm exhausted. The police called me about what happened to you. I panicked, but I didn't say anything. I really feel like I let you down."

"You didn't let anyone down." Stella poured some coffee for Gail and grabbed a Coke for herself. "It was a bad situation. It still is. The investigation may be shut down, but I don't know for sure if that means we're out of harm's way on this."

"You were brave to tell the police what happened." Gail sipped her coffee. "What do we do now?"

"I saved some of the white substance we found at the house. I gave it to our police chief. He's interested because we found some kids who were out here with cocaine."

Gail's eyes got wide. "You're kidding? You didn't *really*, did you?"

"I didn't have any choice. I don't like being threatened and I want to know who killed Barney Falk in my jurisdiction. Did you find anything that would corroborate the explosion I heard before the fire?"

"I did," Gail admitted softly.

"What did you do with it?"

"I still have it." She pulled the blasting cap from her bag.

It was still in the marked and sealed evidence bag. Stella didn't know a lot about explosives. She might be able to find someone who did.

"May I keep it?" Stella asked her.

"I was thinking of it as my protection in case something else came up about it." Gail looked at the charred and mangled scrap of metal. "I suppose you want to give it to someone?"

"It's evidence," Stella reminded her. "If we can prove who started the fire we can also prove the cocaine connection."

Gail shrugged and handed it to her. "I'm sorry. I wish I could help you. I'm not willing to take this any further. I'm only a few years from retirement. I want to live to see it. I don't care who wins the election for state representative."

"So you think it's Barney Falk Jr." Stella nodded. "I got the same vibe when I saw that his driver was one of the men who'd kidnapped me. But why would he kill his own father?"

"I can't imagine. People do things for the oddest reasons. Maybe the old man wouldn't give him his support. A lot of people felt that way when Representative Falk retired right before his son came home. Everyone thought he'd wait so Susan Clark couldn't have stepped in to take his place."

"I suppose that was strange. Maybe they didn't get along." Stella considered what could have happened. "Was he trying to set up his father to look like the drug dealer at the same time?"

"I can give you my professional opinion, off the record. You can't quote me. I won't testify."

"Okay. It might help me find someone else who can identify it."

"It was made by someone with military experience." Gail raised her eyes to Stella's. "Like our candidate friend. You were right. It's very small, probably only enough to set off half a kilogram of C-4. Not enough to take out the house, but enough to make a loud boom. That was the small explosion you heard that triggered the fire. I think the cocaine stash was close to the detonator at the time. That's why the powder was everywhere."

"Thanks."

Gail laughed. "Don't thank me. I wasn't even here. I'm sorry I can't be more help. I wish you well with it. Please be careful. I don't want anything to happen to you. I hope you'll consider taking my place in a few years."

"We'll see."

Gail didn't ask for any details on what Stella had planned to do. Stella didn't offer any since she wasn't sure yet. After a few minutes Gail asked if Stella would take her back down to the firehouse.

"You shouldn't feel bad about this," Stella said as she dropped Gail off. "It was scary. No one should have to go through that."

Gail put her hand on Stella's and smiled. "Good luck. Let's not ever talk about this again."

Chapter 26

Stella watched Gail get in her pickup and leave before she drove back up the mountain. "You heard?" she asked Eric who appeared in the passenger seat.

"I didn't have much choice. Are you going to give that evidence to Chief Rogers?"

"Maybe. I think I'm going to use it like Gail said. If Chief Rogers actually investigates, I'll give it to him. If not, I'll give it to Brad Whitman."

"I see—playing the local cop off the state cop."

"Just hedging my bets. What did you think about what she said?"

"I never believed Falk Sr. would have anything to do with drugs. His son—maybe. It's hard to believe Falk Jr. would kill the old man to hide what's going on. I'm not sure."

"Was she telling the truth?"

"I thought so."

"You must have a ghostly lie detector sense too, right?"

"I wish. It would help with *you* sometimes."

"Meaning?"

"You always keep a little something back. I've learned to expect it."

"I guess we understand each other. Thanks for the coffee and rolls."

"You're welcome."

Stella put on the long brown dress that Molly had created for her. It was made with coarse brown material with tiny pink flowers in it. She put her hair up so it would fit under the bonnet that matched it.

She looked at herself in the bedroom mirror. The only good thing she could say about the outfit was that the hat was small. The last time she'd dressed up for a pepper festival event, the hat was almost bigger than the inside of the Cherokee.

"What do you think?" she asked Eric.

"How did you know I was here?" He appeared to her.

"You know how you said you know me now?" Her gaze speared his in the mirror. "I know *you* too. You're sneaky."

He smiled. "But discreet—particularly since no one but Tagger and you can hear and see me."

"You're forgetting Hero."

The dog barked in the next room when he heard his name. He finally settled down with a whine, his nose buried under the closed bedroom door.

"You're right," Eric agreed. "Sorry, Hero. And I think you look very authentic."

"Is that your way of saying I look stupid?"

"I don't think you'd ever look stupid, Stella. But I think you should wear your hair down. The little hat would still fit. I like it better down."

"Like I asked you." She took it down from its precarious perch on the back of her head anyway and replaced the bonnet. "Better?"

"Much better." He was behind her in the mirror. "I read once in *National Geographic* that males looking for mates like long, loose hair. I think it might help you find a steady beau."

Stella started laughing. "You're kidding, right? Do I *seem* like I'm in the market for a steady boyfriend? You know women today don't always get married. If they do, it might not be until they're fifty."

He looked astonished. "What about children?"

"I can have some of my eggs frozen and have a surrogate carry the baby even if I'm seventy."

"Is that really possible?"

Stella loved teasing him about things he hadn't gleaned from watching hours of late-night TV. Knowing what went on in the world was the only edge she felt she had on him.

"It's possible," she admitted. "I don't plan to do it, but I don't plan to go out looking for a *mate* either. Do you want to come with me tonight?"

His blue eyes gazed into the distance. "I don't know. If you wear your hair that way and a man comes along and sweeps you off your feet do I want to watch?"

Stella waited for his response, not confirming or denying his suggestions.

"You know I want to be there." He finally laughed. "It will be like going to a high school reunion where I still look like I'm thirty-five and everyone else is old."

"True. Except I'll be the only one who can see you."

"Put the badge in your pocketbook, woman. Take me with you."

"Is that how men from your generation talked to women?"

"Of course. We were much more *manly* back then."

"I'll remember to ask my *grandfather* about that. He's about your age."

"*Ouch.* That hurt."

"Sometimes the truth is painful."

After Hero had another jaunt outside in the cold evening air, Stella and Eric said goodnight to him at the cabin, and left for the pepper queen's coronation event.

There was supposed to be an orchestra and dancing as well as a buffet and cash bar. The event was being held at the high school so there would be plenty of room, not to mention a spotlight and a stage.

Stella pulled her brown shawl closer as she got out of the Cherokee. Temperatures had dropped. She wished she'd worn her coat, but that was too modern for the event. She had worn her boots, even though they didn't fit the costume. No one could see them under the large skirt anyway.

"You look like everyone else," Eric said. "I feel like I'm in *Little House on the Prairie*."

"We're out in public. Don't talk to me." Stella smiled and nodded at some people who waved as they went inside.

"Sorry."

Inside the already crowded gym colorful balloons and streamers were everywhere. Stella felt sure there weren't any balloons during the 1800s. She wasn't sure about streamers.

"Oh my God," Eric said suddenly. "Is that Rose Addison? I dated her in high school."

Stella looked at the gray-haired woman who was dressed in a lovely purple gown. She was still very attractive. She held a silver-headed cane in one hand. A shawl that matched her blue eyes was draped across her shoulders.

"I knew it would be like this," Stella muttered. "Do you want me to find out who she married and how many kids they had?"

"No. That would be crazy."

"Okay."

"Well—if you're going in her direction anyway."

Stella laughed and started toward Rose. Before she could reach her Elvita Quick and Myra Strickland cornered her.

"Good evening, Chief Griffin." Elvita smiled, but Stella knew there was something going on. "Just wondering how many new contributors to the recipe contest you've managed to bring in. I haven't received anything from you."

"I have a few. I still have a while to go." Stella couldn't

believe she was making excuses for not having more than three recipes. *Why did I agree to do this?*

"That's wonderful!" Elvita gushed. "I knew you were the right person for the job!"

"I can't begin to tell you how *important* it is to get new recipe contest entrants," Myra said. "It is the heart and soul of the festival. People die, you know. Or they're incapacitated in some way that they can't submit new recipes."

Elvita agreed. "And that's why we depend on someone finding new recipes and possible contest winners each year."

"For this year, that's *you*, dear." Myra smiled and patted Stella's hand. "I know you'll do us proud."

"Thanks." Stella smiled at both of them. "Excuse me. I see Eric's old high school flame over there. I promised I'd ask how she's doing."

Stella walked away from them. She'd left them with their mouths open, watching to see where she was going.

"That was mean," Eric said. "If they think you talk to me they'll never come to the cabin for a meeting."

"I'm counting on it."

Stella waited for Rose to finish her conversation with another elderly man that Eric identified as an old football buddy, Orin Johnson.

"Excuse me," Stella said. "Aren't you Rose Addison?"

Rose smiled and nodded. "I used to be. Now I'm Rose Harcourt. My husband, Wendell, passed last year. I'm afraid I'm not modern enough to take my last name back. And you're Stella Griffin, our fire chief."

"I am." Stella tried to think how she could explain knowing who Rose was.

"Yearbook," Eric prompted as though reading her mind. "You saw her in my old yearbook."

"I saw you in Eric Gamlyn's yearbook. A lot of his stuff is still at the cabin."

Rose's cheeks turned pink. "Eric Gamlyn! I haven't thought of him in so long. We dated through high school. He was such a good man. A little wild, but that was how his daddy raised him. I thought someday he might pop the question, you know? It never happened. I don't think he ever married."

Rose said it in such a sad tone, Stella was sorry she'd asked. It was easy to see that Rose still carried a torch for Eric. She changed the subject and asked her for a recipe. Rose said she'd given so many through the years that she didn't have anything new.

"I guess I'd better move off the floor." Rose pulled her shawl closer. "Looks like they're going to dance. I hope you brought your beau."

"Ask her if she was happy with Wendell. Ask her if they had children." Eric's face looked anguished too.

Stella walked off the makeshift gymnasium dance floor with Rose. "I hope you and Wendell were happy together. Did you have children?"

"We had one son, Eric." Rose blushed again. "It was my idea to name him that. Wendell agreed because he was a very understanding man. We were happy together. He wasn't the love of my life, but he was good to me."

When Rose was seated along the sidelines of the dance floor, Stella tried to find Eric. He was gone. He was only invisible, she knew. Probably needed some time to himself.

Someone tapped her on the shoulder. It was Marty Lawrence, Ben's stepson.

"Somehow you even manage to look good in that getup." He'd opted to dress like a gunslinger—appropriate for the time, but not the occasion.

"Thanks, I think."

"We should dance. You're here alone, right?"

"I don't dance." It wasn't true, but she had no intention of dancing with him. He'd been nothing but a thorn in her side since she'd come to Sweet Pepper.

Stella was fairly certain that he'd meant to have a relationship with her, maybe even something serious—something that would win him the Carson money. She'd learned right away that Marty wouldn't inherit anything from Ben since they weren't related and Ben had no time for him.

"I think this dance is mine." John smiled as he reached for Stella's hand. "Beat it, Lawrence."

Marty glared at John, who looked splendid in his historic outfit. He was dressed like an old-time gambler with lace shirtfront and string tie.

"I'm sorry, Marty," Stella lied. "I forgot that John had already asked me."

"That's okay. Even though I probably saved your life that night when you wrecked your Harley."

"Or caused the accident." John's face was grim.

Marty leaned close and whispered in her ear. "Somebody isn't always going to be there to catch you when you fall."

Stella stared into his steely blue eyes. "I'll worry about that when the time comes."

She and John walked away and slowly swayed to the fiddle music being played.

"What's up with him?" John watched Marty. "I think he's been hitting the punch bowl too hard."

"Sounds like the same old Marty to me." Stella changed the subject. "I like your outfit. Did Molly make it?"

John laughed. "Molly doesn't make men's clothes. This outfit belonged to my dad. He used to drag it out for events like this one."

Stella hoped they wouldn't get into another discussion about his father's death and her grandfather's part in it. "It looks very realistic. I'm surprised you didn't come as a sheriff."

"I would've, but my boss has that privilege." He nodded at Chief Rogers, who'd just come in. "Too many sheriffs make for a bad party."

"I can see that." At least John had been diverted from going into his usual tirade about her grandfather—and her Carson blood.

"You look nice." John looked at her outfit. "That thing is big enough to wear over your turnout gear. You don't have it on under there, do you?"

His eyes twinkled when he was in that mellow mood. Stella was afraid to trust it. John turned on her too quickly.

"What kind of question is that to ask a lady?" Rufus demanded. "I'll take over from here, buddy. It sounds to me like you need to work on your conversation skills."

John didn't seem like he was willing to relinquish Stella's hand for a moment. "You should find your own girl, Rufus."

"I think I have. I could find out faster if you'd get out of my way."

They each had one of Stella's hands. She was about to sit down and leave them both standing when John backed off. "Thanks for the dance, Chief."

Stella watched him get a cup of punch. She diverted her attention to her new dance partner, telling herself it was for the best. She and John could never spend too much time together without an argument. "It's good to see you, Rufus. How are the plans for my fireboat shaping up?"

"They'll be ready for the council meeting. I can't wait to get started on it. It's one of the most exciting things I've done—meeting you being on the top of that list, Stella."

"Why, sir." Stella played the game, fluttering her eyelashes and smiling coyly. "I do believe you're flirting with me."

"You better believe it." He pressed her closer to him as the next song began. "If I were John, I would've made sure a long time ago that you weren't at parties dancing with strange men like me."

Rufus's grin was difficult to resist. He whirled Stella around the dance floor until she was dizzy and laughing at his conversation. When the music stopped, Rufus found her a chair and went to get her some punch.

The gymnasium was crowded and hot by then. Someone had opened both doors to bring in the chilly night breezes. A group of cloggers set up to dance after the gym floor was protected. Everyone seemed to be having a good time, and the big money barrel at the front of the room was already filled with funds to support the festival.

"Chief Griffin." Don Rogers sat down beside her with a friendly nod. "You seem to be the belle of the ball."

"I think that's because I'm the only one here that's not married except for the Sweet Pepper queen candidates and the court."

He didn't look at her. His gaze followed the cloggers' peppy movements. "Just wanted to let you know you were right about the cocaine. I don't know yet why Barney Falk had it in his house. I knew the man my whole life. I never met anyone more against drugs."

"I don't have that answer." She didn't tell him about her conversation with Gail. It seemed Eric, Walt, and John had been right about Chief Rogers. Still, she didn't want to endanger Gail's life in case she was wrong.

"We're investigating. I've got my money on Barney's grandson. The boy has been headed in the wrong direction for some time. It wouldn't be much of a stretch to imagine the kid could've visited his grandfather while he was up here and left the drugs behind for safekeeping. Maybe even meant to kill the old man. Maybe Barney found out what Chip was doing and threatened to turn him in."

Stella thought about the young man she'd spoken with at the coffee shop. She knew a young, handsome face didn't make him innocent. She couldn't see into his heart.

"How do you plan to establish that Barney's death wasn't an accident?" Chief Rogers asked her.

"I have the detonator, and I know what type of explosive was used."

"You have *proof*?"

Stella started to respond, but her radio and cell phone went off. She called the firehouse.

"There's an accident on Pepper Lane," Tagger told her. "A car hit a power pole. People are injured and trapped inside. Chief—it's Banyin."

Chapter 27

~~~~~~~~~~

Stella drove with her siren on and her gas pedal to the floor. By the time the rest of the fire brigade had reached the scene, she'd changed clothes and had a chance to survey the situation.

"Tagger, have you called an ambulance and paramedic unit?" The radio crackled around her voice, masking the fear and emotion that charged through her.

"Yes, ma'am. How does it look?"

"Not good. Banyin and her husband are both unconscious. The power pole landed on top of the car. Live wires are snapping across it like a net."

"God bless her, Chief."

"Call the power company. If they can't have someone out here in the next few minutes, call Elvis Vaughn. I want these wires cut right away."

Stella stood a safe distance from the old brown Chevy that she'd seen Banyin drive to the firehouse dozens of times. She hoped Banyin and Jake were okay. She didn't like standing there, doing nothing, waiting to find out.

When the people at the coronation saw the members of

the fire brigade head out the door at the high school, every-one followed. Cars and trucks began parking everywhere along Pepper Lane. Their passengers spilled into the night to see what was going on.

"Power company on the way?" John asked as he reached Stella's side. He already had the Jaws of Life in his hands.

"I don't know yet. If they don't have a truck nearby, Tagger is calling Elvis Vaughn. There's nothing we can do until they get here."

People pushed closer, gaping like it was the Fourth of July as the power lines sparked. Questions flew as everyone speculated on what would happen to the couple in the car.

"Chief?" Tagger called back. "The power company is thirty minutes away. I can't find Elvis right now. I'll bet he's at the bar."

Stella turned to Rufus, who was in his bunker coat and helmet. "Do you have your uncle's number at the bar?"

"Sure. What's up?"

"Call him. See if Elvis Vaughn is there. We need his help with these lines."

"Okay."

Eric reappeared beside Stella. "This looks bad. There must be something you can use to move those wires."

With John and Rufus beside her, she couldn't tell him that she didn't want to endanger her volunteers that way. *Come on, Elvis.*

"He's there, Chief." Rufus held the phone away from his ear. "Willy says he's in no shape to drive. Should I go get him?"

"No. Have Willy find someone to bring him down here. We can't wait for the round-trip."

"I'm going to move this crowd back until someone gets here to do it," John told her. "Chief Rogers is on his way too."

"We've got Hampton and Bradford in turnout gear." Stella nodded at the two part-time officer recruits. "Let them han-dle it, John. I might need you up front at the car once Elvis gets here."

"I could move those lines for you, Stella," Eric insisted. "They wouldn't do anything to me."

Stella muttered, "I don't think people want proof of life after death tonight, Eric. Thanks anyway."

Jake regained consciousness inside the old Chevy and started pounding on the window. He stopped after being shocked a few times.

Before he could touch anything else Stella went as close as she safely could to the car that was covered in live wires and yelled, "*Live wires!*" at Jake, and hoped he understood. She could see his head and face were bleeding. The Chevy was too old to have airbags.

"I think he understood." Stella stayed where she was near the car. She cautioned the rest of her volunteers to stand back. "We might have to use the hot stick."

"Hot stick?" Eric asked.

"We got one last year from the electric company. They're nonconducting. When they're used correctly with linemen's gloves they can withstand thirty-five thousand volts."

"Sounds better than a broomstick. I have an idea how I could help without people knowing a ghost is involved."

Jake was trying to wake Banyin. She wasn't responding. Stella needed to make a decision. Banyin and her family were her top priority.

"Allen!" Stella called back to the volunteer. "Get the hot stick and gloves off the back of the truck."

John advanced toward her as Eric told her his plan.

"I don't know what you have in mind, Chief," John said. "If it's what I think, you can't do it. Even if you are able to separate the lines they could still turn back on you."

"We have to try something," Stella said as Allen brought her the hot stick.

"Chief," Allen also protested. "You can't do this. One line, maybe. There are at least three up there. Let's wait for Elvis."

Rufus yelled out, "Chief, Willy says Elvis is too drunk to work with sewer line much less electric line."

"I guess we're up," she whispered to Eric. "Step back," she yelled at Allen and John.

Stella put on the linemen's gloves—she'd had more training with them than anyone else in the group. She picked up the bright orange hot stick and stepped toward the car. At the same time, Eric moved beneath the wires. Half of his body was in the car, the other half sticking out the top.

"Ready?" he called out.

"Yes." Stella used the hot stick to hook the first line and move it off the car. John had been right. Like a dangerous snake the wire twisted back and would've hit the car on the hood, but Eric was there to catch it. Together they moved the wire a few yards away from the car. "Two more to go," Stella said as much to herself as Eric.

"We can do this," he said.

Eric picked up the second line at the same instant that Stella grabbed it with the hot stick. There was no noticeable time lapse between them. As they moved the wire to the street the crowd was applauding and encouraging her.

Stella took a deep breath. Her heart was pounding and her hands shook, but she managed to move the last wire from the car to the street with the help of Sweet Pepper's first fire chief.

John and Allen wasted no time getting in the car. Jake's door opened easily. Rufus helped him out of the Chevy.

Banyin, on the passenger side, was a different story. She was still unconscious. Her door had been damaged when the car had hit the pole. John stepped in with the Jaws of Life and pried the door open. JC and Rufus peeled the metal away from the opening so John could reach Banyin.

"She's okay," John called out. "We have another problem."

Stella joined him. "What's wrong?"

"Her water broke. She's gonna have the baby."

"Tagger? Where's our ambulance and paramedics?" Stella shouted on the radio.

"About twenty minutes away," he replied. "Is Banyin okay?"

"She's fine, as far as we can tell," Stella said. "But she's going into labor."

Banyin woke up with a dozen faces staring at her. "My head hurts. What are you all doing here?"

"Keep still," Stella said. "You were in an accident, and you're going to have your baby."

As though she'd suddenly realized it, Banyin let out a loud wail. "What's wrong with me? It feels like I'm ripping apart."

John grinned. "Welcome to motherhood. Now lie back and let's hope the paramedics get here in time to deliver this baby."

"What about Doc Schultz?" JC asked. "We could get him. Probably have him back here before the ambulance."

"Go!" Stella flipped him the keys to the Cherokee as she took off the linemen's gloves and put down the hot stick.

They leaned back Banyin's broken seat and made her as comfortable as they could.

"Maybe we should put her on the street," Kent suggested as he cleaned her cuts with a first-aid kit.

"I think it will be easier with her on the car seat." John put on latex gloves.

"Have you ever delivered a baby?" Eric asked Stella.

"Yes. Twice."

"Did you say something, Chief?" Rufus asked, standing beside her.

"Yes. We're not going to need the pumper. Kent, when you're done over there, you can take it home. Royce and Bert, you stay here in case we need you."

Kimmie said, "Chief, I can get a couple of blankets so Banyin doesn't have to have her baby with the whole town watching."

David agreed as he held Hero and Sylvia from investigating the scene.

"Good idea," Stella said. "Then you and David take the dogs back to the firehouse. Will you take Hero home with you tonight?"

"Sure, Chief," David agreed and then led the dogs back to the pumper.

Banyin gritted her teeth. "We were on our way to the hospital. I want something for the pain. I don't want to have my baby in the car."

Stella came in close. "Don't panic. That baby is going to come no matter where you are. We'll get through it. Take my hand."

Banyin had another contraction, and Stella took the latex gloves John handed her.

"I'm going to make sure everything's okay," she told Banyin. "Let's see how close we are to delivery."

Stella timed how close the contractions were—less than a minute. "Let's hope JC can find Doc Schultz."

"I thought he didn't practice anymore." Jake winced as Banyin's fingernails made impressions in his hand.

"He doesn't practice, but he'll help now and again with an emergency," Allen said.

Banyin let out a loud cry. The crowd that had been waiting to see if the baby would be born there caught their breaths at the sound.

"Where's the ambulance, Tagger?" Stella asked him on the radio.

Petey answered. "Sorry, Chief. There was another accident. They had to stop on the way. The injuries were more serious. I don't know when someone will be there."

The Cherokee squealed on the turn coming to the scene. JC yelled at the people in the crowd. "Get out of the way—doctor coming through."

Chief Rogers had helped Clyde Hampton and Nancy Bradford try to clear a path for the vehicle, but it was taking too long.

JC almost lifted Doc Schultz out of the vehicle. "She's over there."

"Of course she is," the doctor remarked. "Otherwise everyone would be turned in the opposite direction, wouldn't they? I'm old, not stupid. Get out of my way."

Doc Schultz was in his eighties, his wispy white hair standing on end. He was medium height with a round body and spindly legs.

"Doc!" Chief Rogers greeted him. "Glad you could come out."

"What a night for this baby to be born," Doc Schultz complained. "Why is it that this always happens when the weather's bad? I've probably delivered five hundred babies—all during awful weather."

The old doctor was known for his constant complaining. He'd been the only doctor in Sweet Pepper for the last fifty years. The closest clinic was in Sevierville. The town had tried to recruit a doctor since Doc Schultz had announced his retirement, but no one was interested in working there.

"Get out of my way." Doc Schultz pushed through the members of the fire brigade standing beside the car that were holding up the blanket that Kimmie had put in their hands. "What's all that for?"

"We're trying to give Banyin some privacy," Allen told him.

"Don't be ridiculous. Having a baby is the most natural thing in the world. I can't get in here with you all standing around. Go fight a fire or something."

Kimmie directed the volunteers. "Move back a few feet."

Doc Schultz looked disgusted as he got near Banyin. "You can worry about people seeing a woman give birth but not about an old doctor's knees on this cold, wet pavement? I'm not into replacement surgery. Find me something to put on the ground."

Royce scrambled to do the doctor's bidding and returned with another blanket.

"That'll have to do," Doc Schultz said.

Banyin screamed again. "Get this thing out of me!"

"Calm down, young woman," Doc Schultz said. "You've got a ways to go. Just lay back and rest. I'll let you know when it's time to push."

Stella got out of the way. A tow truck was on the street

waiting to take the car. John instructed him to cut his engine and be patient as he also kept pushing the interested crowd back on the street.

Chief Rogers joined Stella away from the group. "Nice work, Chief Griffin. Very creative. You know if you'd accidentally touched one of those hot wires, or let one of them fall on the car, we'd have a much different scenario right now."

"Blowhard," Eric dismissed him.

"There wasn't another way," Stella said. "Willy said Elvis was not only too drunk to drive, he was too drunk to handle these wires. Let's hope the power company gets here soon."

"We were interrupted at the dance." He stared at her. "Did I understand you right? Did you say you have a detonator from Barney's house?"

"That's what I said. I wasn't sure if I should give it to you or to Agent Whitman."

"Maybe you *should* give it to Whitman since he's down here," Chief Rogers drawled. "But I'd rather see this case through myself, if you don't mind."

Stella wouldn't have told him about the device if she hadn't been willing to give it to him. "I have it back at the cabin. I'll bring it to town hall tomorrow."

"Sounds good." He nodded. "I can't figure why anyone would want to kill Barney. I sure don't understand what's up with the cocaine. I'll never believe he was involved in that."

"I didn't know him as well as you," Stella said. "Maybe he needed the money. It can get expensive living an extravagant lifestyle with your son running for state representative."

"I guess that's true. My gut tells me that there's more to it."

"What about Falk Jr.'s driver? Did the police get anything out of him?"

"No. Junior bailed him out. Maybe he and Chip are both working to protect their drug trade."

Banyin yelled again from the interior of the car. People from the surrounding houses on Pepper Lane began to bring out urns of hot chocolate and coffee for the crowd.

"Looks like we kept the party going, just moved it out of the gym." Chief Rogers grinned. "I gotta get going. I'll see you tomorrow."

Stella agreed.

"And thanks, Chief Griffin." Don Rogers touched the brim of his costume hat. "I'm beginning to think there might be a way we can work together after all."

Smiling, Stella repeated her orders for the pumper-tanker to go back to the firehouse. There was another loud scream from Banyin that made everyone pause. In the silence, they all heard her baby's first cry. A loud cheer went up from everyone on the street.

"It's a girl!" Doc Schultz shouted. "Now someone take me home."

Chapter 28

~~~~~~~~~~~~~~~~~~

The ambulance arrived at the same time as the power crew. People began going home after the excitement. Banyin and Jake rode to the hospital in Sevierville to have both mother and daughter checked out.

Stella and Eric were some of the last participants to leave.

"It's too bad no one will ever know the truth about moving those electric lines." Stella watched the power crew cleaning up the mess. The pole would need to be replaced from the impact of the Chevy.

"It's for the best," Eric said. "Like you told me, no one needs to know what's waiting for them when they die."

"You're still a hero." She smiled at him as she drove away from Pepper Lane. "I didn't realize I'd have such big shoes to fill when I came here."

He laughed. "Yeah. It's a life and *afterlife* commitment, I guess."

Stella stopped at the firehouse to let Tagger and Petey know what happened. The pumper and the engine crews were still there cleaning the equipment and packing away their gear.

She changed clothes. It had been difficult and uncomfortable to stuff the large dress under her turnout gear. She packaged the dress and bonnet in a shopping bag and traded it for jeans and a sweater that she kept in her locker.

They sat around the big table in the kitchen talking about Banyin's baby and Petey coming back to work.

"That was amazing the way you moved those live wires, Chief," Petey gushed. "I want you to show me how to do that."

Tagger snickered. "I got a feeling I know how she did it." He winked at Eric.

"It wasn't a big deal," Stella said. "We had to get into the car. All of you need to be trained with the hot stick. How'd you find out about it?"

Petey took out her cell phone. "Are you kidding? Royce texted me a picture as you were doing it. Probably half the state knows about it by now. You might go viral, Chief."

Stella laughed. "I'm not sure if that's a good thing. Everyone should put a caption on the picture—'Don't try this at home.'"

Talk turned to the crowning of the new Sweet Pepper Festival queen and her court. Foster Waxman had dominated for another year. Everyone wondered who would take the crown next year when Foster went to college.

After half an hour or so, Stella yawned and decided to go back to the cabin.

"Goodnight, Chief," Tagger said. "I hope the rest of the night isn't so exciting."

"Me too," she agreed. "Good job everyone. Let's remember to get something to the hospital for Banyin tomorrow."

In the Cherokee, going back up the mountain, Eric said, "We make a good team. I do the work, you get the glory. I like it."

"I don't know if that's a fair assessment, but we do make a good team."

Stella parked the Cherokee next to the cabin. She started to get out and then noticed Eric staring at the cabin, not moving. "What is it?"

"You know, I lost some memories from when I died. They kind of come and go. I think I just remembered something from my will that might help save the cabin."

"What is it? Do you have a copy of the will?"

"I think so. Probably upstairs with the rest of my stuff. I can't recall exactly, but there's something about the cabin and the firehouse."

Stella went inside with Eric. She took off her coat and started upstairs.

"Where are you going?" he asked.

"To help you look for your will."

"I can look without you. You must be exhausted. Get some rest."

"I've been up here before, you know." She kept going up the two flights of stairs that led to the loft. "I've seen your stuff."

"You've only seen what I *let* you see."

Stella turned on the light in the room upstairs. It was cluttered with pieces of furniture, books, and other items that had once belonged to Eric. There was a double bed she'd made use of for company, a chest of drawers, a rocking chair like the ones on the back deck, and a hand-carved cradle.

"Why the cradle?" She made it rock with a gentle hand.

"Hoping to have a family someday, I suppose. I never meant to live alone all my life. I just thought the right woman would come along." He smiled at her. "I guess I thought it would be *before* I died."

Stella didn't know what to say to that so she busied herself going through papers that were on the table beside the bed. "If we both look we can probably find it faster."

"I have some personal items I might not want to share." Eric stood slightly above the hardwood floor. "I think you should go back downstairs."

"That's not going to happen, especially now that I know there are other things up here that you're hiding. Why do you think the town didn't throw all of your stuff away after you died?"

"There was talk of a museum."

"Dedicated to *you*?" She grinned. "That would be interesting. The stories I could tell."

"Okay. You can stay. Just don't touch anything."

Stella sat on the bed while Eric rummaged around in a few crates and metal file cabinets. She knew he'd made the bed, the chest, and the cradle, as well as the rest of the furniture downstairs. He'd been a wonderful craftsman and a well-loved fire chief. That's why the people who'd known him hadn't gotten rid of the things that were important to him. As time had passed, people had probably forgotten what was up here. Then they were afraid of his ghost.

"I think I found it." Eric was suddenly sitting beside her on the bed.

"Your will?"

He handed the document to her. There was that familiar feeling of having been zapped by static electricity as their fingers met. "The last will and testament of Eric Gamlyn."

Stella studied the yellowed paper and scrawling handwriting. Most of it was about bequests he'd made to various community groups. "I guess you really *did* find gold up north, huh? Or being fire chief paid better back then."

He laughed. "It didn't pay anything. Fire chief was a volunteer position too."

"Good thing that changed or we wouldn't be having this conversation." She smiled and shook her head. "Eric! You were *wealthy*. You spent all your money on Sweet Pepper and then gave them this property."

"What else was I gonna do with it? There was no wife, no children, to think about."

"Still. No wonder everyone loved you." She continued to read his will. "This is a huge piece of property—two hundred acres. You've got a lot of river frontage too. That's expensive now."

"Look at the bottom part." He pointed a lightly glowing finger at the paragraph she was reading. "See the conditions set for the town to keep the property?"

Stella scanned the words. "So the town has to keep the whole two hundred acres intact, including the cabin and the firehouse? They can't sell it at all?"

"That's what I thought I remembered. I can't explain it, but it gets a little confusing sometimes between when I was alive and now."

"You *did* die in between. I think we should allow for that being traumatic."

"Don't you think that should take care of the problem? What was the town council thinking anyway?"

Stella shrugged. "Maybe they haven't read this. It's been a long time. I'll call my grandfather's lawyer tomorrow and let him take a look at it."

"Sounds like a good idea."

"What else is over there in your boxes?"

"Pictures. Medals. Things people collect over a lifetime, even a short lifetime."

"Well, I promise not to snoop—at least as long as you're here." She got up from the bed. "I'm going to sleep. We'll talk about this tomorrow."

"Where's that detonator?"

"It's downstairs. Why?"

"I thought I'd look it up on the Internet."

"Knock yourself out. Goodnight, Eric."

"Goodnight, Stella."

She could hear the sadness in his voice. Sometimes he was depressed about how his life had ended and the things he'd meant to do that would never happen. Probably finding his will again had made him a little mopey about the past. Seeing his old girlfriend hadn't helped either.

"You know you did more in thirty-five years than most people do in eighty. I know there are lots of things you regret not being able to do, and I'm sorry for that. But you're still a great man. Thanks for your help again tonight."

Eric didn't reply. Stella went to bed, leaving him upstairs with his stuff. Sometime during the night she heard music, an old song she remembered from when she was a child.

She listened to the slow, sad verse and then went back to sleep.

Hush, hush, sweet Charlotte, I'll love you till I die.

It was Friday morning. Thick frost covered everything, glistening in the sun like diamonds. Stella grabbed a Coke and a Pop-Tart, stuck Eric's badge in her pocket, and went out to the Cherokee.

"Anything on that detonator?" she asked when she saw him beside her as she scraped the windshield.

"Not that I could find." He blew hard on a side window and wrote his name in the frost. "The Internet is a wealth of information, though. Did you know you can clean rust stains with tomato juice?"

She grinned. "I had no idea."

Despite the workout the fire brigade had the night before there was still practice and drills to go through. The birth of Banyin's baby and their success rescuing their colleague made everyone slightly sassy as they came into the firehouse.

Stella was glad to see her volunteers appreciated in the newspapers and on TV. They worked hard and deserved the praise they got. They even deserved the back-slapping and high-fiving they gave one another as they came in for practice.

Walt Fenway came to the firehouse as they were getting on their gear. He congratulated them on their good work, but he also came with bad news.

"The police are holding Jake responsible for the accident last night. They say people heard him and Banyin arguing at Scooter's. He was drinking too much too. He didn't stop for the right of way and he was weaving. Chief Rogers says he wasn't looking where he was going."

Royce whistled between his teeth. "Tough break. Was he drunk?"

"Not drunk, I guess." Walt shrugged. "Banyin and the

baby went home from the hospital early this morning. Her mama picked her up and took her home to where she lives in Frog Pond."

Petey shook her head. "That's even worse news. I know they've been arguing a lot about Banyin going back to work at the library and starting back here. Jake doesn't get her commitment."

Petey rerouted the firehouse basket she'd sent to the hospital so it would go to Frog Pond. There wasn't much more to say.

Stella reminded everyone that they were there to practice, not to gossip. "Let's get out there. We have a show to put on tomorrow at Beau's. We can't sit around on our butts all day."

Petey, Stella, and Tagger watched the new recruits get in some time with the hoses. Walt laughed at the part-time officers, Clyde and Nancy. It wasn't easy getting a handle on how to control the high-pressure hoses.

Nancy, with her red hair going gray, laughed back. Stella liked the easy-going new recruit who had a love of reading and was always looking for the next cruise she and her husband could go on.

"Hey, Walt," John yelled. "Why don't you come up here and show them how it's done?"

"Give me a gun, and I'll shoot it," Walt said. "That's the only thing I know."

"That's what I thought," JC fired back.

By the end of the drill, Hampton and Bradford were doing better with the hoses. Stella started them on carrying the sixty pounds of hose up the ladder to the second floor.

"What are we supposed to show off tomorrow, Chief?" Petey asked. "Hose practice?"

"I hope not." Tagger grinned. "Maybe we could wax the trucks real pretty and people would admire them enough to give us some money for the fireboat."

"Yeah," Walt added. "How's that coming, by the way, Stella?"

"I'll let you know tomorrow."

"The chief has a date with Rufus tonight." Tagger smiled and rolled his eyes. "Guess we'll know what's what when he gets all the good jobs."

"Are there any *good* jobs?" Petey asked.

"Not from what I've seen," Walt agreed. "But I think it's good that the chief has some male companionship."

Stella could tell Eric was enjoying the conversation. It was probably a lot like being with his fire brigade forty years ago, standing in the sun, watching the drills. She was glad to see him smile again after they'd found his will.

"The chief has plenty of male companionship," Tagger said. "She lives with Eric. She doesn't need anyone else."

"I'm right here," Stella reminded them.

"I don't blame the chief for wanting to have dinner with Rufus." Petey's smile was dreamy. "I wish he were here right now. He could ask me out anytime."

"Where is Rufus anyway?" John asked.

"He couldn't make practice," Petey said. "But he called in."

"I have a good idea about tomorrow." Stella changed the subject. "If we can find a practice car, we could let Hero and Sylvia rescue a few of you."

"Light a car on fire with all those people standing around?" Petey asked. "Would that be safe?"

"I wasn't thinking about saving someone from a fire," Stella said. "We could practice an accident scenario, like rescuing Banyin last night. People will love watching the dogs."

"Good idea," Walt said. "I have a junk car you could use. Max Morrison over at the towing shop owes me a favor. I'll have him tow it to Beau's for the show."

"It's all settled then." Stella blew her whistle and changed drills.

She wanted as many people involved with the pretend rescue as she could. She wasn't worried about the older members of the group. They knew what to do. It might be best to put Clyde and Nancy—the newest members—inside the car to be rescued. She wasn't worried about Rufus—he seemed to be a natural.

Stella explained to the group that she needed as many

fire brigade members at the event as possible. "We could bring in some new recruits with this event and raise money for the fireboat and other equipment." She explained her idea to show off their skills. "This is a good opportunity to raise awareness for everything we do."

"It doesn't hurt that it comes right after what happened last night," JC said. "Heck, my grandma called from *Knoxville* because she saw me on TV."

Everyone agreed with him. It sounded as though most of the volunteers would find a way to be at Beau's.

David wouldn't be present. He had to go out of town for work. Kimmie would be there with Sylvia. It was agreed that Stella would bring Hero to Beau's too.

"Okay then." Stella smiled at her volunteers. "You guys did a great job last night, but you always do a great job. Keep that in mind for the times that we aren't so successful. I'll see all of you tomorrow. Don't forget, I need your reports if you were on the scene last night."

There was further back-slapping and self-congratulation ringing through the firehouse as the fire brigade members changed clothes and got ready to go. Stella smiled as she heard them while she worked on her report in her office.

Walt knocked at her door. "You got a minute for me?"

"Sure. What is it?"

"I've heard a few rumors about what happened out at Barney Falk's place." He closed the door and sat in a chair. "Just wondering how true they are."

Stella sat back in her chair. She knew Walt always had his ear to the ground. As the former Sweet Pepper police chief, he knew everyone and liked to keep up with things.

"What have you heard?" she asked.

He grinned. "We're gonna play it that way, huh? You don't tell me anything unless I already know about it."

"I'm in the middle of this, Walt. My life, and the lives of others, have been threatened. I don't want anything going out of here that might make it worse."

"Stella, are you saying I'm a gossip?"

"Not exactly. I'm saying that I'm not sure who to trust. That means I'm not sure who *you* can trust either."

He nodded. "All right. I have a good source who tells me that Barney crossed the wrong people. It has nothing to do with drugs. That's only the cover-up. There are people who don't want to see Barney's son at the statehouse."

Chapter 29

"Who are these people?" Stella asked him.

"I think it's probably best if you and I don't know exactly who they are."

"Walt—"

"Here you are telling me you don't know if you should say what you know about this whole mess. Why do you think *I* should say?"

"What is he talking about?" Eric perched on the edge of her desk.

"Eric wants to know what's going on too." Stella smiled at Walt. "Did I mention he can leave the cabin now?"

"No way!" Walt looked around the room as he always did, hoping he could see his old friend. "That's amazing, and good news too, since Bob still wants to tear it down. This way Eric can live anywhere."

"We may have good news on that front too." Stella showed him Eric's will. "The town can't sell the property to Bob. It says the whole tract of land—with the cabin and the firehouse—has to remain Sweet Pepper's property."

Walt took a quick peek at the will. "That's great too. I'm

glad he can't kick you out, buddy. I sure wish I could see you. From what I hear, you saved Stella from whatever those men had in mind for her. I guess that explains the whole magic of her moving those electric lines too. That video is beating the devil out of a lot of people right now."

"Eric is happy about it too."

"I didn't say I was happy about it," Eric argued.

"But you are," she told him.

"If I have a choice when I die, I'd rather live at the police station." Walt winked at Stella. "My old cabin can get pretty boring sometimes. How'd you figure out how to get Eric out of there?"

Stella explained about Eric's badge. "I guess that was why he couldn't go to the firehouse after they'd moved his body. He could only go to the firehouse because the badge was there. When they gave me the badge, it meant he could go anywhere the badge goes."

Walt frowned and shook his head. "That's good news for sure." He looked at Stella. "I think you should keep your fingers out of this pie the powers that be are making of Barney's family. I wouldn't want to see them get cut off. I don't know if Eric can handle this situation. Don't press your luck."

"Just tell me one thing—is it someone local behind this?"

"Nah. It goes further up. Nobody around here would do this kind of thing to old Barney."

"Is that all you can give me?"

"I'm afraid so."

Stella toyed with the idea of letting Walt take a look at the detonator Gail had given her. If he was right, knowing about it could be a bad thing for him. Or he'd tell the wrong person and that would be it.

"He's bluffing," Eric said. "I've played poker with him too much not to know. He doesn't have anything else. He wants to know what you've got."

"I have to get back to work. Thanks for stopping by, Walt."

He put on his old hunting hat and glanced around again. "Good talking with you, buddy. See you later, Stella. Watch yourself. Don't take any chances."

When he was gone Stella started again on her report for last night's incident.

"I think you should give someone else this detonator," Eric told her. "Walt could be right about you staying out of it."

"I'm going to give it to Chief Rogers later. As soon as I finish this report we're going to my grandfather's house to tell him about your will. I'd like to get that obstacle out of the way."

Eric agreed. "Would you mind if I stay in the car? I don't want to go in there. I managed to avoid it while I was alive. I'd like to continue that tradition."

She shrugged. "That's fine with me."

When Stella called Ben, he told her he was at town hall.

"You should be here too," he said. "Steven and I are meeting with Hugh Morton, Bob Floyd, and Mayor Wando. Steven thinks he has something that will make a difference about that old cabin."

Stella agreed that she should be there, even though technically she wasn't really part of the debate. She wanted Eric to be present too and told her grandfather she wouldn't miss it.

"Do you think your grandfather's lawyer found the same clause?" Eric asked as they went out to the Cherokee.

"I hope so. That would make it easier."

Stella drove quickly through light traffic into Sweet Pepper. She had to park a block away from town hall but walked quickly back to the old building.

"They're in the big conference room," Sandy Selvy told her without raising her head. "Go on in."

As soon as Stella walked into the room, Bob raised an objection, holding his broken arm in the air. "This is *town* business. There's no way Chief Griffin figures into this."

"Since the chief is living in the cabin *and* runs the fire brigade I believe her presence should be allowed." Steven

Morrow, her grandfather's attorney, was very smooth and professional.

Hugh Morton, the town's attorney, whispered something to Bob that made him sit down. "We don't have a problem with Chief Griffin being present," Mr. Morton said.

"That's good." Eric stood behind Bob's chair. "I could probably pick him up and throw him out the window."

"It wouldn't help," Stella muttered. She hoped Eric wouldn't do anything that would validate Bob's claims. She even felt sorry for the man as he still bore the bruises and cuts from being beaten.

"Chief Griffin?" Hugh Morton asked. "Do you have something to say?"

"Not right now."

Steven Morrow began the presentation. Stella didn't see a copy of Eric's will on the table. She had to assume the attorney had gone in another direction.

"We believe the town agreed to allow Chief Griffin to maintain a residence in the cabin on Firehouse Road—as they agreed to allow the fire brigade to work out of the firehouse on the same piece of property."

Mayor Wando cleared his throat. "That is accurate. But we never stipulated how *long* Chief Griffin would be allowed to live there."

"That land has been up for sale for the last twenty years. Now that I want to buy it, it suddenly has to remain Chief Griffin's home," Bob argued. "She doesn't pay rent. There are other properties where she could live close to the fire-house. I already have a loan for the property. I think I should be able to do what we've wanted to do forever—get rid of that haunted cabin."

Hugh Morton took a sip of water and leafed through his papers.

Steven Morrow continued. "Because Chief Griffin was not informed that the cabin and land were for sale we maintain she must be given time to find another suitable location to live."

"That's fine." Bob grinned, as though sensing victory.

"She can take all the time she wants—as long as she's out of there in the next thirty days."

Ben wasn't happy with that. "I think we should talk about Bob's mental state that made him try to bulldoze the cabin without letting my granddaughter know what was going on, even though he was ordered by a Sweet Pepper police officer to stand aside."

"I had the right to do what I wanted to my property." Bob defended his actions.

"You mean to get rid of the ghost of Eric Gamlyn." Steven picked up on where Ben was leading. "You truly believed a man you disliked, who has been dead for forty years, is inside that cabin? You believed you could get rid of him by tearing down the cabin. Is that *right*?"

"Yes, that's right." Bob got painfully to his feet again, a cane in one hand. "We all know it's haunted. How many people, besides Chief Griffin, have been able to stay there more than one night? That's why the town put the property up for sale in the first place. If it was bringing in money it would be a different story."

Mayor Wando dropped his pen on the wood floor and spent the next few minutes searching for it. Bob sat down again with a smirk on his face that reminded Stella of the Grinch.

Steven conferred quietly with Ben and then offered, "Suppose Chief Griffin were paying rent on the cabin?"

"What? Where did that come from?" Eric asked.

Before Hugh Morton could answer, Stella intervened. "I think I have another answer. Have any of you checked Eric Gamlyn's will?"

"I'm afraid his will was lost a years ago." Mayor Wando answered her query as he finally managed to retrieve his pen. "It was the *only* copy, as far as we know."

Stella took the will out of her bag. "You might want to have Sandy make a few copies of it this time."

"Where did you find that?" Hugh Morton asked. "How do we know it's legal?"

"Well first," she explained, "you can see the old notary

stamp. I found it with some of Chief Gamlyn's personal effects in the cabin—the cabin Bob wanted to get rid of right away. Maybe he remembered that the chief only *willed* the property to the town. It could never be sold. He stipulated that it was always to be used for the fire chief and the fire brigade."

Steven assessed the old will and then passed it to Hugh.

"It looks valid to me." Ben had read the clause while his lawyer studied it. "I'd say Stella gets to stay in the cabin as long as she's the fire chief."

Bob snatched the document from the town attorney. "This can't be right. I've never laid eyes on Gamlyn's will before. I think we should have this carbon-dated. She could've made this notary seal on it herself. She'd do *anything* to keep his ghost up there."

Hugh Morton called Sandy into the conference room. "I recognize this seal," Sandy said. "Bonita Wando was this town's first clerk and notary. I'm sure you recognize her name don't you, Mr. Mayor?"

Mayor Wando took a peek at the faded blue seal. "That's my aunt. You remember, Bob? She clerked for the town before we could even pay someone to do it."

Bob threw the document on the floor. His face was dark red with rage and frustration. His coloring made his facial bruises stand out even more prominently. "I don't *care* who put their seal on this paper. I bought the land. It belongs to me. The cabin is coming down."

Sandy had already joined them in the conference room. She leaned down and retrieved the document. "I'll make a few copies, Mr. Morton."

Hugh Morton turned back to Mayor Wando. "You'd better get him some help or I'll start a petition to have him removed from the council. Good day, Mr. Carson. Steven."

Stella nodded back to the town attorney before he left the room. Bob was actually crying in one of the chairs. Mayor Wando seemed embarrassed, but he didn't leave his friend's side.

Ben hugged his granddaughter. "You have to let me buy

you lunch to celebrate even though I'd rather buy you a new house so you wouldn't have to live in that tiny old thing."

Stella agreed to lunch. "I'll have to meet you somewhere. I need to have a conversation with Chief Rogers before I leave."

"Not a problem." Ben glanced at his watch. "I'll meet you at the café in thirty minutes."

Steven Morrow shook hands with Ben and then with Stella. He seemed a little befuddled by what had happened. Maybe he wasn't as sharp as she'd thought.

"That's done at least," Eric said. "Are you sure you want to stay there? We could move somewhere else. I know the cabin is small."

Stella smiled at Sandy and stepped into the ladies' room. "I don't care if the cabin is small. It's got plenty of room and it's cozy. Besides, it has great views and it's only two minutes to the firehouse. And where else could I live that Hero could run up and down the road without getting into trouble?"

"Thanks." Eric grinned. "I could hug you."

He proceeded to do just that. Stella's feet were a few inches off the floor when a woman in a purple suit emerged from one of the bathroom stalls. Eric hurriedly put her down.

"Oh my!" The woman adjusted her glasses and glanced at Stella again. "You won't believe what I thought I just saw. I've been putting off the appointment with my eye doctor for too long."

Stella washed her hands and left the bathroom. "Next time make sure we're alone before you try something like that."

"Are you suggesting I should check to see if there are women in the stalls?"

"Never mind. Let's get this over with."

Chief Rogers was in his office as Stella walked by. She knocked on the open door.

He motioned for her to come in. "I believe you know Agent Whitman."

Brad Whitman nodded to Stella and got to his feet. "Stella."

"We were just talking about the analysis of the cocaine you found in Barney's house." Chief Rogers gave nothing away. Stella kept her mouth shut, unsure if it was a good idea to speak freely about the investigation.

"What I don't understand," Brad said, "is why the state arson investigator is denying all knowledge of finding cocaine during her investigation of the site."

Stella glanced at Chief Rogers. No matter what, she wasn't giving Gail away. "I'm more familiar with drugs being found in fire investigations. We had special training for that in Chicago. Gail Hubbard is very good at what she does. I took it on myself to have the powder tested by Chief Rogers."

Brad smiled at both of them. "I don't understand why you didn't simply point out the powder to Mrs. Hubbard and allow the investigation to proceed through *her* office."

Chief Rogers nodded. "I think I can help with that. I asked Chief Griffin to keep a look out for anything unusual that had bearing on us here in Sweet Pepper. She was only respecting my wishes. I'm sure you understand that we don't want to be known as the Tennessee capital for drug dealers, don't you, Agent Whitman?"

Stella thought it was plausible, though no such conversation took place between her and Don Rogers. They had never worked together in that manner.

"Smooth," Eric said. "See? I told you. You have to give the good guys a chance to be good."

Brad rubbed the back of his neck. "I thought Chief Griffin and I had a similar understanding at the start of this investigation. You should've come to me with this. The TBI will take it from here."

Chief Rogers shrugged. "That's fine as long as I don't meet up with some drug dealer on the streets of Sweet Pepper. This is our town, Agent Whitman. It's up to me, and Chief Griffin, to keep our citizens safe."

Eric laughed. "Okay. Don't faint, Stella. I think he's *really* on your side now."

"I understand." Brad turned to Stella. "Is there anything else I should know about that came out of the investigation? There was no evidence turned in by Mrs. Hubbard. I hope that means that you found no sign of foul play."

Stella's words were guarded. "The investigation was abruptly shut down. We may never know the truth."

"I guess what we have here will have to do then." Brad shook hands with Chief Rogers and Stella. "I'll be talking to both of you soon."

Stella waited for Brad to leave the office. She closed the door before she took out the detonator in the plastic evidence bag.

"What was that all about?" she asked.

"I don't know for sure." He took the detonator from her. "I'll have someone take a look at this. It won't be someone from the state, I can tell you that. Something else is wrong here. I can't put my finger on it, but my gut is screaming at me to keep digging. Have you heard anything else?"

Stella wasn't sure if she should repeat what Walt had told her. She decided to tell Chief Rogers what she knew, but not how she knew it.

When she'd explained what Walt had told her, he whistled and sat back in his chair. "Why'd they pick my town to mess up?"

"It seems to me it was the only place they could take care of Barney Falk, his son, and his grandson. What are you going to do?"

"Darn if I know. Let's keep a lid on this. It's probably gonna get worse before it gets better."

Chapter 30

~~~~~~~~~

When Stella arrived at the Sweet Pepper Café there were colored streamers and balloons everywhere. A sign at the door said "Free Cake for Everyone."

Eric wondered what the celebration was.

"Did you hear?" Lucille Hutchins's face was wreathed in a huge smile. "My Ricky got parole. He's coming home in a few days. I'm so excited. I can't tell you how hard it's been without him. Once he gets back you can have Little Ricky again for the fire brigade."

"I asked you not to call me that," Ricky Junior protested, holding a gray tub full of dishes. "I know you and Dad like to think of us like the old TV show, but we're not."

Stella was surprised at his unhappy tone. She congratulated Lucille and she followed Ricky into the kitchen.

"What's up? Where's your excitement? You wanted to get back to the fire brigade. You'll get your chance."

Ricky continued rinsing plates that were bound for the dishwasher. "I don't know. I wanted him to come back. I've missed him as much as Mom. And you know I want to drive the engine again. I don't know what's wrong."

She looked at him with the elbow-high yellow rubber gloves on his hands. "You know sometimes getting to the end of something can be depressing, even if something good is happening. You don't know what's next and you're not sure what to do."

He put down the plate he was holding and turned off the faucet. "That's the thing. I've been thinking this whole time that I wanted to break away from the café. I've worked here since I was nine. I want to do something else—make more money, for one thing."

"You should do it. Once your father gets back and is settled in, tell them. Do something else—as long as it leaves you with time to work on my trucks. They miss you."

"See? That's what I'm talking about." He glanced around the busy kitchen and lowered his voice. "Ben Carson offered me a job working on his cars. He's got a buttload of them, all classics, except the new ones. It's good money, and I'd be my own man for once, not just *Little Ricky*—busing tables and flipping burgers."

"Bad idea," Eric commented. "Don't let him get mixed up with the old man."

Stella considered the proposition. *Why not?* Ricky was right about the big garage full of cars that had to be serviced. He was really good with engines. Maybe that was his calling.

"Ricky?" His mother popped her head in the doorway. "There are three tables that need cleaning. Quick now. We can't fall down on the job because we're excited."

"Thanks, Chief." He smiled at her when Lucille was gone. "I appreciate the pep talk."

"This could be a good opportunity for you," Stella said. "Good luck. I'm looking forward to you coming back to the team."

"Yeah." He rolled his eyes. "I bet JC isn't. He's giving up my engine. That's all I have to say. It's good to have backup for emergencies, but *I'm* the main driver."

She laughed as she left the kitchen. She really didn't believe it would be a serious problem between the two men.

"That's a mistake," Eric said again. "Nothing good will come of it."

She ignored him.

"Stella!" Her grandfather hailed her from a booth near the front windows. "Over here."

"I'm going to wander around the café," Eric told her. "I don't want to have lunch with him."

Stella watched Eric disappear and then sat down across from her grandfather, surprised to find he was alone. She'd expected Steven Morrow to be with him. She ordered sweet tea, a grilled cheese sandwich, and a salad.

"No fries?" the waitress asked.

"Not today. I have to cut back on the fried foods." Stella wasn't surprised that the waitress knew her eating habits. She ate at the café several times a week.

"Wise choice." Her grandfather patted his flat stomach. "It's good to eat fresh vegetables."

"Good *for* you. Not necessarily good tasting."

Ben laughed, his face wrinkling at the eyes and lips. He was picking up a tan from working in the new vineyards, where he hoped to turn a profit in a few years.

"Didn't your mother tell you not to eat so much junk food?"

"If she did, I didn't listen." The waitress brought Stella a large Coke.

"Good job today with the will," Ben commended. "I'm sorry I let you down. I didn't realize what a loser Steven was. At least he won't be a loser on *my* payroll anymore."

"You fired him?"

"I pay well for good service. I don't pay anything for bad service." Ben sat back and smiled at her. "Which reminds me—I've offered Ricky Hutchins Jr. a job servicing my cars. My mechanic left suddenly a few days ago. I know you think highly of Ricky."

"I do," she agreed. "I'm sure he'll do a good job for you. I'll be happy to get him back at the firehouse too. I hope you realize he'll need time for practice and calls."

"By all means. You know I'm a backer of the fire brigade.

I plan to make a hefty donation tomorrow at the barbecue. I'm intrigued by the fireboat idea. I look forward to a tour when it's ready. Kudos on that project too. Bob Floyd and Nay Albert must be off somewhere licking their wounds. Are you sure I can't convince you to come to work for me too?"

"Not as long as Sweet Pepper wants me for their fire chief."

Their meals came—Ben ate only a large salad.

Stella looked at her salad and started on her sandwich.

"I wasn't happy about someone kidnapping you up off the road like that. I wish you'd let me hire a bodyguard for you. You're the heir to everything I own—you and your mother. People could want to get at me through you."

"I appreciate that, Ben. In this case, it had nothing to do with my being your granddaughter." She thought about how frightening Eric had been that night. "I can take care of myself in most situations."

"All right. I know better than to argue with you by now." He smiled at her. "You're good at making deals. So am I. I guess we get along best that way."

"I think so."

"What's the news on your investigation into what happened to Barney? I've heard some crazy stories about that."

"I can't really talk about it right now. I'm sure you know as much as I do anyway. I've heard you have spies everywhere."

"I'm not the king of Sweet Pepper," he reminded her. "I hear things like you do. Talk gets around in a town this size."

She couldn't argue with that. She sipped her Coke and finished her sandwich. A few bites of leafy green made it into her mouth before she stopped eating.

"I *did* hear a rumor that you're dating Rufus Palcomb." Ben finished his salad and patted his mouth with his napkin. "The Palcomb family has always been hardworking. Their boats are known all over the world."

"I hear a 'but' in there somewhere."

"Stella, let's face it—he'll never amount to much. I think

he's a fine young man from what everyone tells me. But he's not the right man for you. You could do so much better."

This was always the part that made Stella angry. Ben manipulated so much in world. She knew he wanted to manipulate her life too—from where she lived to the job she did and the man she was dating. That wasn't going to happen.

"I like Rufus. I don't know how far that will go. Right now I'm not serious about anyone. I can't be. I'm very focused on making the Sweet Pepper Fire Brigade the best it can be. I'm a career firefighter, Ben. I don't think that makes for good climbing up the social ladder."

"I understand, although I should mention that no granddaughter of mine would have to climb *anything* to have her pick of the wealthiest and most powerful men in Tennessee."

"Thanks anyway." She took out her wallet.

"Put that away. You know I'm not letting you pay for lunch."

"Thanks. Just so you know, buying me lunch doesn't give you the opportunity to decide who I'm dating. I'll see you later, Ben."

"What?" He got to his feet in a lithe move for a man his age. "No hug?"

Stella hugged him. It was getting easier. He was so thin she felt like she could break him. "Take care of yourself. Don't eat so much green food."

He laughed and left a hefty tip on the table.

Stella spent the rest of the afternoon collecting recipes. Eric had joined her as she left the café. She had ten pepper recipes for the festival from new people who'd recently moved to the area.

"Are you trying to get more recipes than anyone else ever has?" Eric asked as she went from place to place.

"You saw how happy they were with three recipes. Imagine how happy they'll be with a hundred."

"No, that's not right. You have to start thinking slower and smaller. This is Sweet Pepper, Stella. No one is competing with you. They'll be happy with whatever you do."

"I don't have speeds—just an on and off switch."

"You're going to set standards that other people who follow will hate you for."

"Look who's talking. The man who built a dam on the Little Pigeon River by himself in his spare time while he made a tunnel through one of the Smoky Mountains."

"Do they *really* say that about me?"

She laughed. "Something like that. You're definitely mythological."

"I kind of like that."

"That's what I mean. Get out of my way. I'm getting another ten recipes before I head back."

Stella only ended up with three more recipes. Her mother called from Chicago. Her father had hurt his back trying to catch a child who'd jumped out of a second-story window during a fire. He was on medical leave for a few weeks.

"Tell him he's supposed to go up and rescue them *before* they have to jump," Stella joked.

Her mother relayed her message. Her father threatened to take back the Harley he'd let her bring to Sweet Pepper.

Stella told them about the barbecue and demonstration to raise money. She also told them about everything that was going on in the investigation of Barney Falk's death. She left out the part about being kidnapped. She didn't want them to worry about her any more than they already did.

"You know it was the oddest thing," her mother said. "While we were there I took several pictures of the cabin so your aunts and uncles could see where you were living."

"Let me guess—they couldn't believe I could live someplace like that."

"No. Everyone thought it was darling. Your Uncle Jamie wants to know when he can come down there and go fishing."

Stella laughed. "That doesn't sound so bad."

"It was your Aunt Maura. She looked at one of the pictures around the stairs in your cabin. She swears she saw a ghost there. I looked at it. I don't see anything. But I told her about the ghost haunting the cabin. You know she's always claimed to have the 'sight'. This time I'm not so sure."

Stella had the phone on speaker so Eric could hear too. "What did she claim to see?"

"She said it was the ghost of a big, blond-haired man with his hair tied back. He was wearing a red shirt and boots. Kind of detailed, huh?"

"I'll say," Eric reacted.

"And you can't see anything?" Stella asked her.

"Not a thing. But you know your father's family—always full of Irish blarney. Anyway I only mention it because Aunt Maura says she's sending you a ghost charm. I don't know if it's supposed to protect you or what. It's some kind of root wrapped with twine. Just a heads-up in case you want to put it right in the trash."

Stella said she'd take a look at it and they talked about Stella's date with Rufus. She promised to send pictures of him, and of the new fireboat.

"I have to go," her mother said with a sigh. "You know what a baby your father is when he's hurt. I love you, Stella. Call me when you can."

Stella had been walking through Sweet Pepper's municipal park as she spoke with her mother. There were a few joggers, but otherwise she was alone.

"Maybe that's why *you* can see me," Eric said. "Maybe it runs in your family. You could start a business like Madam Emery. You'd have to change your name though. Madam Stella doesn't sound right."

"I think I'll take a look at the ghost charm Aunt Maura is sending. Maybe it's a charm that will make a ghost do and say only what you want."

"What fun would that be? Living with a ghost should be full of excitement and a little fear. I *am* a supernatural creature, you know."

"Yeah. My grandmother in Chicago called that kind of supernatural creature a buttinski."

They'd reached the Cherokee and the end of Stella's quest for recipes. She had to get home, take a shower, and get ready for her date.

"What are you wearing tonight?" Eric asked after they were in the truck and she'd started the engine.

"When did you become a fashionista?"

"A what?"

"Never mind. What do you think I should wear?"

"I think you should wear something demure for your first date. You don't want him to get the wrong idea. Nothing too tight or low-cut. Don't forget—you're after marriage, not a fling."

Stella laughed long and hard at that. Tears ran down her cheeks as she stopped at the stoplight going out of town.

Cindy Reynolds, whose claim to fame was that she had once seen a headless ghost on Second Street was in the car next to Stella's. She made a cranking motion with her hand to get Stella to roll down the window.

"Are you okay?" Cindy asked.

"I'm fine. Why?"

Cindy shrugged. "I saw you on the news and I was worried about you."

"Thanks. I'm fine. How are you?"

"I'm hanging in there. Worried about my mother's old house being haunted. She can hardly get a wink of sleep for all the moaning."

"That sounds bad," Stella remarked.

"We'll figure it out," Cindy said. "Just an unhappy ghost, I guess. Probably my uncle. He was always miserable when he was alive."

Stella waved and closed her window before she drove through the intersection when the light had turned green.

"Sounds like an unhappy ghost who wants people out of the house," Eric remarked.

"You want to talk to him? Maybe you can help."

"No, thanks. I have my own problems."

"Like what? The cabin is safe now."

"You." His answer was blunt. "Keeping you safe is turning out to be a full-time job."

Stella laughed. "You and my grandfather. He offered to hire security people for me."

"Maybe you should let him. I don't like the idea of you being out by yourself with everything that's been going on."

"I'm not taking your badge with me tonight. Nothing you say is going to convince me that you should go on a date with me."

They argued about it all the way back to the cabin. Stella picked up Hero at the firehouse. He bounded out of the Cherokee as soon as she'd opened the door at the cabin. Eric ran around with him outside in the woods while she went inside to get ready.

Eric's notions of what a woman should and shouldn't do on her first date with a man prompted her to dress a little more provocatively than she might have otherwise. After her shower she pulled on a scoop-neck black sweater that hugged her body and teamed it with tight black leather pants. She zipped up her knee-high black boots and used a little more makeup than normal. She wore her bright red hair loose on her shoulders.

Eric's face was hilarious when he saw her. He stopped inside the doorway and stared at her. Hero jumped around barking trying to get their attention.

"Well?" She turned around slowly. "What do you think?"

"Where's that big brown dress you wore to the coronation dance?"

She laughed at him. "Women don't really dress like that anymore."

"Women don't really dress like *that* either, do they?"

"I guess you don't watch as much TV as I thought." She put on a short black jacket and picked up her bag. "Don't wait up."

Eric and Hero watched her leave. Eric could feel that she'd left his badge behind as soon as she was gone. He found it lying on her dresser in the bedroom. He picked it up and rubbed his finger over the face.

"I hope she knows what she's doing," he said to Hero. "Neither of us will be there to help her if she needs us."

Chapter 31

~~~~~~~~

Stella was glad she didn't dress up too much for her date with Rufus. They took a look at several boats moored in his family's marina. One of them, a large sailboat, was where Rufus lived. They ate sandwiches and drank coffee while he showed her plans for the new fireboat.

"Maybe you should wait to put any more time into this until the town council approves it." She looked at the elaborate plans and hated that they might go to waste.

"No problem. I have the inside track on this now. Uncle Willy told me that Phil Roth put up a large chunk of money for the fireboat. So did your grandfather. The council hasn't voted yet, but with that kind of financing they'll vote for the project. That's how things get done."

Stella felt a little disappointed that Sweet Pepper was small but corrupt. It didn't surprise her exactly—she *was* from Chicago. She'd thought it would be different here. It wasn't.

Rufus had claimed to be a great cook, but his refrigerator was bare when they got to his boat. "I meant to make a cheesecake and a nice grilled chicken for tonight and really impress you. I got so busy I forgot."

Stella accepted a pudding cup from him with a smile. "That's okay. You know I'm not into cooking either. If you have hot peppers in that cheesecake, though, I'd love to have the recipe for it. I'm collecting for next year's festival."

"Sure. I can write it down for you. Doesn't everything around here have peppers in it?" He grabbed a pen and a piece of paper. "No. I love to cook. *Really*. I get carried away with projects sometimes. I'm really excited about the fireboat. What do you think of calling the boat *Sweet Pepper Teardrop*?"

"You mean name it after the pepper everyone grows around here?" Stella wasn't sure it was a great name for a fireboat—*Sparky* or *Fire Jumper* sounded better to her. But she didn't know anything about naming boats. "That fine. I'm sure the council will like that idea."

"That's what I thought. I have a friend who works at the pepper plant. He's also an artist. He's willing to paint a teardrop pepper on the side of the boat with the fire brigade logo. He'll do it for free to get his name on something."

"I think that would be great."

He looked across the tiny table at her. "Have I told you how awesome you look tonight? Maybe that's not appropriate since you're the fire chief and I'm a volunteer. I don't know."

"I'm not the fire chief right now." She smiled. "Thanks. You look awesome too."

He got them a drink. "I didn't mean to make you feel awkward about being the fire chief. You do a great job."

"I don't feel awkward at all about it." She took the rum-laced hot cider from him. "It's part of me now. Probably like you building boats."

"Yeah." He held his drink in one hand while the other was in the pocket of his jeans. He didn't sit next to her.

She couldn't tell if he felt awkward about it now that she was there or if this was his normal dating behavior. He barely spoke answering any attempt at conversation that she made with monosyllables.

Stella wasn't sure how to break through that barrier.

She suggested listening to music. She wished they could sit out on the deck and look at the stars too. Rufus reminded her that it was colder with the winds coming off the lake this close to the mountains.

They found some common ground talking about the fireboat. Rufus liked it when she suggested he show her around the future fireboat.

They put on their jackets and trudged over to what would be the *Sweet Pepper Teardrop* when he was finished. He pointed out where the hose brackets would go to allow for greater coverage and range of spray during a fire and described how he was shoring up the front end to hold the weight of the water cannon.

Rufus laughed when Stella called it the rear end of the boat. "It's the stern. I can tell you're a landlubber. Have you been on a boat before?"

She described her tour of duty on the fireboat in Chicago. She didn't mind being corrected about the boat. She didn't really know much about boats or even firefighting on boats. She was going to have to do some research. While Rufus might be in charge of any firefighting the team did on the *Teardrop*, she was still the chief and needed to know her subject.

They walked through the galley and a small sitting area below the deck. The boat wasn't as large as the one Rufus lived on, but Stella could see the potential for making the craft work for them when it came to fighting fires in the lake community.

As much as she enjoyed talking about Rufus's plans for the fireboat she was a little disappointed that the time wasn't spent getting to know each other better. As dates went this was more like a working dinner.

About nine thirty, after Rufus had showed her everything on the fireboat, Stella thanked him for the tour and said she had to go home.

"We all have an early morning tomorrow to get in some practice before the barbecue. I hope you'll be there."

"I wouldn't miss it. I plan to pull the *Teardrop* up on a trailer and haul her out to Beau's for the event. I even made up a little box where people can put donations." He took out the cardboard box he'd painted red.

"Great idea." Stella picked up her jacket. "Thanks for dinner."

Rufus put down the box. "I'm sorry. This wasn't much of a date. Like I said, I get carried away when I'm working on a project. Thanks for putting up with me."

He helped her put on her jacket and kissed her cheek. "I enjoyed spending time with you anyway, Stella. Maybe we can do this again sometime."

"Definitely. Goodnight, Rufus."

She left the boat and walked toward the Cherokee. Rufus was a nice guy—maybe a little preoccupied with his work, but so was she sometimes. She'd be willing to give him another chance.

As she reached the Cherokee, she saw Phil Roth. He appeared to be waiting for her.

"Good evening, Stella. I saw your truck out here."

"Good evening, Phil. What can I do for you?"

"I wanted you to know that the fireboat is in the bag." He went on to explain his part in the proceedings. "I know this is going to be good for the community."

Stella wasn't sure *why* he'd waited for her. It sounded like he wanted her to be impressed with his generosity. Okay, she'd be impressed.

"I've heard that. Thanks so much for your donation. Between you and my grandfather, I think we'll have a fireboat up and running in no time."

"I was wondering if you'd like to go and have a drink to celebrate." He smiled at her as the overhead light shadowed his face.

"Not tonight, but thanks for asking. I hope you'll be at Beau's tomorrow for the barbecue. We're trying to raise money for the fireboat and other necessities. Maybe you'd even like to volunteer."

He moved very close to her and touched a long strand of her hair. "I hope you plan on having a kissing booth there. I'd be willing to pay a lot for a kiss from *you*, honey."

Stella maintained her dignity. She wasn't worried about him trying anything with her. She also didn't want to alienate a big donor. "As far as I know there's no kissing booth. If there were Willy would be doing the kissing." She tried to make a joke out of it.

Phil didn't laugh. He moved even closer to her wrapping the strand of her hair around his finger. "Maybe you could help me out right now. I *am* giving a lot of money to your fire brigade."

She took a step back pulling her hair away from him. "I hope you didn't donate to the fireboat because of what you'd get from *me*. It's *your* fire brigade too. I'm happy to have lunch or dinner with you, but if I've led you to think there was something more between us, I apologize. Excuse me. It's getting late and I'm tired."

He looked her over with lazy insolence. "I don't want you to feel obligated, Stella. Have a drink with me. Let's see where it goes."

She didn't know how much plainer she could make it without knocking him down. "Maybe some other time. Goodnight."

Stella walked around him and got in the Cherokee. She was glad when he stepped aside. He was still standing at the side of the vehicle when she started the engine and turned on the headlights. He even waved to her as she left.

Creepy. She shuddered and left the marina. Phil Roth was a man to avoid in the future no matter how many large donations he made to the fire brigade. She didn't appreciate feeling like he was stalking her.

She drove back to the cabin after a quick stop at the firehouse. Allen, Kent, and Petey whistled and made a big deal about her makeup and how she was dressed. They wanted to know how her date had gone with Rufus. She told them the dinner was fine.

"What's wrong with that boy?" Kent asked. "When I was his age I wouldn't show a woman like you a bad time!"

Stella blushed and changed the subject. Her volunteers—and Eric—were a little *too* interested in her love life.

Petey was on communications that night. Her doctor had told her she could be on light duty starting next week.

"Maybe that means I could get in gear and come along on a call. I could look for pets if a house is on fire. I could relay orders. I'm sure there are dozens of things I could do even if I can't climb a ladder, carry people out of a house, or knock down doors. It means a lot for me to start feeling like part of the team again, Chief."

"Okay. We'll figure it out," Stella agreed. "It'll be good to have one of my assistant chiefs back again." She told her about Ricky coming back soon.

"Oh well." Petey frowned. "Nobody said it was a *perfect* life."

Allen slapped her on the back. "Cheer up. It's not as bad as poor JC fighting for the engine!"

Stella laughed. "Come on. Everyone works together."

She listened to twenty minutes of why Ricky and Petey didn't work out as a couple outside of the team. It wasn't just her lovelife under scrutiny. They all drank a couple of Cokes together. Kent and Allen went on with their game of chess.

"Sorry about your date with Rufus," Petey sympathized. "I'm beginning to think it's a mistake to ever date a good-looking guy. They never seem to get it, you know?"

Stella agreed and then said goodnight. She drove back to the cabin. Lights came on inside and the door opened as she got out of the Cherokee. Hero ran outside barking happy to see her as always.

"Where in the world have you been?" Eric ranted as he worked on frosting a cake. "This is way too long for a dinner date. Did you go out for drinks or something? Hero and I were worried."

Stella took off her boots and jacket. She went to warm her

hands by the fire in the hearth. "Housemates don't ask those kinds of questions. Only my parents get to ask those things."

"If you would've taken my badge with you I wouldn't have to ask." He looked up from the cake. "How was it? Did you have a good time?"

Stella went through the whole tale with him too. She also added the odd note to the evening when Phil Roth had appeared.

"I hope he gets over it." She stuck her finger in the frosting. "I won't feel comfortable with him again."

"Too bad." Eric smoothed out the frosting where she'd poked it. "He's mature. He has money and standing in the community. Not to mention that he gave money to the fire brigade."

"All things I look for in a man."

"Take me with you next time and I can tell you what's going on with him."

"Using your ghostly powers?" She rolled her eyes as she got a plate from the cabinet. "Can I cut a piece?"

"No. I'm not done with it."

"You're not going to eat it. I might as well have some."

He slapped her hand when she came close to the cake with a knife. The static zing made her pull her hand back.

"*Ouch.* What was that for?"

"I didn't just bake this for you to eat. I made it for you to take to the barbecue tomorrow."

"Willy is catering that, remember?"

"I know. It doesn't matter. Other people will bring desserts because he won't have any. It's the way we do things around here. No one has to know that you can only microwave food. They'll be impressed."

Stella got out some crackers. "You threw me off, buying all that food that I won't make. Now I don't have anything to eat."

"You're not eating the cake tonight. Go to bed. You have to get up early for practice. I'm sure your sandwich and pudding cup was enough for one night. If you're still hungry you can eat some cheese. I'm sorry you didn't get to put your sexy pants and sweater to good use. Sometimes things don't work out the way we plan."

Stella ate her crackers and opened a Coke. "You're right. I need to go to bed. You're crazy, even for a ghost."

"Like you've known so many."

She started toward the bedroom with her snack but turned back to him when she reached the doorway. "So you think I'm hot in these pants, huh?"

He looked up and grinned. "I think you look hot in everything. But then you're a fire chief so I'm prejudiced."

"Goodnight." She laughed as she closed the bedroom door.

"You wouldn't have to ask if I wasn't dead," Eric muttered. "I think I need more frosting."

Saturday dawned cold and clear. Even the fog couldn't hide the startling blue sky that was a backdrop for the dark mountains that surrounded Sweet Pepper.

Stella was up at five a.m. She showered quickly, before the hot water tank ran out, and wore layers of clothing since the afternoon was supposed to be warm. She brushed her hair and tugged on her boots. All the while there was this amazing aroma coming from the kitchen.

She walked out of the bedroom and stroked Hero's spotted coat. He was still asleep on the rug in front of the hearth.

"What are you making now?" She sniffed the fragrant air.

"I was thinking last night that I could make some egg biscuits. You could freeze them and take one out each morning to put in the microwave. It would be better for you than a Pop-Tart, and yet you wouldn't have the feeling that you had to cook anything."

"You know I have a soft spot for biscuits." She groaned as she sat down at the table in front of a flaky, hot biscuit stuffed with egg. "But all I'll be is one giant soft spot if I eat them every day."

"At least they have some protein."

Stella sniffed the biscuit and then nibbled on it. "Okay. You convinced me."

"It was harder to convince Hero to eat his new dog food than it was to convince you to eat that biscuit." He laughed. "Speaking of Hero, let's go out, boy."

Hero wagged his tail. Eric opened the door and the dog bounded outside barking at squirrels and birds before his paws hit the frosty ground.

Stella had to acknowledge that the warm biscuit was really good. Eric had made it smaller than the ones at the café. Maybe that would be the equivalent of two Pop-Tarts.

There was always a lot more food in Sweet Pepper than she normally had in Chicago. She'd never kept food at her apartment. There were some large spreads sometimes at the firehouse. They were never as attractive as what she faced here every day.

Stella picked up Eric's badge when she was done eating and put it into the pocket of her jacket. She knew he'd want to be at the barbecue.

She looked at the cake he'd carefully put into a plastic carrier. He'd managed to create a decent likeness of the Sweet Pepper Fire Brigade logo on top.

Rose, or some other woman, had missed out on marrying Eric. It seemed as though he would have worked hard to make a relationship successful.

"Are you ready to go?" He was standing half in and half out of the closed kitchen door.

"I think so. Thanks for making the cake. No one is ever going to believe I made it."

"What choice do they have? Besides Tagger and Walt, I don't think anyone suspects that you have a ghost that cooks for you."

Stella started to agree with him when the phone rang. She debated about answering it. She got more sales calls on her landline than she did on her cell phone.

"Hello?"

"Stella? It's Gail. I didn't know who else to turn to. I think someone is *following* me."

Chapter 32

"Where are you now?" Stella asked her. "I can meet you. Have you called the police?"

"I called last night when I saw this SUV parked outside my house. It left before the police came. They said it was nothing. I *know* something is going on. The fire marshal talked to me yesterday about the Falk investigation. I didn't tell him anything. He was upset that we didn't find much. I thought I did the right thing. Now I'm not so sure."

"I'll meet you, Gail. Tell me where."

"I'm on my way out to Sweet Pepper. I'll be fine. I guess I only needed someone to talk to."

Stella told her that they'd be at the firehouse practicing their drills. "Stop there. Let's talk."

"Okay. I'll be there in about twenty minutes. Thanks."

"Gail Hubbard?" Eric guessed.

"Yeah. She sounded scared. I think she was crying. She's on her way out here. Let's get down to the firehouse."

Hero jumped into the Cherokee with them. He sat in the backseat with his head held proudly surveying the woods and letting out small growls when he saw a deer or a squirrel run by.

All the fire brigade members were eagerly waiting for them when they arrived. There was a lot of talking and good-natured joking about the mock drills they'd be doing that afternoon.

During that initial group get-together at their lockers putting on their turnout gear Tagger slipped up next to Stella and whispered a friendly hello to Eric. Eric waved back to him, and Tagger laughed out loud.

"What are you laughing about?" Royce asked him after he was suited up and ready to go. "Are you coming along today?"

"Yep. Petey said she couldn't participate so she'd stay here on communications."

"You're not participating either are you?" Royce looked uncomfortable with the idea.

"The chief said I could be in the car for you all to rescue." Tagger grinned happily. "I'm glad it's an accident and not a fire."

Royce and JC laughed and fist-bumped each other. They grabbed their pry axes and went outside.

"Are we taking the trucks with us to the barbecue?" Kent asked Stella.

"You better believe it. Rufus gave me a good idea about getting donations too. We'll leave a box on each vehicle so people can drop money into them as they take a look at the trucks."

Allen shook his head. "I don't like the idea of asking for charity. We get money from the town and the state. Why do we need other donations?"

"Because the money we get from the state is barely enough to pay for two runs a month," Stella said. "That leaves the town funding most of our needs. We could do with all the help we can get. Don't forget, the better equipped we are the better the chances that we can be ready for an emergency."

"Like getting this beauty." Bert pulled out the Sawzall.

"This, and that new Jaws of Life, are gonna make a big difference when we have to rescue people from wrecked cars."

"Hey! That's not fair," Petey protested. "I was supposed to get to use that first."

Bert laughed. "Next time don't fall off the ladder."

Petey made a growling sound and went back to the communications room.

"It's not nice to remind people that they've been injured." John came out of the locker area in his bunker coat and pants. "Otherwise we'd all be talking about how *you* managed to break your ankle before we went out on our first run."

That brought a lot of laughter and anecdotes about their first run when they'd put out a fire in a henhouse. Bert took the ribbing and promised he'd apologize to Petey—but he didn't put down the saw.

When everyone was assembled in the parking lot Stella started them on drills. Not all of them were going to show off their skills. There wasn't enough time and they really needed the best volunteers on the ladders. A mistake would be costly to their fund-raising efforts.

Rufus pulled up with the fireboat behind him on the trailer. He'd managed during the night to paint *Sweet Pepper Teardrop* on the side, nothing really artistic but it was there. He'd also added a hose mount—no hose yet, but people would get the idea.

"Are you starting without me?" He climbed out of his pickup.

"Only two of us are going up the ladder with hoses," JC told him. "You might as well take your boat and go on to the barbecue."

"Don't dismiss me because I'm new," Rufus said. "I can beat you and Royce up the ladder with two hoses."

He flexed his arms and laughed at them.

"I think a small wager might be in order," John added. "Because *I'm* gonna be one of the two going up the ladder."

Everyone, except Kimmie, who didn't approve of gambling, tossed some money into four boots, one for each man.

Stella agreed to the friendly wager. She decided that the two with the fastest times would be the ones to go up the ladder at the barbecue.

"My money would be on Royce and JC," Eric said.

Stella put a couple of dollars into each of their boots. "There you go."

"Who are your favorites?" he asked her.

"I'm neutral. I think any of the four of them would make me proud."

"What do you say, Chief?" Bert asked. "Can I be in on this?"

She nodded to the saw in his hand. "You can't do everything, at least not at the barbecue. You've got the saw. You cut the car."

He agreed. Allen and Kent put up the ladder to the second-floor window. Tagger went upstairs to make sure each man went all the way.

Walt pulled in the parking lot as they were getting started. "Max Morrison already hauled that old car over to Beau's. It's a wreck. I hope you can get people out of it once they're in it."

Stella had started the first man up the ladder. It was Royce. He was medium height with a wiry-strong build. Even with the sixty-pound hose he was up the ladder and back down again in record time. The group applauded for him when Stella called out his time.

Rufus was next. He picked up the hose and got ready to climb as Stella called out for him to start. Rufus was six-foot-two and heavily muscled from his long hours building boats. He should've been sure-footed too, but he lost his balance going up the ladder and fell back to the ground.

The group rushed toward him to make sure he wasn't hurt. He was fine—unless you counted his pride. He waved as he put down the hose for the next volunteer.

"It's fair this way," he said to Stella. "After all I get the boat."

She laughed and called for the next contestant. John got the hose and started up the ladder when she gave the word.

John was about six-foot with a light, muscular frame. He had no trouble running up and down the ladder with the hose. His time was two seconds slower than Royce's.

"Okay," Stella called out. "Last but not least, JC. Get ready."

JC was built like his friend, Royce. He was thin but sturdy and fast-moving. He'd been one of the first recruits to figure out how to handle a high-pressure hose.

He ran quickly up the ladder and got to the top even faster than Royce or John. He looked back at his friends, grinned, and dropped the hose.

There was a loud groaning sound that came from everyone on the ground.

"I guess John and Royce will be climbing the ladder at the barbecue," Stella decided. "Share the winnings if your man won."

"At least I got one right," Eric said. "They're all good men."

Walt was watching Stella. "Is Eric here now? What did he say?"

"He thought Royce and JC would win."

"I thought John would be one of them." Walt laughed and slapped his thigh. "I'm glad I never had to do something like that to be a police officer. I couldn't run up a ladder like that *without* a hose."

Eric agreed with him and laughed at the idea.

While the volunteers were making sure both the engine/ladder truck and the pumper were shiny clean, Stella glanced at her watch. It had already been forty-five minutes since she'd talked to Gail at the cabin.

She confided in Walt about Gail's phone call.

"Oh?" He raised his thick, gray brows. "I guess you trust me *now*."

"It wasn't that I didn't trust you before. You know how these things get out of hand."

Walt sniffed. "That's okay. I suppose I forgive you. Which way was Mrs. Hubbard coming from?"

"What's going on?" John joined them as though he could sense what they were discussing.

"I'm about to go look for Stella's friend from the arson investigator's office," Walt said. "Want to ride along and make it official?"

"Sure. I'm not on duty. I don't have my vehicle. And we'll probably be out of my jurisdiction." John grinned. "I'm ready."

Walt slapped his shoulder. "Don't worry, Stella. We'll find her for you."

"Let me know what happens. Thanks."

After making sure everything was ready for the barbecue, Rufus left with the fireboat. The rest of the team went into the firehouse for coffee.

This was frequently a time the volunteers asked Stella questions about what it was like being a firefighter in Chicago. They were eager to hear stories of fires she'd fought and other aspects of training.

She was happy to share. She'd grown up with family members talking about their exploits over Sunday dinner every week at her grandmother's house. By the time she was ten she could recite the details of every major fire that had ever been fought in the area.

"How are we going to decide who works on the fireboat?" Kent asked. "Are you going to choose a team and those people are the only ones to work the lake fires?"

"I don't like that idea. I want each of you to have experience with the fireboat. If we only have one group doing the job we risk not being prepared if something happens to one of those team members."

She went on to explain her plan. Everyone would have training on the fireboat. The team would work a rotating shift when it came to calls.

"As soon as everyone has some time on the fireboat we're going to tackle swift water rescue. We've got the Little Pigeon River almost running through town and other local waterways where boaters could need help. There's also a nice stipend from the state once we get that certification."

"More training?" Allen groaned. "I don't want to say I'm too old, but I think I'm too old."

The rest of the team assured the fifty-something barber that he wasn't too old to go out on calls and learn new skills.

Banyin and her husband, Jake, stopped by with their baby on the way to Beau's. Everyone was excited to see her and the new baby they'd rescued. Banyin handed her little girl to Stella.

"We're calling her Meagan Stella Watts." Banyin smiled. Tears came to her eyes. "Just a way of saying thanks, Chief."

"She really wanted to call her Fire Brigade Watts since that's about all she can think about," Jake told them. "Her mother talked her out of it."

Stella looked down into the baby's wrinkled face. "Thank you, Banyin. I'm glad you and Meagan are fine."

"Never mind that," Petey said. "Pass the baby."

While most of the volunteers were making cooing sounds at the newborn, Banyin and Jake approached Stella.

"Jake has something he wants to say to you, Chief." Banyin nudged her husband with her elbow. "Go ahead."

Jake hung his head a little. There were bright spots of color in his cheeks. "I'm sorry I've been such an ass about Banyin working here. I didn't want her to get hurt."

"I understand. Everyone feels that way when their spouse, brother, or sister go on calls and could be injured."

"I was out of line about it." Jake smiled at her. "I'm hoping you'll give me another chance. Banyin says I have to join up so we can worry about each other—if that's okay?"

Stella shook his hand. "I'm always glad to have a new recruit."

"He can't drive right now," Banyin said with a nervous smile. "He lost his license because of the accident."

"Not a problem. Ricky is coming back to work. I'm already going to have to work out a schedule for him and JC to drive the engine. You know there's plenty to do around here without driving."

"Thanks, Chief." Banyin hugged her. "It's gonna be great. I can't come back for six weeks, but Jake can go ahead and start training. Right, Jake?"

"Right." He put his arm around his wife. "I'm gonna be the best firefighter you've got, Chief Griffin."

"You'll have to take a seat behind me." Banyin looked at Petey. "Oh yeah. And you can't mind when Petey shows you up all the time. She's small, but she's fierce."

Once everyone was finished talking and looking at the baby it was time to head over to Beau's. Stella wanted to get everything set up before the crowd arrived.

She was too late. The cold morning was giving way to a warmer afternoon. The blue sky and dry weather had already brought out a crowd for the event. Stella wasn't happy that they would have to set up between groups of people, but she had no choice.

"It won't matter," Eric said. "And look at that dessert table. Aren't you glad you brought my cake?"

The team was unloading the ladder and taking Clara and her family to the old car that Walt's friend had brought for the occasion. The silver Thunderbird looked as though it had rolled down the side of a mountain. The windows were smashed and there was damage done to every part of the vehicle.

"I'm glad we didn't have to really rescue people from that wreck," Stella said.

"You should be." A man with a mass of curly gray hair came up beside her. "I'm Max Morrison. This here was my car. I missed a turn and took a little tumble. Lucky I was alone. My father tanned my hide, even though I had a broken leg and a couple of cracked ribs to learn from. He didn't let me drive again for a year after that."

Eric laughed. "I remember that. It was a mess and no Jaws of Life to get him out either."

"You're the new fire chief, right?" Max asked.

She held out her hand. "Stella Griffin. Nice to meet you."

"That's right. You're the old man's granddaughter. Quite a ruckus when you first came to town."

"A woman likes to be noticed."

Max and Eric both laughed at that.

Stella's cell phone rang. It was John.

"We found Gail Hubbard. Someone ran her off the road. The highway patrol is out here with the Sevierville Rescue Squad. I can't tell what kind of condition she's in right now, Stella. It doesn't look good."

Chapter 33

~~~~~~~~~~~~~~~

Stella thanked John for the information. She offered to go out there, but he told her there was nothing she could do. He promised to keep her updated on the situation.

"You might have to let Rufus or JC take my place on the ladder," John told her. "I don't want to leave until I hear about Gail's condition."

She understood. "I knew something was wrong. Whoever was following her is probably responsible for the accident."

"Hold up on that," John said. "People run off the road on their own all the time. She could've been looking back too much and missed the turn. Let's wait and see what the highway patrol says."

Max had wandered away to look at the dessert table that had been set up in Beau's parking lot.

"I feel like I should be there," Stella said to Eric. "That could've been me."

"The fire brigade needs you here. The rescue squad can handle the accident. It's not even your jurisdiction. Let's take the cake over to the table."

"I think you're more worried about the cake than what happens around it." Stella got the cake out of the Cherokee.

"I worked hard on it to make *you* look good. I get no appreciation. It's not easy harnessing my energy to make things move."

"You're right. I don't appreciate you enough. Thanks for making the cake that you don't believe anyone will think I made. What *do* you expect them to think?"

He shrugged. "That you bought it from a store."

"That's what I thought."

People were already walking around the fire trucks asking questions of the volunteers who'd kept their bunker gear on despite the day heating up. Rufus took questions and donations at the fireboat. The smell of hickory-smoked barbecue filled the area.

It looked as though half of Sweet Pepper was coming out for the event. Even before they'd started the demonstrations the boots, boxes, and bags were filled with donations.

Stella saved what she considered to be the best demonstration for last. With the ladders on Beau's roof, Royce rushed up and down like a pro with a hose across his shoulder. People in the audience applauded enthusiastically.

Next up was JC. He was fast and a little showy. He got to the roof and held up his hose, doing a little dance that could've come from an NFL touchdown. More people crowded in to watch what was happening.

Stella called out the names of all of the volunteers. Each person came up with their pry ax, looking tough and ready to handle anything.

Banyin came up with Jake and Meagan to take her bow.

The people of Sweet Pepper were wonderfully appreciative of their fire brigade. As one man told Stella later, having the volunteers made him feel safer and made his wife happy when she wrote out the check to pay for homeowner's insurance.

Stella would have moved on to the next event, but Kent stopped her. "Let's give our fire chief, Stella Griffin, a big hand. She brought all of this together. We know we're doing the right thing because she tells us when we're not."

The large audience laughed and applauded. Stella doffed her helmet, a surge of pride and happiness running through her.

As they set up for the next event—having a tug-of-war with a three-inch-diameter hose—people from the community asked for autographs from Stella and the rest of the fire brigade.

The first group to try the tug-of-war consisted of police officers versus firefighters. There was a small runoff ditch that still had a little trickle running through it. The police officers stationed themselves on one side, firefighters on the other.

Stella could tell where their new recruits' real loyalties lay when she saw Clyde and Nancy with their comrades on the police side. She didn't let it bother her.

She'd noticed that Chief Rogers was absent from the event. She was hoping things were better between them. Maybe she was wrong.

The whistle blew to start the tug-of-war. The two teams began pulling as hard as they could.

"Look at those puny police officers," Eric remarked. "My money is on the firefighters."

"Big surprise." Stella took off her jacket and left it on a chair near the fireboat. "When *wouldn't* you choose the firefighters?"

But Eric was right in his choice. The firefighters pulled the police officers into the runoff ditch. There was laughter and some wet feet, but everyone seemed to be having a good time.

"Are we ready for Hero and Sylvia yet?" Kimmie asked. Neither dog was happy with waiting, but both had maintained their positions at Kimmie's feet. They whined a little, eyes shifting left and right, feeling the excitement around them.

"Let's get the car set up," Stella said. "Where's Tagger?"

Tagger was putting Clara and her family into the old

Thunderbird. Bert was standing by with the new saw. JC and Royce joined them with Kent and Allen getting ready for the demonstration.

"Do you need us, Chief?" Nancy asked.

Since she and Clyde weren't in their turnout gear, Stella decided to go with the volunteers who were dressed.

"I don't need you this time, but make sure you pay attention. We'll be practicing this soon."

"Thanks, Chief Griffin." Clyde touched his hat and moved back from the car.

To set the mood, Rufus sounded the siren on the engine and turned on the lights. This got everyone's attention. A large group wandered away from the tug-of-war.

"Let's suppose the fire brigade has been called to the scene of an accident." Stella addressed the crowd with a handheld microphone. "There are people trapped inside the car who need to be rescued. We have some new tools and our certified rescue dogs, Sylvia and Hero, who can get the job done."

Rufus turned off the siren and lights. Tagger was behind the wheel of the Thunderbird. He was moaning pitifully and had even squirted ketchup on his forehead for effect.

"Okay, ready?" Bert looked at his proud parents and turned on the saw.

Rufus and Royce stood by the driver's door ready to assist Bert as soon as the door was cut away from the car.

Sylvia and Hero took their instructions from Kimmie. The two dogs raced into the backseat of the car to save the dummies. Each dog dragged one person by carefully holding a sturdy part of their clothing with their mouths. The dummies were heavy enough to make this a realistic task for the dogs.

Mayor Wando and his wife immediately began applauding Bert's job with the saw. Most of the other people were clapping and cheering the two dogs as they dragged their victims to safety.

There was one victim left in the backseat. Before Sylvia could turn around, Hero leaped over her and headed back to the car for the last dummy. Even Kimmie laughed at that. Hero brought his dummy to safety with thunderous applause from the audience. He sat down at Kimmie's feet and barked twice, eagerly wagging his tail.

Tagger had been rescued by Bert, Rufus, and Royce. Kent and Allen immediately brought out the basket stretcher to take Tagger to safety. JC checked his injuries.

When the applause had died down Banyin took the microphone from Stella. "I want to say that I don't know if my husband, daughter, and I would be here if it wasn't for the time and training the fire brigade volunteers receive. I want to publicly thank all of them for saving our lives." Banyin started crying and hugged Jake.

"Let's see you do that trick with the electric wires again, Chief Griffin," Doc Schultz yelled out from the crowd.

"Yeah," Max Morrison agreed with him. "I'd pay good money to see that."

Stella thanked them and everyone else for coming that day. "I think lunch is probably ready. The fire brigade appreciates all of you. Our job is to protect Sweet Pepper."

More applause followed her words. She stepped away from the microphone.

"Have someone cut some wires," Eric said. "We could do it again."

"No thanks." She turned her head to the side. "I'm going to eat."

While Stella waited in line for lunch, Eric went to watch the tug-of-war competition that continued with the hose and the runoff ditch.

Stella found herself in the food line with Flo and Matilda Storch. They both had too many questions about how she'd managed to move the electric wires. The event had been captured forever on a YouTube video.

"You could make Sweet Pepper famous all by yourself," Flo told her. "I've watched that video a dozen times. There were more than a million views last time I was there."

"Curious how that wire seems to float away from the

pole you're holding," Matilda observed. "Sometimes it looks like you're not touching it at all."

"That's because you're looking at it on the Internet." Despite Stella's decision not to comment on what had happened that night, she felt trapped into saying something. "It looks different than it really was."

"People who were there said the same thing," Flo pointed out. Her very blond hair was covered with a flowered scarf and her dark blue gaze stared curiously at Stella.

"Let's admit it," Elvita Quick chimed in from behind them in the food line. "It was Eric Gamlyn. He was out there helping her. We all know it."

Flo looked back at the short, stout sisters who wore bright pink dresses and matching pink hats with daisies on them. "Elvita, you know a ghost can't leave their residence. I believe Eric stopped his cabin from being bulldozed by Bob Floyd. But no way was he out on Pepper Street."

Other people in the line, before and after them, began to join in the discussion. Stella was surprised and happy to see Ricky Senior and Lucille from the café at the event.

Ricky Senior clasped her hand tightly and then hugged her with tears in his eyes. He looked older and thinner than he had when he went to prison. Even though it hadn't been long, she could see it had changed him.

"Stella! It's good to see you! It's good to see *anyone* without tattoos and shaved heads," he joked. "To be here today in the sunshine with everyone is a blessing."

"Thanks, Ricky. It's good to see you too. I'm glad you're back. Where's Ricky Junior?"

"He's around here somewhere with Valery from the coffee shop." Lucille raised her expressive brows as though to let Stella know what she thought of *that* idea. "Nothing good can come of it."

"You want my son and his mechanic skills, I hear." Ricky Senior stood back and smiled. "Thank you for putting in a good word with your grandfather. A young man shouldn't be washing dishes and cleaning tables at his age."

Lucille called her husband's attention away from Stella to the food laid out on the long tables. "Let's eat. It's not often someone makes food for *us!*"

Stella couldn't take credit for Ricky's new job with her grandfather. She didn't argue though. They could always talk later. Ricky Senior was right. It was a good day to enjoy the sunshine and the company of friends.

Stella was glad to finally see the barbecue, coleslaw, and desserts come into view. She was starving. She could still hear Flo and Matilda whispering about the possibility that Eric had helped her with the electric wires on Pepper Street. She was ready for her fifteen minutes of fame to be over.

She reached for a plate, and Brad Whitman appeared at her side.

"Please tell me you aren't planning to cut in line," Flo said tartly.

"No, ma'am." Agent Whitman inclined his head, wearing a faint smile. "I'm here to borrow Chief Griffin for a few minutes. I'm sorry. Duty calls."

Stella gave Flo her plate. "I'll be back. Don't let everyone eat it all."

"You want me to make you a plate, sweetheart?" Flo asked. "I can make one for your friend too."

"Thanks." Stella appreciated the gesture.

"That would be nice of you, ma'am," Brad said. "We won't be long."

Stella got out of the food line and walked away from the crowd as some local musicians were setting up and tuning their instruments. She was looking forward to coming back and enjoying a lazy afternoon.

She looked around for Eric. He was still standing at the tug-of-war area. The runoff ditch had become muddy— which meant everyone who'd lost was walking away covered in red mud. Eric was laughing so hard he'd drawn Hero and Sylvia to his side. She thought he might as well enjoy himself. She could talk to Brad by herself.

"Chief Rogers is waiting for us at his office," he said. "I told him I'd get you and bring you there to finish the meeting."

"I was wondering where he was. People thought he'd stayed away because he doesn't like me."

"No." Brad smiled. "There's been a break in the Falk case. He called me early this morning. We both realized we needed you there for details about the fire. It shouldn't take long. Think you could drive?"

Stella looked around for his vehicle. "How did you get here?"

"I hitched a ride from one of the police officers in town."

They were standing beside the Cherokee. Stella took out her keys.

"I guess I should tell someone." She looked around to see who she could leave a message with.

"It won't be that long. They won't even miss you with all this going on," Brad assured her. "Would you like me to drive?"

"No thanks. They probably won't even notice I'm gone."

All of the fire brigade members and the police officers she knew seemed to be eating or watching the tug-of-war. She got into the Cherokee as Brad got in on the passenger side.

"What kind of new information did Chief Rogers find?" Stella put on her seat belt and started the engine. She was glad she'd parked away from the crowd and the other vehicles. It might be hard to get out otherwise.

"According to your friend, Gail Hubbard, she gave you a detonator she'd retrieved from the Falk house. Chief Rogers said you were going to turn that piece of evidence over to him. I told him it belongs to the state investigation."

Stella faced him. Something was wrong. Chief Rogers knew what had happened to the detonator—he had it. Was this some weird game he was playing?

"I'm not sure what you're talking about." She reached for the keys again to turn off the Cherokee until she could find out what was going on.

"I didn't want it to be this way, Stella." Brad pulled out a nine-millimeter Glock. He held it high against her side. "Just drive. We can talk on the way."

Chapter 34

~~~~~~~~~~~

There wasn't much else she could do. Stella carefully nosed the Cherokee out of Beau's parking lot. No one could save her from a bullet that would do a lot of damage very quickly unless she went along with whatever Brad had in mind.

"The only way Gail told you about the detonator was under duress." Stella kept her eyes on the road. "You ran her vehicle off the road this morning, didn't you?"

"You two were quite a team. Good work. The only thing is that the people who pay me were hoping you and Mrs. Hubbard would keep your mouths shut. What didn't you understand about our warnings?"

Stella kept the Cherokee moving at a slow rate of speed as they approached the town. She thought something would come up—a distraction of some sort—so she could get away without taking the bullet that seemed to have her name on it. She was scared. Her palms were sweaty. What could she do?

"You should've told me how serious you were about it. I would've paid more attention."

"I don't think so. You're the heroic type, I'm afraid. People like you tend to live short lives."

Stella stopped at the red light on Main Street. The whole area was deserted. Many of the stores and restaurants—even the coffee shop—were closed. Everyone was at Beau's.

"Just park over there at town hall. Chief Rogers is waiting for us." Brad nodded toward the parking area. The Glock was still pressed into Stella's side.

She parked the Cherokee and waited to see what came next. When he got out she might have a chance to get away. She wondered if Chief Rogers was still alive. Had Brad killed Gail too?

"Let's get out now," he said.

The door beside Stella opened, and Barney Falk Jr.'s driver was standing there with another gun in front of him. Brad pushed up against her to slide out of the Cherokee. He was right behind her. It was the perfect setup. She didn't think she could get away without losing a kidney.

Timing. It all came down to waiting for the right time.

Eric felt a sharp tug, as though he was involved in the tug-of-war he'd been watching. But this was something different.

He looked up as the taillights on the red Cherokee were disappearing out of Beau's parking lot. It seemed odd that Stella would leave without a word. He saw her jacket still on the chair where she'd left it. He tried to follow her to find out what was going on.

He couldn't. She'd left the badge in her jacket pocket. He was stuck at Beau's.

It was probably nothing. Stella probably went to run an errand, maybe pick up something for Willy. Maybe she went to talk Chief Rogers into making an appearance.

But his gut, or what was left of it, told him something was wrong.

Hero was standing where the Cherokee had been parked. His nose lifted as he sniffed the air and whined. Eric went to him and asked what was wrong. Hero responded by barking sharply several times, not taking his eyes off the road.

Kimmie heard him and walked through Eric to speak to Hero, reminding the dog that he was supposed to be on his best behavior.

Eric looked around. He couldn't follow Stella and he couldn't tell anyone else that there might be a problem. Hero was the only one that could hear him.

He whispered in the dog's ear and told him to forget what Kimmie had told him and follow Stella. Hero took off running, with Kimmie and Sylvia in hot pursuit.

"Hey, Chief." Tagger scratched his head as he came up behind him. "Why'd you want to get Hero in trouble like that?"

Eric suddenly remembered that Hero *wasn't* the only one who could see and hear him. "I think Chief Griffin is in trouble."

"Why didn't you say so?" Tagger looked across the crowded area and yelled, "Hey, Kent! I think Chief Griffin is in trouble."

Stella walked into town hall with the driver on one side and Brad on the other. The place was completely empty—except for Chief Rogers, who was tied to a chair in the big conference room.

He had duct tape across his mouth. There was a nasty bruise on his forehead and right cheek, blood and dirt on his uniform.

"As you can see Chief Rogers wasn't forthcoming about how the three of you worked this out." Barney Falk Jr. strode into the room. His expression was as pleasant as it was on his posters.

"Worked what out?" Stella realized where she'd made her mistake. "You mean that you killed your father?"

"I knew you were sharp for a fire chief!"

"What I can't figure out is why."

"Let's say that my father was old-fashioned. He didn't

approve of selling drugs to finance our lifestyle or my campaign. When he found out he said he'd put an end to it. He left me no choice. Our family's legacy must continue."

"And it didn't bother you to use your son as part of this either?"

"I'm preserving his future too. He doesn't understand right now, but he will later."

Brad asked Stella to sit in one of the chairs that were set around the table. "I thought about using a small amount of C-4 here in town hall. That seemed messy and unnecessary."

"What have you decided to do?" Stella refused to take a seat. They were obviously going to kill her. Placating them didn't seem important.

"I believe Chief Rogers is going to shoot you with his gun and then take his own life." He shrugged. "Tragic really. Both of you are such *good* people. Everyone knows you two don't get along. They were all speculating about it at the barbecue. I don't think anyone will be surprised."

"Good idea," Barney Falk Jr. approved. "That's why I hired Agent Whitman. He thinks on his feet!"

"I don't understand why an agent with the Tennessee Bureau of Investigation would get involved in something like this." Stella tried to reason with Brad.

He smiled. "Do you know what retirement is for a state investigator?"

"So it's all about the money?"

"I've been an TBI agent for ten years, Stella. I think *you* might make more money than I do."

"Why not just get another job?" She tried to keep him talking in what she was beginning to think was a vain effort to stay safe. "I'm sure private security pays better."

"I chose another path, a very *lucrative* path." He carefully made his way around the table to take the chief's gun from his holster. Chief Rogers made some strangled talking noises that were muffled behind his gag.

"This wouldn't have happened if you'd given me all the evidence as I asked you to at the cemetery that day," Brad persisted. "I could've handled the whole thing. It was you,

Mrs. Hubbard, and Chief Rogers who stepped out of line. You get what you ask for."

"What do you want me to do?" Falk's driver asked from near the door.

"Wait outside," his boss said. "I'll be out in a few minutes. We have a plane to catch."

Brad's eyes never left Stella's face as he walked around the table holding Chief Rogers's service revolver.

"It would be easier if you sat down," he said to her. "I don't see any reason for you to fall on the floor. Both of you could be sitting here, arguing like always, when Chief Rogers's temper gets the better of him."

"Just do it, Brad," Falk urged. "I'll be outside. Don't take all day about it either."

Chief Rogers's attempts to be heard got louder as Barney Falk left them. He rocked back and forth in his chair.

Stella heard a commotion at the front door. Falk swore, and his driver started yelling at someone. She heard a familiar bark and growl. Had Hero followed her? She didn't want him to get hurt.

"What's that?" Brad's gaze slid away from her toward the front door.

Stella didn't wait for another chance. She threw herself at him trying to knock his gun hand to the side. He yelled as the gun went off.

Hero found his way into the conference room through the door the driver had left open. He jumped on Brad, clamping onto his hand as though he meant to pull him out of a wrecked car.

The gun went off again before Stella could knock it out of Brad's hand. She was terrified Hero was going to be hurt. Brad kicked at Hero, but the dog wouldn't let him go.

Stella pulled back her right hand and punched Brad as hard as she could. It wasn't enough to knock him out, but it staggered him. He dropped to one knee, shaking his head.

Chief Rogers knocked his chair over on top of Brad, pinning him to the floor.

There was a cracking sound. Stella didn't wait to see

what it was. She untied Chief Rogers and pulled Hero away from Brad.

"Are you okay?" she asked Don Rogers as he ripped the duct tape from his mouth.

"I'll live. Thanks."

Brad was in too much pain to struggle much—probably a few broken ribs.

Several Sweet Pepper police officers and members of the fire brigade ran into the conference room.

"I think we've got it under control," Stella said to their erstwhile rescuers.

Chief Rogers's voice was gritty and strained as he demanded, "Where the hell were all of you ten minutes ago?"

"Stella." Eric was next to her. He'd had Tagger bring her jacket with them.

"It's okay," she whispered. "We're okay."

Kent's face was white when he looked at her. "I don't think so, Chief."

Stella looked down at the rapidly spreading bloodstain on her shirt. "I just had this cleaned."

Chief Rogers caught her as she fell.

Three weeks later, Stella was getting ready for her second date with Rufus. Her arm was still a little sore from the bullet that had grazed it. There had been no major damage done though.

Everyone had treated her like an invalid since the event. She'd ignored them for the most part. There were no stitches, but the rules said she had to be off duty until the doctor released her. That was today.

"Are you sure you're up for this?" Eric asked when he saw her struggling to get her arm into the jacket sleeve.

"I'm fine. It's a little stiff, that's all. Besides, I thought you wanted me to go out and find a husband. I shouldn't miss this chance with Rufus, right?"

"That's fine. Now that we know Agent Whitman is put away somewhere and Chief Rogers is your bosom buddy, you should be safe enough. I'm going to work on this new pepper recipe I found in one of the old Sweet Pepper cookbooks my mother left behind."

"Sounds good. Don't wait up for me. I might be very late in choosing my appropriate mate."

"That bullet didn't slow you down." Eric manipulated a bowl and the electric mixer out of the cabinet. "Your mythology is starting to get as big as mine."

She laughed as she headed out the door.

Eric and Hero had been great while she'd recovered. Everyone from town had brought her food until she had to beg them to stop. She couldn't eat any more and there wasn't enough room to store it. Most of it had ended up at the firehouse.

Gail Hubbard had taken early retirement. She was injured when Brad Whitman had pushed her car off the road, but she'd recovered. She'd come to see Stella in the hospital, and the two of them had talked for a long time.

"I could put in a recommendation for you to take my place as state arson investigator," she offered. "It's a good job—if you can stay out of the politics."

"Thanks. I'm still getting used to being a chief. I think I need a little more practice."

Stella and Gail had hugged, carefully since both of them were injured, and parted. Stella didn't expect to see the other woman again. It was too bad. She was sure there was a lot she could have learned from her.

The night was balmy. It would change quickly as winter set in.

They'd scheduled a test of the new fireboat for the next day. Rufus was supposed to take her out on the boat tonight. She hoped, despite him wanting to show off the improvements, that they could actually take some time to get to know each other.

She pulled the Cherokee into the marina, where the fireboat was docked next to Rufus's boat. She put on her most winning smile and got out to look for him.

"Rufus?" She stepped onto his boat. He wasn't there.

She shrugged and went on board the fireboat, admiring

the chrome fittings that held the water cannon and the hoses on each side.

"Rufus? Are you here?" She went below, but he wasn't there either. "Rufus?"

There was no sign of him on either boat. His truck was gone too. Maybe he had an emergency. Cell phone service was always spotty in and around Sweet Pepper. She looked for messages anyway. There was nothing.

So much for the second date. She realized it was possible that he'd forgotten their date completely. Stella got back in the Cherokee and started the engine. Eric was going to have a field day with this.

She stopped by the firehouse in case Rufus had left a message there for her. Petey and Tagger were playing checkers in the kitchen as they monitored communications. They'd heard nothing from Rufus either.

"Stay and have some root beer floats with us, Chief," Tagger invited. "I'll beat Petey at this in a couple of minutes. I think people have forgotten how to play regular games instead of those Internet games."

"Thanks, but I'm going home and having an early night. Good luck, Petey. I don't think there's anyone that can beat Tagger at checkers."

"Chief Gamlyn always beat me," Tagger whispered to Stella with a wink and a smile. "You should challenge him sometime. He'll show you."

Stella went back to the Cherokee. She yawned as she drove up Firehouse Road. Three deer ran across the road in front of her. She waited a moment in case more followed. It was still a thrill to see wildlife after living in the city, but frightening too after hearing stories about the animals jumping in front of vehicles.

The light was on at the front porch, but the door didn't open as Stella approached. That was odd. *Eric must be so caught up in his new recipe that he doesn't even notice I'm back.*

Two men forgetting about her in one night might be a little much for her ego.

Hero was sleeping in the middle of the kitchen floor. She called his name, but he didn't move.

"Hero?" She shook him, but he stayed asleep. She checked his pulse. It was slow. So was his heartbeat.

She looked around the kitchen. The bowl and mixer were still out. Ingredients were scattered on the cabinet too. "Eric?"

There was no response. She called him again, a little louder.

Still nothing.

She ran into the bedroom and looked at the chest next to her bed. Eric's badge was gone. Stella lifted Hero. He was a heavy weight for her injured arm, but she got him out to the Cherokee to take him to the vet.

When she reached the end of Firehouse Road, she called Walt.

"Eric is gone. It sounds crazy I know, but I think someone may have kidnapped him."

The Sweet Pepper Difference

~~~~~~~~~~~~~~~~~~

Sweet Pepper, Tennessee, grows the hottest, sweetest pepper in the world—the Tennessee Teardrop Pepper! It's a combination of our soil and our proximity to the Smoky Mountains that makes our jalapeño peppers better. Sweet, but with a bite that makes your eyes open. Not too hot—but not too tame either.

These are some of the award-winning recipes from our annual pepper festival. Try a few, or some of your own, with our peppers. We're sure you'll agree that our peppers are the best! Enjoy!

Know Your Peppers

Because knowing the strength and taste of the peppers you use with your foods can make or break your meal, it's best to know your peppers!

The featured pepper is Bhut Jolokia (the Ghost Chili Pepper).

This popular chili pepper has been named the hottest

pepper in the world. It is 2½ to 3 inches long, with a red-orange to hot red appearance. Its Scoville rating, which grades the amount of heat you feel when you're eating it, is 855,000 to 1,050,000. These are naturally grown peppers, not synthetically developed. Now that's hot!

The normal jalapeño is 2,500 to 5,000. Proceed with caution if you eat a ghost pepper.

Recipes

~~~~~~

AWARD-WINNING HOT SAUCE

by Darcy Eldridge

5 chili peppers, minced. Try to use a variety of pepper
    types for best flavor.
1 tablespoon minced onion
1 tablespoon minced garlic
Olive oil
1 small can tomato paste
1 cup vinegar
½ teaspoon black pepper
1 tablespoon lemon juice

Sauté peppers, onion, and garlic in a little olive oil.

Stir in the tomato paste and ½ cup vinegar.

Bring the mixture to a boil. Add the remaining ingredients as it cools.

Store in the refrigerator. Serve with anything from chicken to ribs.

AWARD-WINNING HOT PEPPER
CORN MUFFINS

by Elsie Winnapoor

2 cups self-rising yellow corn meal
1 cup self-rising flour. If you don't have self-rising, use 1
    teaspoon baking powder.
2 eggs
1 cup milk
¼ cup cooking oil
1 tablespoon sugar or sweetener
4 jalapeños

Mix first six ingredients together. This makes the basic
muffin batter. Now add jalapeños, chopped, seeded, and
stems removed, and mix with the batter.

Add hotter peppers to your own taste. Add a mixture of
red and green peppers for a prettier look!

Be sure to coat the pan first in either case so the corn-
bread won't stick. Bake at 350 degrees for 20 minutes or
until toothpick comes out clean.

AWARD-WINNING SWEET AND
SOUR CUKES

1 cup vinegar
1 tablespoon mayonnaise
½ cup finely chopped onion
½ cup finely chopped, seeded, and stemmed jalapeños
1 tablespoon sugar or sweetener
2 long, narrow cucumbers. These should be cut diagonally
    in thin slices.

Combine first five ingredients in a bowl. Add cucumbers and stir. Add salt and pepper to taste.

BLUE-RIBBON-WINNING RECIPE FOR STUFFED HOT PEPPERS

by Fire Chief Stella Griffin

For this recipe, you will need 1 loaf of homemade bread with candied fruit added. Also add an additional ½ cup sugar to your normal bread recipe. If you're using a bread machine to make this, follow the instructions for raisin or fruit bread.

You will need 12 large jalapeño peppers with the seeds and stems removed. These should be intact, so be careful how you handle them. Create a candy glaze for the peppers by mixing 1 cup water with 1 cup sugar to create a syrup. Dunk each pepper into the glaze mixture, making sure they are well coated.

When they are dry and the bread is cool, push the bread mixture into the peppers until they are full.

Put each pepper on a cookie sheet and bake at low heat for about 5 minutes. The glaze should get hard.

Serve cold. Excellent with ice cream!

FROM NATIONAL BESTSELLING AUTHOR

J. J. COOK

DEATH ON
Eat Street

A Biscuit Bowl Food Truck Mystery

Struggling restauranteur Zoe Chase turns an old Airstream into a food truck, and in no time she's dishing out classic Southern food throughout Mobile, Alabama. But when the owner of a competing food truck winds up dead inside her rolling restaurant, Zoe needs to find the real killer before she gets burned.

Includes recipes!

jjcook.net
facebook.com/authorsj.j.cook
facebook.com/TheCrimeSceneBooks
penguin.com

J. J. Cook

That Old Flame of Mine

A Sweet Pepper Fire Brigade Mystery

Meet Stella Griffin, former Chicago fire fighter turned small-town fire chief. When Stella's dear friend Tory dies after her gingerbread-style Victorian house is set ablaze, Stella suspects arson and foul play. What she doesn't suspect is that the ghost of Eric Gamlyn, Sweet Pepper's old fire chief, is about to help her smoke out a killer.

PRAISE FOR THE SERIES

"Dark family secrets, a delicious mystery—
and a ghost. What reader could ask for more!"
—Casey Daniels

*Includes delicious hot and
sweet pepper recipes!*

jjcook.net
facebook.com/authorsj.j.cook
facebook.com/TheCrimeSceneBooks
penguin.com

M1557T0814